STONE FIELD

STONE FIELD

A Novel

Christy Lenzi

ROARING BROOK PRESS
New York

Text copyright © 2016 by Christy Lenzi
Published by Roaring Brook Press
Roaring Brook Press is a division of Holtzbrinck Publishing Holdings Limited Partnership
175 Fifth Avenue, New York, New York 10010

fiercereads.com

Library of Congress Cataloging-in-Publication Data

Names: Lenzi, Christy, author.
Title: Stone Field / Christy Lenzi.
Description: First edition. | New York : Roaring Brook Press, 2016. | Summary: In
  this loose retelling of *Wuthering Heights* set in Missouri during the Civil War, when
  free-spirited seventeen-year-old Catrina discovers a mysterious young man with amnesia
  on her family's sorghum farm, they fall passionately in love, scandalizing intolerant
  family members and neighbors.
Identifiers: LCCN 2015027143 | ISBN 9781626720695 (hardback) |
  ISBN 9781626720701 (ebook)
Subjects: | CYAC: Love—Fiction. | Amnesia—Fiction. | Toleration—Fiction. | Racially
  mixed people—Fiction. | Missouri—History—Civil War, 1861–1865—Fiction. |
  United States—History—Civil War, 1861–1865—Fiction. | BISAC: JUVENILE
  FICTION / Historical / United States / Civil War Period (1850–1877). | JUVENILE
  FICTION / Love & Romance.
Classification: LCC PZ7.1.L445 St 2016 | DDC [Fic]—dc23
LC record available at http://lccn.loc.gov/2015027143

Our books may be purchased in bulk for promotional, educational, or business use. Please
contact your local bookseller or the Macmillan Corporate and Premium Sales Department
at (800) 221-7945 ext. 5442 or by e-mail at MacmillanSpecialMarkets@macmillan.com.

First edition, 2016
Book design by Elizabeth H. Clark
Printed in the United States of America

1 3 5 7 9 10 8 6 4 2

For Alexandria Juliet Lenzi,
the first person who ever asked
me to please tell her a story

1

I'M A LOADED GUN.

Henry knows. He thinks he and Jesus can save me from myself.

"Catrina, what you want is discipline." Henry pushes aside the new issue of *Farmer's Almanac* on the breakfast table instead of picking it up like usual, to show the gravity of the situation. "I know you were wasting time daydreaming in the woods yesterday and up in the cave again last night."

If he knew I wasn't daydreaming but creating my wild work in the woods, it wouldn't make any difference. He'd still call it a waste of time.

"If Father won't tend to you, somebody has to. Whoever heard of a girl roaming up and down the hills at all hours? Look at you—wearing boys' pants and your hair hanging loose and tangled. It's not proper."

I don't give a damn about being proper. It's just a mess of rules that people make up so they can have a say in other people's business. But I don't waste my words on Henry. I tear off pieces of my biscuit and crumble them in my fist while he preaches his sermon. Since Papa's off working in the barn, I'm the only one left in Henry's congregation.

He crosses his arms over his chest, looking at me like I'm dirt on a stick. If the high slant of his cheekbones and the soft curve of his lips didn't belong to our dead mother, I would slap his face. Mother had never minded what I wore and would never have talked to me this way.

"Plenty of girls are courted or already married at seventeen, but there's not a man in his right mind who'd want to chase down and tame a wildcat like you. You should be here at home." He tilts his chin up as he talks so the righteousness he spouts will fall on me like manna from Heaven. "When you feel troubled or restless, you should turn your idle thoughts to the Bible and your idle hands to work. That'll sweep the wickedness out of any girl's heart." He nods, agreeing with himself.

But Henry and Jesus don't know a thing about a girl's heart. And they don't know what it feels like to have a soul bent on wandering through dark places, looking for the missing piece of itself. They can't help me.

"You'll stay home today and set your mind toward improvement." Mistaking my silence for acceptance, Henry opens the *Almanac* and shuts the invisible door between us. He doesn't realize his words are bullets dropping into the barrel of my soul. I wonder what he'll do if someone pulls the trigger.

Henry didn't always treat me like the enemy. Less than a year ago, Abraham Lincoln was elected president of the United States, and Mother left the land of the living. That's when Henry pulled away from me and Papa, just like the southern states drew away from the Union. Last year, the old Henry had a bright look on his face when I showed him the new weather vane I designed for our barn. Instead of making a horse or a rooster, I made two naked wind nymphs soaring on the breeze, their wings outstretched. Back then Henry didn't call me wicked—he called me clever. Seems ages and ages ago.

I make a decision. If Henry glances at me over the top of the *Almanac*, I'll smile at him. If he lowers the *Almanac* and smiles, too, then that means there's a chance we can find our way back to how we used to be before Mother died. I stare hard at the cover of the *Almanac* and chant inside my head, *Look at me, look at me, look at me.* I don't take my eyes away from him so I won't miss my chance. But Henry's already forgotten about me. He finishes his coffee, biscuits, and molasses without glancing up.

"I'm traveling to Rolla today to get the papers and see how things are. We should be hearing more about the battle at Lexington by now. Damned Confederates and their Missouri Guard—they're ripping the state in half. And not a hundred miles northwest of Roubidoux Hollow!" He slaps the *Almanac* down as he shoves away from the table. Dirty dishes are women's work.

Right now I'd rather jump off a cliff than scrape another plate, churn another tub of butter, or scrub one more load of wash. A lump grows in my throat and I can hardly swallow. When the back door shuts behind Henry, I stretch my arm across the table and slide it over the surface in a great wave. The wave pushes the *Almanac* and the clattering tin plates and cups over the edge like God sweeping the Egyptians into the Red Sea. They tumble to the floor with a crash. I step over them and out the door. By the time Henry gets a quarter of the way to Rolla, I'll be sitting on top of the world in a place where dishes, Bibles, and battles don't exist.

The fresh scent of rain and wet cedar fills the air from a late-night shower that scrubbed the earth clean. It's September, that twilight month between the heat of summer and the chill of autumn. In my mind I think of it like Missouri, the hazy border between the northern and southern states. They are uncertain, in-between times and places that aren't quite one thing or the other. Yet.

I part the bushes at the edge of the ravine, and a small flock of thistle birds takes flight. The flutter of their wings sets the pace of my heart. A rush of cold dank air from the cleft in the rock lifts the hairs on my arms and finds its way under my clothes like icy fingers. I shiver and close my eyes, imagining the lonesome spirit of a dead man sliding its hands over my body, beckoning me inside the cave like a long-lost lover. The rim of the cave is as high as my hips, but I pull myself up easy without any fool skirts to tangle my legs.

The cave's main tunnel is long and winding and leads to my secret place, a small opening high in the bluff overlooking Roubidoux Hollow. Henry doesn't understand the darkness that settles over me, and why I need to come here, but Papa does. When Papa needs to escape his pain, he locks himself in his study with the books Mr. Lenox orders for him—they come all the way from St. Louis. Most people in Roubidoux only read if they have to—the *Almanac*, the newspaper, or the Bible sometimes—but Papa has always had his stories and poetry, and I have my tunnel to the sky.

Henry doesn't open Papa's books or climb into my cave to learn where it goes because he doesn't own the patience or curiosity for it. Not anymore, anyway. Ever since Mother died, he doesn't like to think too hard about anything he doesn't understand. If he can't wrap his mind around an idea in a heartbeat or see all there is to see of a thing in a glance, he can't abide it. That's why he's turned cold toward me—he knows I'm a quiet cave with secret tunnels and open rooms beneath my stone face—dark places he doesn't want to find. And Lord, how I want to be found. I ache for it. But not by a coward like Henry. I want someone who will climb right into me and explore every inch, knowing they might never find their way out.

I breathe in the smell of cool wet rock and mud as I crawl in the dark to my secret place. Nobody knows about it but me. Well, a couple years ago, Frank Louis, who's older than me and mean enough to bite himself, followed me to the cave opening without me knowing. But I threw rocks at him and he ran away bleeding. Now I make sure nobody follows me.

I creep up through the muck and mire till I see a blue spot of shining sky. When I reach the opening on the edge of the high bluff, I lean against the damp wall of the tunnel. No one can see me way up here. Cold water drips from the top ledge onto my eyelid and slides down my cheek.

The gray snaky curves of Roubidoux Creek glint silver as the sun climbs over the hills. The stream winds around the slope of Hudgens Cemetery and slips through our cedar grove toward Stone Field, where our sorghum cane grows.

But I don't look at the grove or the field. Today I see only the cemetery.

My eyes linger on Mother's small mound of earth. Last night when I went there, a silver-dollar moon floated over the graveyard, casting black shadows and blue light around her grave marker. I considered getting a shovel and digging a tunnel down to her coffin. I wanted to break it open and crawl in beside her like I used to climb into her bed after I had a bad dream. Even though her arms are cold and stiff now, I still want them around me. I want to believe she forgives me for being the one who killed her. Papa says it was an accident. But I was still the cause of it. That was the day my darkness settled over me.

I thought about throwing myself in the ground with her. But it wasn't the fear of going down into the grave that kept me from getting the shovel—I was afraid I might decide to never come back up. And I don't want to break what's left of Papa's heart.

Soon the worms that have slipped into her coffin will chew her body into dirt. I imagine them crawling through her crow-colored hair that looks like mine and eating away her lovely skin that was once smooth and white as a new-laid egg. My friend Effie Lenox thinks I shouldn't say such things. I said, if the truth is wrong, then what the Hell is right? Effie thinks I should imagine Mother in the next world, Heaven, dancing around on streets of gold. I love Effie and know she's sharp as needles, but that's bull.

When I die, I'd rather wake up here inside this world, become a part of it like the roots of the black walnut trees. Like the wild pawpaws and persimmons with their sweet smell as they rot in the ground, turning back into dirt, becoming something different, something new. I'd be the creek water that changes into mist and lingers in the hills, then rains on the fields, trickling down into the cracks where all the seeds hide. I don't want to leave this world. I want to go deeper into it.

Two hawks swoop over the rocky ledge above. They call to each other like old friends or lovers and glide in circles together over the valley, picking out their breakfast down below. Their hungry cries pierce me near the heart in the spot behind my ribs where my loneliness festers. Watching them soar side by side makes the wound throb, and I screech my own wild birdcall into the sky. It ricochets off the hills.

Then, down below in Stone Field, someone returns my birdcall. I about jump out of my skin. When I look toward the sorghum crop, my heart stops beating. I forget how to breathe. I'm struck like a slap to the cheek when I see the field.

I blink, but it's not my imagination. Great swirling lines curve and spiral through the rows of stalks as if God's played a boys' game, drawing giant circles in the cane field with His finger. The design stretches across five acres, as if it were meant to be seen from somewhere up high. It's beautiful and terrible at the same time. I wonder—did I make it myself when my mind was too dark last night to think straight? I don't think so. What does it mean?

My breath escapes me. A stranger sits on the black boulder in the middle of Stone Field, surrounded by cane. He's naked as Adam and Eve. And he's staring straight at me.

2

OUR DOG NAPOLEON STARTS BARKING FROM THE edge of the cane, warning Papa about the man in the field. Soon all our dogs join in. Their urgent voices bounce off the hills and crisscross over the hollow, howling for Papa to get his gun.

No.

I scurry back through the tunnel like a mole on fire. But the cave floor is slick, and I fall flat on my stomach, scraping the side of my head against the wall. I push the hair out of my face with my wet hands and crawl the rest of the way out. I race toward the field. Mud coats me like a second skin, drying and cracking as I run. I push myself faster so I can get there before Papa finds out what the stranger did and shoots him dead.

But when I round the hill, Papa's already standing in front of the field, ramming black powder and a bullet down the barrel of his gun. The stalks are too high for him to know about the crop design. He sees only a gap in the rows like a path entrance cut into the cane. He steps into the opening.

"Papa."

He glances over his shoulder. "Where've you been, Cat? Looks like the dogs dragged you under the porch."

"There's a man in Stone Field."

Papa pulls the hammer half-cocked and slips the cap into place.

I keep walking, hoping I can get ahead of him, into the gap. "But he doesn't need shooting—he needs dressing. And feeding, most likely."

Papa pauses as he holds the rifle. "I'll take care of this, Catrina. Get to the house."

"I can't." Something pulls me to the center of the field like iron to lodestone. I push the barrel of Papa's gun aside and pass by him, but at the last second, I grab it from his hands and run ahead of him into the narrow maze.

"Damn it, Cat!" Papa barks like the dogs at his heels. "Careful!" His heavy footsteps follow me into the gap.

The path is smoother than I thought. Padded. The stalks haven't been cut or removed, just bent near the bottom and pressed to the ground. The man didn't destroy any of Papa's cane. A path splits off to the left, but I keep going. I imagine myself moving through the design I saw from the bluff. Papa's footsteps hesitate behind me at the division, and I push my legs faster, trying to reach the bend ahead. As soon as it curves, a narrow branch splits off to the right and I take it.

My heart beats my blood so hard it comes thumping on my eardrums begging for mercy. The sharp blades of the cane slash my face and arms, but I keep running. Napoleon leads the other dogs to follow Papa past the split, away from me. They're headed into a spiraling circle. Papa's curses ring out from the northwest corner of the field when he realizes it's a dead end, but I'm almost to the black rock in the center of Stone Field.

I slow down when I hear singing. It comes from up ahead—a deep rumbly voice:

"Come, live with me and be my love
And we will all the pleasures prove
And if these pleasures may thee move
Then live with me and be my love."

The tune's strange, but I've read those words somewhere before, in one of Papa's books. His low voice sends a chill curling up my spine like a snake slithering up a pole.

I stop walking and peer through the stalks, straining for a glimpse of the stranger. For a moment I think I see him, his head and shoulders above the tall cane only a dozen paces away. I stumble several steps before I realize it's only the scarecrow that Henry put up last March.

"There will I make thee beds of roses
With a thousand fragrant posies
A cap of flowers and a kirtle
Embroidered all with leaves of myrtle."

As soon as I round the bend, I see him—a madman, sure as I'm born. He's naked and pacing around the rock like a restless mountain cat. I never saw a man with no clothes on before, and I can't stop staring at the parts of him I'm not supposed to see. He doesn't seem to notice. But even the parts of him that aren't private, like the place where the line of his neck turns into the slope of his shoulders, look like holy things that only gods and angels should be allowed to look at. I've never seen anyone as beautiful as him.

He's not much older than me. Little leaves twine through his black tangled hair, which hangs in his face and covers the back of his neck. His skin's neither pale like mine, nor midnight black like Effie's. He's dark but golden, like a copperhead glistening in the sun. I want to touch his sleek skin to feel if it's hot or cold. I want to see if he'll strike me like a snake. Lord, I'm mad as he is.

The stranger's voice rumbles like wheels on a gravelly road, traveling straight to me.

"A belt of straw and ivy buds
With coral clasps and amber studs
With gray feather of the dove
Oh, live with me and be my love."

He stops singing and turns his head toward me. I look up quick from glancing at his private parts, and his wild eyes meet mine. They speak a foreign language, but I understand it clear as day—they can see straight through me to the inside. They tell me I'm more naked than he is and the secret things inside my heart are showing.

The shock of it sends a thrill through my body that feels like both pleasure and fear. I've always wanted someone to look at me that way, but I never knew it would be so dangerous. My fingers remember the gun they clutch. The little hairs on my neck lift the way they do when there are lightning charges in the air from an approaching storm, but the sky is cloudless. I raise the rifle and point it at the madman's chest. "Who the Hell are you?"

He doesn't blink. He steps forward, as if the gun's an invitation, not a warning, and stands five paces from me. " 'We know what we are, but know not what we may be.' "

I've read those words—Ophelia says them in Papa's copy of *Hamlet*. My thoughts spin like a weather vane, and I can't tell which way the danger's coming from—him or me. I place my thumb on the half-cocked hammer. "I don't know what you are." I pull the hammer all the way back till it clicks. "But I know you may be a dead man mighty easy."

My heart pounds. Ophelia went mad and killed herself—she walked right into the river. I know how it feels to want something like that, wanting to walk right out of your troubles, to walk right out of your life. Is that what this stranger wants— to walk into my bullet? My fingers shake. I don't want to shoot him, I just want him to come closer to me like he did when I first raised the gun.

He does.

He steps so near to me that one shot would blow his troubled heart clean out of him. His eyes are deep water. Lord. I can see myself in them. Something makes me quiver as if an invisible spirit's running its fingers across my soul. My arms tremble, the rifle shakes in my hands. I'm not afraid of him anymore, I'm afraid of me. I want to put the gun down, but my fingers have clenched up tight and won't work.

"Catrina, put the gun down!"

Papa's voice strikes me like a bolt of lightning, and I feel like I'm exploding. But it's the gun in my hands, firing with a loud *crack* that splits the sky and echoes across the hollow. *Oh God.* My fingers turn numb, like they don't even belong to me, and the rifle slips away, falling to the ground with a soft thud. The smell of burnt sulfur fills the air. Black smoke hangs like a curtain between me and the stranger. As the smoke rises, the man sinks to his knees, his beautiful body crumpling at my feet like a dropped handkerchief.

In my stomach, a stone falls. Its weight drops me to the ground beside the madman. He's so near, I can smell the salt and sun of his body. I stare at his eyes. I saw myself in them, but now they've rolled back in his head, showing only the whites. Did I kill him? My hand shakes as I reach out to touch his face.

His golden skin burns hot as hellfire. Or is it mine? I can't tell the difference between us.

Papa kneels beside me.

"I didn't mean to—" My throat swells up.

"I know, Cat, I know." Papa's breath comes fast as his big hands travel over the hills and hollows of the man's muscles and joints, searching out the wound. "He ain't shot." It sounds more like a question. He says it again, stronger, to feel the truth of it better. "He ain't shot."

I didn't kill him. My body goes limp and shaky. I didn't kill him.

"Poor fellow. He's no thief—it's a mad fever that's got ahold of him. He's burning up." Papa shakes his head. "I'll get him to the house and you take the mule to fetch Effie Lenox to come doctor him."

"I won't."

"Cat—"

"I'll tend him myself." I don't care if Henry gets mad at me for disobeying or not being proper. I don't care about anything except saving the man I found in Stone Field. When I thought I killed him, it was like seeing Mother dead on the ground by the molasses press. If I can fill him back up with life, he can fill me up, too—I know it in my bones. He won't have to die like Mother. And neither will I.

I glance up at the hawks, still circling together above the bluff. "Don't try to stop me. I want to be with him."

3

PAPA DOESN'T TRY TO STOP ME, BUT AS SOON AS WE lay the man on the cot in his study and he covers him up so I won't see him naked anymore, Papa still runs off to fetch Effie. I start brewing some willow bark tea, using Mother's recipe for Fever Cure that's always helped Papa in his bouts of throat sickness. While the tea boils, I wash the stranger's burning face and neck with cool water from the well and prop his head up with a pillow. I pull Papa's reading chair up next to the cot and stare at the man from Stone Field.

The leaves in his hair make me think of Puck, the sprite from Papa's Shakespeare. But he doesn't look like a pesky little nature spirit. He looks strong and human. And handsome as the Devil. More like King Nebuchadnezzar from the Bible, who went crazy and wandered around naked in the wilderness like an animal because God got mad at him. Maybe God was jealous.

I pick the leaves out of his hair one by one, and stick them into mine like a wreath around my head as I cool his face again with the water. After I strain and cool the tea, I dip a clean rag in it and squeeze the drops between his lips. He's quiet and still as a dead man and it makes me all-overish. I grab Papa's pipe and pace the floor as I fill it with tobacco and light it with a stick from the stove. Papa used to try to keep me from smoking, but he knows it helps calm me when my darkness settles over my moods, so now he lets me be. I puff on the pipe as I scan the shelves for *Hamlet*.

The cover's worn soft from Papa's fingers. I sit down close to the Stone Field man with my knees up against his bed and look for the words he spoke to me in the cane. *We know what we are, but know not what we may be.* I blow a smoke ring toward him. His face fits perfectly inside the white round frame, just like a tintype photograph. I wish I could slip his image into the deep pocket of my trousers where I keep things I might need one day. The rings begin to fade as the smoke fills the space between us.

Damn it, God, don't You let him die. I pull and puff more smoke and read out loud the line I already know by heart. " 'To be, or not to be—' "

A low voice rumbles, " 'That is the question.' "

I can't see him through the smoke, but as it fades away, his image slowly appears. He opens his eyes and blinks at me. His eyes are the golden brown of barley ale, sweet molasses, dark honey. "I saw you." His voice is dry and rough like a croaking frog's. "In the cliff. You looked like a bird ready to fly away. I didn't want you to leave."

My hand shakes as I dip the rag in the cold water and squeeze him a drink. He's going to live. He has to. The man's eyes don't leave me once. They still have a glassy fire and look lit up from the inside. The fever's still got him. As I give him water, his hot lips brush against my fingers and make everything inside me shake and rattle like a tornado coming. "Who are you?" I ask.

"I don't know yet."

"Well, what's your name?"

His eyes scrunch up and he holds his head like it hurts to think. "I don't recall it. I don't recall a thing."

When the fever took him, it must have stolen his memory. But he remembers seeing me up in the cliff. I take another puff on the pipe and stare at him.

He blinks at me, and then props himself up on his elbow. "Who are *you*?" He stares at me strong and steady, like I'm the one who's the mystery, and he's the one to solve me. Lord. Maybe he is.

I glance out the window, not knowing how to answer. "Why did you make the circles in the cane?"

"So you'd look at them." He speaks slow, like he's trying to find the words. "I saw you up there . . . yesterday? I think it was yesterday—I'm not certain. It took me all night. The moon helped." He reaches out and takes the pipe from my hand. I feel a tiny charge of lightning when his fingers brush against mine. He puts the pipe in his mouth and takes a long pull. When he blows smoke rings, it looks like he's kissing the air between us. Soon it's full of swirls and spirals like the ones in Stone Field.

I take the pipe back. "You should rest."

"But what if I wake up and find out I only dreamed you and you're not real?"

My face feels strange when I smile—it's been so long, I'm surprised I remember how. "If I'm not real, then poor me." A leaf slips from my hair and falls into my lap.

He picks it up and tucks it back into my hair. "It'd be a poor situation for us both. I'd just have to go back to sleep and keep dreaming." His smile is slow, like deep water with a current so strong it pulls me right under. Everything in the world disappears except for him and me, and even when our words are gone, his eyes still speak.

His lips don't move, but I hear his rumbly voice in my head saying, *If the question's "to be or not to be," then the answer's "to be." As long as it's to be here, with you.*

My heart beats faster. His voice is in my head so strong, saying the exact same thing his eyes are telling me. I know it's him talking silent to me, and not my mind making things up. He wants to be with me, and I nod because I feel the same way.

His eyes get heavy and I know he needs resting. "Go to sleep. Let the Fever Cure work on you. You'll need to sleep ages, but when it's done with its work, you'll be all right." I reach out and squeeze his hand so what I said feels true and certain for him and for me, too. His eyes slide shut, but his smile stays put.

I hold his hand and gaze at the smooth golden skin of his arms and chest until I hear Papa and Effie ride up outside, and then I slide away to meet them on the porch. Papa looks worried and lost, but Effie's clutching her bag of fancy medicines that she won't even need now, and has that look of determination she always wears.

"Effie, he's asleep. We should let him rest. I gave him Mother's Fever Cure—that's all he needs for now."

She nods, but I know she won't be at ease until she's set eyes on him and decided what's what. I move aside and let her into the house. "Well, he's in the study if you want to see for yourself. But don't wake him."

Papa and I follow her through the house. The heels of her boots click like a timepiece against the wood floor. Wherever Effie is, without even saying a word, she makes people feel like she's in charge, and she's only twenty—three years older than me—and black as the slaves who live beyond the hills of Roubidoux. She marches right up to the man and feels his forehead. He doesn't move a smidgen, and keeps sleeping.

She clucks like a hen as she pulls the blanket back up over his naked chest and feels the sides of his neck, under his chin.

"His fever's still dangerously high. His glands are slightly swollen, too. We'll have to be diligent to keep his temperature lowered through the night, but if we can, he'll be fine, Lord willing."

I nod. Effie Lenox is the smartest person I know. She talks just like a book and she showed me how to read and write when I was five and she was eight. She's the one who got Papa interested in reading her father's library full of novels and poetry.

She's read the thick doctoring books that Mr. Lenox orders for her, cover to cover. If God had made Effie a man and given her paler skin, she'd have gone off to a fancy school to be a real doctor, sure as I'm sitting here. But even God can't stop Effie from learning more about doctoring than Him, if she sets her mind to it.

She's an expert on being proper and good, too, because her papa, Mr. Lenox, was a missionary. He met and married Effie's mama in the Congo, but the woman died there giving birth to Effie's little sister. Mr. Lenox is white as paste, but Mrs. Lenox had the same curly hair and black skin as Effie—her tintype's inside the locket that's hanging from Effie's neck, dangling over the Stone Field man.

"Hm." Effie peers at the man. "He looks as though he might be Mexican or perhaps Indian. In either case, I imagine he's far from friends and family." She holds her locket between her fingers with an anxious look on her face. "I hope he's able to leave soon and join them again. People here in Roubidoux won't know what to make of him and that may mean trouble for—"

I snort. "I don't give a damn what they—"

"My goodness!" Effie lifts the pan of Fever Cure I made. "What an odd concoction."

Lord, I hate when she interrupts me and changes the subject for no reason.

She sniffs the brew. "You come up with the strangest tonics, Catrina."

I cross my arms proud over my chest and sit back in the chair to smoke some more. "Well, who cares if it's your expensive store-bought pills or a witch's brew, as long as it makes him well?"

Stone Field man's eyes flutter open. For a moment, he smiles at me as if he heard what I said, and then his eyes slide shut again. Papa and Effie didn't even see. It makes me laugh out loud.

"Catrina Dickinson." Effie shakes her head and almost smiles. "You *are* a witchy girl—you think it's funny, carrying a strange man who wore next to nothing in from the field—"

"It wasn't 'next to nothing'—he was bare naked. And Papa helped me. Stonefield was too heavy for me to carry on my own or I would have done it."

"Stonefield?" Papa and Effie say it at the same time.

"He lost his name somewhere in the field. Maybe he can borrow that one till he finds his memory."

Stonefield mumbles, "I like it."

Effie looks at him like she smells a skunk, but Papa beams when he hears Stonefield's voice. I swear I never loved Papa more than I do right now. He smiles and pats the man on the shoulder. "Good to meet you, Stonefield. You can stay with us as long as you like."

Stonefield's eyes open again, looking past Papa and Effie at me for just a moment before his breathing turns heavy with sleep. And in that moment the look on his face lights up the whole world, like when lightning strikes at night turning everything clear as day. I could almost forget what my darkness feels like. And I'm so happy, I hardly even think about what Henry will do when he finds out.

4

STONEFIELD SLEEPS ALL DAY WITHOUT WAKING AS Effie and I keep his temperature lowered by changing the cloth on his head and bathing his arms and chest in cool water. Effie handles his body as if he's just an ordinary person with ordinary skin and muscles like you see every day. Doesn't she notice the strange weight of his arm in her fingers? It feels smooth as water and firm as stone at the same time. I'm surprised she can't sense the strength bottled up inside his shoulders. I feel a quiet power resting inside every muscle my hand brushes.

Every couple hours I give him another dose of Fever Cure. By late afternoon his fever breaks. Lord. Looks like God finally went and did something right. When Stonefield wakes and sits up with his dark hair ruffled and his eyes all sleepy, I want to reach out toward him, but Effie's watching, so I just speak to him in my head, without using my voice.

Stonefield, you fought the fever off. You came back to the Land of the Living.

He looks at me like he sees something written on my eyes, like he's reading words there.

I had to come back—you're here.

He heard me talking with him in his head, too. I'm certain it's real. Hearing him this way is a quicker path to my heart than hearing through the ears. His voice shoots straight to the center of me like an arrow.

Effie adjusts his pillow. "I've brought you some broth—it will help your strength return. All you need is some rest and you'll be perfectly fine."

I reach for the bowl. "I'll do it."

Effie says, "Catrina, you need to rest, too. You look . . . rumpled."

She glances at the mud still caked in my hair and on my clothes. I washed my hands and face earlier, but I don't have time for a bath. I take the bowl from her before she can sit down beside him.

"I think I know better than you when I need resting and when I need to keep on doing a thing."

Effie rolls her eyes as I sit down and start feeding him, but I just mind Stonefield. I like the way he leans in slow toward the spoon and takes it in his mouth as he looks steady at me. I don't know why, but every time I slide the spoon from his lips and he swallows, it sends my heart a-quivering.

As Stonefield finishes the broth, Papa walks through the door. He left earlier for the field to see what could be done about the bent stalks. When he sees Stonefield's well enough to eat, he nods and grins. Papa always says thousands more with his smile than he does with his words, and I know he's relieved to see that Stonefield's going to be all right. When Papa saw him lying like a dead person in the field, it must have flooded him with memories of finding Mother that way. All those painful thoughts gathered again over Stonefield. But now that he's alive and safe, it's like Stonefield saved Papa, not the other way around.

Stonefield starts looking sleepy again and lies back against his pillow. Papa shoos me and Effie from the study. "So the boy can sleep and the man can read in peace."

I don't think Papa even hears Henry's horse and wagon tearing into the yard a couple hours later. I jump up from the sitting room floor where I started dozing off while Effie read Proverbs out loud from the Bible like she does sometimes when she visits, because she knows I skip those whenever I read the Good Book.

When Henry walks through the front door, he's madder than hornets. "Damned insurrectionists won the battle! The Union troops retreated—they're headed back to Fort Rolla at this very moment. The whole nation's going to Hell." He throws the newspapers into the fire. I stare at them burning, the words curling up and melting. Henry always saves the papers so when we're done reading them we can stuff them in the walls for insulation or use them to cut sewing patterns.

"And have you seen Stone Field?" He wrings his hat like a dish towel. "Some kind of fool's been playing tricks in our sorghum. Looks like the work of a lunatic!"

I nod and glance at Effie, who's sitting quiet in the corner rocking chair listening, with the Bible open on her lap. Henry's so worked up he hasn't even noticed she's behind him.

He keeps going. "Bill Hoss was shooting rabbits up on his oak knoll this morning and saw the circles in our cane all the way from there. He rode down to tell me when he saw me coming home just now. Said it looked like the Devil's work, and now everyone around thinks our farm's been marked with an evil sign." His voice rises like it's climbing a mountain, getting higher and higher as he goes.

I know when he reaches the top he'll blow. I move to the window and sit on the sill with one leg in the house and the other outside so I can get away quick. But that only makes him madder.

"And look at you. You can't even sit properly. You're covered in mud and you've got leaves in your hair like you sleep in the woods. Damn it, I told you to stay home today, Cat! No wonder everybody's tongues are wagging about you, too."

"What do I have to do with it?"

Henry throws his hat into a chair and glares at me. "Bill's sister says you wooed the Devil and that's why he blazed a sign in our field—to show that you're his."

Lord, I can't help but laugh at that. "Dora Hoss is just a mush-minded girl." I get up from the window, pick up Henry's crushed hat, and press it back into shape. "She's got nothing in her head but nits." I put Henry's hat on my head, down low, over one eye. "What does it matter, anyway?"

His hands ball into fists. "Blazes, Catrina! You think Father and I can bring in the sorghum, the corn, and the barley all by ourselves? You know his heart's weak. If people say our farm's cursed, they won't want our help at harvest and they sure won't help us with our crops. It could ruin us." His face turns the color of a ripe red apple.

"Oh." My voice sounds tiny like the squeak of a mouse. I hadn't had the chance to think it through.

Henry looks like he wants to fling me out the window, or at least send me to my room without supper. But before he can yell anything else, Effie clears her throat and stands up from the rocking chair. That's all she has to do, and I know Henry won't do anything like that now.

When Henry turns toward her, the tension in his shoulders loosens just a whipstitch. He lets out a deep breath. "Oh, I beg your pardon, Miss Effie. I didn't realize."

She gives him a little nod and sets the Bible on the chair. She knows how to calm him down with just a look. It's always been that way. If Henry was a girl, Effie would be his best friend, not mine.

She walks over and takes the hat off my head and hands it back to him. "It wasn't the Devil who made the circles in the field, Henry. It was a young man, delirious from a dangerously high fever. Catrina saved his life—because of her care, his fever just broke. Your father's taken him in like a Good Samaritan. When everyone hears what really happened, they'll stop talking nonsense and forget all about it. Don't worry."

I love Effie for smoothing all the wrinkles from her voice and not telling Henry about me bringing Stonefield in naked. I want to hug her, but I just stand next to her and nod.

Henry stares at the hat in his hands. A line forms across his forehead like somebody plowed a tiny furrow in it. "Father should have spoken to me before taking in a stranger. What sort of man is he—a drifter? The Union Army's conscripting folks in St. Louis—maybe he's a secessionist, trying to run away to Springfield to join the Confederates. Or he could even be a criminal or a murderer for all we know."

I snicker.

"You won't think it's so funny, Cat, if he creeps to your bed in the middle of the night and slits your throat."

I imagine Stonefield coming to my bed in the middle of the night. But he doesn't creep. He walks tall and naked through the moonlit room. And instead of a knife, he's holding Papa's Shakespeare. I smile.

Effie narrows her eyes at me before turning to Henry. "We don't know what kind of man he is, and apparently, he doesn't either. He says he lost his memory from the fever. But he looks strong and able. When he's feeling better, he can earn his keep by helping you and your father take care of the farm."

Henry shakes his head and sighs heavily. "That must be what Father was thinking when he took him in—we could use a hand." The furrow on his forehead is still there, but it isn't quite so deep. He puts his hat back on. "I'll go over to the Hoss place and set them straight. Allow me to give you a ride home on my way, Miss Effie." He smiles at her, and when she smiles back and says, "Yes, thank you very much, Henry," he starts whistling a tune as he heads toward the front door.

Effie snaps her bag of medicines shut and turns to me before leaving. "I'll come by tomorrow to check on your guest."

I almost say that he only needs my care and a little sleep, and I want him all to myself, but I swallow those words. I just nod my head and make myself say what Mother would have said. "Thank you, Effie. That's mighty kind of you."

5

STONEFIELD SLEEPS THE REST OF THE EVENING AND into the night. I get up with a grease lamp every so often and poke my head into the study, quiet, just to look at him. I like to watch when his eyes move back and forth under their lids. I wonder what he dreams about if his memory's still gone. I wonder if he's dreaming about me.

Even though Stonefield's still sleeping in the morning, Henry makes Papa wait until Effie arrives late in the day before they go mend the sorghum field. He says it's not proper for me to be home when there's a strange man in the house unless we have a chaperone. After they greet Effie and she checks on Stonefield, Henry invites her to stay for supper later. Of course she accepts, and when Papa and Henry head to the field, I'm stuck with her. I love Effie, but Lord, I just want her to go.

I can't stop fidgeting. I glance toward the study. I feel him tugging me back to him like there's a rope between us with him tied on one end and me on the other. I move toward the study door.

Effie sighs. "Catrina." She shakes her head. "Stonefield isn't going anywhere. Let him rest. Sleeping is what his body needs to get his strength back. I'm sure he'll surprise us all with his improvement when he wakes up. I can tell that you want to make a friend of him, but he's a complete stranger. It's important that he find his family and friends as soon as possible. The newspapers are full of talk about Indians lately and it causes irrational fears. There are people in Roubidoux who might treat someone like him, someone different, as a novelty, but most people will just want him gone."

"Oh, Effie, how do you know? You always think bad things will happen. What does it matter to those people who Stonefield is? He can stay here with us and do whatever he wants—they can't stop him."

Effie just shakes her head like she's continuing her argument in her mind but won't say it out loud because she thinks I'm too dense to understand it.

It burns me up.

She clears her throat. "If we're going to have supper ready by the time your father and brother get back, we should get started. What are we having?" Effie's always suspicious of my cooking, for no good reason.

"It's a surprise." I head toward the back door, anxious to find a way to see Stonefield without her knowing.

"Well, where are you running off to?"

"I have to go hunt down some ingredients." I turn the doorknob. "How about you make the cornbread and potatoes while I'm gone."

"How about you hurry back and help. And you still haven't taken a bath! You should wash the mud off yourself—you look like a pig."

Before she can say anything else, I slip outside and shut the door behind me. I watch Effie through the window as she walks to the kitchen, shaking her head at the mess she sees. As soon as she gets there, I run around the house to the study window and peer through the pane. Stonefield lies on the cot with his back toward me.

I drum my fingertips against the glass and Stonefield turns right around like he knew I was coming. His hair's ruffled and his eyes are bright as he sits up. He grins at me and starts to get out of bed. I point to the set of Henry's old clothes that I laid next to the pillow and I watch as he puts them on. Every muscle and tendon in his body's strung tight as a fiddle string, yet he moves so slow and easy. Lord, how can the same pants and shirt that hung on Henry's body look so different on Stonefield? It's like the clothes were sleeping and now they're awake. Watching the way he moves makes something inside me tremble like a blade of grass in the breeze.

He comes to the window and presses his nose flat against the glass. I clamp my lips shut so Effie can't hear me laughing at the face he's making. He lifts the window and leans out.

"Catrina."

I hear my name every day, but not the way he says it. He makes it sound like a precious jewel cradled in the palm of his hand.

"Stonefield. How do you feel?"

"New. Like I was just born."

"Then come with me."

Before I finish the words, he's climbing out the window. He doesn't even ask me where I'm going, but that rumbly voice of his that I hear in my head says he doesn't care as long as we're together.

I grab a gunnysack from the shed and take off through the backyard toward the woods. He's right behind me. Dry leaves crunch under our feet until we reach the quiet of soft moss. We're almost to the creek. I feel him reach out and touch the ends of my hair, whipping in the wind, and he catches hold like it's a horse's mane and pulls me back against him. I laugh at the sharp-alive feel of it. We've stopped running, but still, we can barely catch our breath. His fingers get tangled in my hair, but he doesn't try to get loose. He holds on tighter. The stern lines of his face make him look wild as a wolf. He could break my neck with a jerk of his hand, but his eyes and his touch tell me he'd never hurt me in a thousand years.

"Stonefield." I like to say it. The name sounds hard and gentle at the same time. Dark cold rock and soft warm earth like our sorghum field.

He smiles. I want to run my fingers over his lips to memorize it. I want to keep him smiling like that forever.

"Effie says I'm dirty as a pig."

He laughs. "Effie sounds very observant."

"There's a swimming hole under that weeping willow."

Stonefield glances at the creek and laughs again. "Looks like a good place to wash a pig."

I laugh, too, as I work at pulling his fingers from my hair. He tightens his grip. "But what if you're a water nymph, trying to escape me?

> *"'You nymphs, call'd Naiads, of the winding brooks,*
> *With your sedged crowns and ever-harmless looks,*
> *Leave your crisp channels, and on this green land*
> *Answer your summons; Juno does command:*
> *Come, temperate nymphs, and help to celebrate*
> *A contract of true love; be not too late.'"*

"If you don't let me go, I'll be too late to help Effie and she'll want to skin me."

"Well, I don't want to be the cause of a water nymph's gruesome death." He loosens his fingers on my hair, and I pull away, still laughing.

I bolt to the willow, part its branches like a curtain, and duck inside. When the curtain falls back into place, light seeps through the little gaps and I see Stonefield staring back at me. I want him to see all of me, the way I saw him naked in the field. I take off my shirt and pants as we watch each other. I like the way he looks at me, like his eyes are touching me. I can almost feel his gaze on my skin. But when he moves toward the willow branches, my heart starts thumping hard and sudden like it wants free from my ribs. It startles me and I step quick into the cool shady water of the creek under the willow's canopy.

It's like stepping into another world. The water laps at my thighs, beckoning me in. It drinks me up like cold ale and swallows me as I sink to the pebbly bottom. I push off and swim underwater until I think I've cleared the willow's sweeping branches. When I come up and feel the air kiss my skin, the world seems more alive than I remember.

Stonefield's unspoken words float over the water into my head. *What are you doing, water nymph?*

He watches as I swim to a log jutting across the middle of the creek. A giant bullfrog sits there with its back to me. I'm a cottonmouth snake, gliding up behind it slow and quiet. I strike, sweeping the stunned frog off its perch, and hold it up for Stonefield to see.

"Catching some supper. Throw me the gunnysack."

He grins and throws it to me. "I should've known naiads would serve something like frog legs for supper."

I hunt down more bullfrogs while Stonefield watches from the bank. He hums the tune he sang in the cane field, the one asking the girl to come live in the wild with him and be his love. They'll make their clothes out of leaves and feathers and sleep in beds of flowers.

I smile to myself. The song reminds me of my wild work. I've never shown it to anyone before, but maybe I will show it to Stonefield. Maybe tomorrow. My heart beats faster at the idea of sharing my secret with him.

It takes me a while, but I catch four more fat frogs to put in my sack and swim back to the willow tree. As the cool air hits me, my whole body tingles, but it's not just the breeze over my skin, it's Stonefield's gaze that makes my breath come faster. Under the canopy, I hum Stonefield's song and smile at him as he watches me wring out my hair and tug my clothes on over my wet skin. Before I can do up all my buttons, his strong arm shoots through the branches and hooks my waist. Stonefield yanks me through the curtain into the sunlight, just as easy as I snatched the bullfrogs out of the water.

"I caught the biggest one." He loses his balance from pulling me toward him and we both fall down on the mossy creek bank, laughing. I like the firmness of his arm around me and the rise and fall of his chest on my back, and the moss under my side. I lie against him, feeling his heart beat under his bones and skin. It's the same rhythm as mine.

"Stonefield." I turn to face him. "When you walked toward my gun in Papa's field, were you wanting a bullet to stop your heart from beating?"

Stonefield stays quiet for several moments, thinking. Waiting to hear what he says is torture. I've never wanted to know someone's thoughts as much as I want to know his.

He props himself up on one elbow. "I didn't care about the bullet," he says. "There was something I wanted more."

"What was it?"

"The same thing you wanted when you pointed the gun at me."

"I wanted you not to go," I say.

"It was the same for me. I would rather you had shot me dead than have to leave you behind."

"Stonefield, I feel as if I know you."

He nods. *From ages ago*, he says to me without his voice. He moves a strand of wet hair away from my eyes. "I think I must have been looking for you."

I smile. The things he's telling me are so similar to what I feel, it seems as if he's speaking my own thoughts for me.

He plucks a little pebble from the bank and turns it over in his fingers.

"What do you have?" I uncurl his fingers. The creek stone has a tiny hole through its center.

"I think it's a magic seeing stone. It finds the beauty in the world, no matter where you are." He lifts it to his eye and smiles as he looks at me through the opening. "Yes, this is definitely a magic seeing stone." He hands it to me.

I lift it to my eye and squint through the opening. Everything else in the world disappears at once except for Stonefield's earnest face framed in the circle. His tangled hair hangs in his eyes, and his grin is the happiest, most peaceful thing I ever saw. I place the image, the moment, into the treasure box of my memory. In the future, whenever I raise it to my mind's eye, I'm certain everything else will vanish just as it does now.

I rummage in my deep pockets to find a piece of yarn and thread it through the pebble's hole. When I lift it to my neck, Stonefield takes the ends from me, and I hold up my hair so he can tie the necklace for me in the back. As I let go of my hair, it falls over his arms like water. He gathers it gentle and lets it run through his fingers, his hands trailing slow down my shoulders as if he doesn't want to be done with his task.

I close my eyes, wishing I could feel it all over again. When

I turn back to him, the world seems to have shifted just a speck, like I can see things I've never noticed before. Everything seems different, clearer, now that his seeing stone rests over my heart.

"Listen," I whisper.

For a moment, all we hear is the rush of the water and our own breathing, coming fast and heavy. But then I hear it again—a voice in the distance calling my name.

"It's Effie." I get to my feet. "She'd skin you if she saw you running around so soon after having a fever. She thinks you should sleep for days."

Stonefield waves the idea away like he's shooing off a fly. "I can sleep when I'm dead." He smiles, and the corners of his eyes crinkle up. I want to touch his face.

Effie calls my name again, closer this time, and Stonefield gets to his feet.

I pick up the gunnysack. "I'll go first, and you wait here a few minutes. I'll get her to the kitchen so you can get back into bed." Water from my hair drips down my forehead to my lips. I lick the bead and taste the wet earthy tang of river and grass on my tongue. *I don't want to go.* I say the words to him without speaking.

Neither do I.

Feeling him say it sends a thrill up my spine. He takes my hand. "But adieu, sweet water nymph. Until we meet again."

When he kisses my fingertips, the whole world trembles. No, it's just my knees shaking. Lord. I turn and run back through the woods, my wet hair slapping my back and my heart pounding my ribs like a fist against a door.

Effie's hands are on her hips when I get to the yard and she frowns at the undone buttons on the old shirt of Henry's that I always wear and how I never bother wearing any underclothes beneath it. "Catrina, Henry's home. He's putting away the wagon."

"Already? Seems like I just left."

"Where have you been? I could have finished having dessert and tea with my father and sister by now if I'd gone home for supper."

"You can have dessert here—I made shoofly pie the other day." I try to catch my breath. "I bet your sister doesn't even know how to make shoofly pie."

Effie doesn't seem impressed. "I could be playing 'Heavenly Bliss' for them on my father's pianoforte this very minute."

Lord, she's crabby today. I wish I could make her happy as I am, make her feel what I feel—like I'm flying in a sky of sunshine. "You can still have some music after supper, Effie—I'll play the fiddle for you." I laugh as I imagine Effie and Stonefield dancing a jig.

She sighs. "Catrina, there's no butter churned or linens washed for the table. Sometimes I wonder if you ever think of anybody but yourself."

The heaviness of her words hits me like a blow to the heart. I want to tell her I've been thinking of Stonefield ever since I first saw him and there's been no room in my head for anything else. But I swallow up my excuse and say, "I'm sorry, Effie," and give her a peck on the cheek as I hurry past her into the house to make it up to her. I start whistling "Oh! Susanna" and grab the slop bucket and a knife.

Effie follows me in and crosses her arms over her chest. She raises an eyebrow when the sack moves. "Catrina Dickinson, what in Heaven's name are you making for supper?"

6

*A*T THE SUPPER TABLE, HENRY AND EFFIE keep glancing at Stonefield like he might steal the spoons or sprout another head when they're not looking. And Henry won't stop badgering our guest about his memory.

"Now, you say you don't recall a thing about yourself or anything before Catrina found you, not even how you came to be in our field, is that so?"

Stonefield's eyes always find mine. Even when he answers, he says it to me, not Henry. "'Memory, warder of the brain, shall be a fume, and the receipt of reason a limbic only.'"

I laugh, and Papa smiles at the book-words, but Henry frowns and keeps going. "Well, it seems a person would remember *something*. I don't understand how a whole life could be washed away like it never even happened."

"Henry." Effie moves her drumstick to the side of her plate with her fork. "It's a real condition caused by trauma to the brain, called amnesia. Stonefield's extreme fever is probably to blame. It's possible that soon his memory will return to him."

I spoon a heap of Effie's creamed potatoes onto Stonefield's plate. "Well, what matters is he's here. Maybe it's not so bad to have the past emptied out of a person's head—it might make more room for the here and now." I wish I could empty my past from my head. If I could forget what I did to Mother, then maybe all my darkness would spill out and leave my mind clean and free like Stonefield's.

Henry sounds annoyed. "I'm just surprised he isn't more upset about it."

Stonefield looks up and says in his low voice, " 'What's gone and what's past help should be past grief.' "

Henry looks like he just sucked a lemon.

But Papa's face turns thoughtful and a little sad. He nods and says, "Mr. William Shakespeare told the gospel truth when he wrote that, but it's not always easy. Memory makes it hard."

I can tell he's thinking of Mother, and it causes something sharp to rise in my throat, so that my eyes water when I try to swallow. Papa pats Stonefield's shoulder. "If your past was full of grief, then losing your memory could be a blessing, son." Papa never pats Henry on the shoulder like that. Henry's turning so hot at hearing Papa call a stranger *son*, I swear I can almost see steam coming out his ears and nose.

He stiffens up and sets his jaw all tight, but Stonefield just smiles at Papa and reaches for another fried frog leg. Effie wrinkles her nose as he takes a big bite.

"Catrina." Stonefield's voice is quiet. "This is the most delicious thing I ever tasted." He grins and adds, "Well, at least it's the most delicious thing I *remember* tasting."

Papa's face lights up and he laughs. It's been so long since I've heard him laugh that my heart swells and I think it might burst. Stonefield makes everything brighter than it's been for ages.

Except Henry's not laughing with us. He's glaring at Stonefield, his body rigid but shaking a little. He turns to Effie, like he's looking for a steady place to find his bearings. Effie's hand moves toward Henry's on the table like she's going to touch him, but she flattens her palm next to her plate and clears her throat. She turns to Stonefield instead. "It appears you're familiar with the works of Shakespeare. That's extremely rare in these parts. My father has collected a nice library over the years and offers his books to anyone in Roubidoux, but I'm afraid only Mr. Dickinson has ever taken him up on the offer."

Papa nods at Effie. "Cat sometimes reads the books your father gives me, but Henry never seems to find the time."

Henry winces.

"It is strange that Shakespeare's words survived Stonefield's memory loss," Effie says when she sees how Papa's gentle words hurt Henry, moving the conversation away from him. "Perhaps he is a student of literature, or a tutor."

Henry sniffs. "Or a traveling stage actor." He talks about Stonefield as if he isn't even here. "From down south, near Mexico, I expect."

Effie tries to make her voice soft and pleasant. "It may be true that he is far from home. Perhaps Mexico or the Indian Territories. It's impossible to know at this point."

But Effie's words only give fuel to my brother's fire. "You

know, down in Alabama, there's talk of building a whole in-sane asylum just for Indians. I read about it last week. Seems Indians can't figure out how to be civilized like normal folks and the effort of it makes them go crazy."

His rudeness turns my skin hot.

"Now, son—" Father starts.

"Henry—" Effie's eyes plead with him to stop.

Lord. I drop my frog leg on my plate. "Not everything is a story out of one of your newspapers!" My voice is so loud, it makes Effie jump. If Mother were here, she'd never let Henry treat a guest this way. And he's the one who's always saying that *I'm* not being proper!

Effie, who never fidgets, looks as nervous as a long-tailed cat in a room full of rocking chairs. She clears her throat. "I've heard St. Louis is quite a diverse city—people from all over the world live there, yet it's only a couple days' journey from Roubidoux. It's possible that Stonefield's from there."

"Who knows where he's from or who he is," Henry mutters.

Stonefield acts like he doesn't hear him. He takes another bite.

I know who you are, I say to him in my mind.

His voice is as close as my own thoughts. *I'm Stonefield.* He reaches his hand across the table and touches the tips of my fingers.

Henry leaps to his feet, knocking over his chair, making me jump. "How dare you take liberties with my sister!" He looks like he's going to grab Stonefield right out of his seat, but he stops when Effie rises and comes to my side.

She slides my hand away from Stonefield's and holds it. I know she can tell that I want to touch him as much as she wants to touch Henry and I brace myself for the sermon she'll give us, but instead, she squeezes my hand real gentle and says, "Henry, I'm sure Stonefield didn't mean any harm. Catrina did save his life. A person would surely have warm feelings after such an experience and want to express their appreciation." She turns to Papa. "Don't you agree, Mr. Dickinson?"

Papa blinks, flustered. He's not used to having to make decisions. Mother was always the one to say what's what. "Well." He scratches his head. "I suppose if I'd been whisked away from the edge of death . . . Yes, I'm sure I'd want to kiss the hand that did the whisking."

Henry's face is red, but he sets his chair upright and turns back around slowly, nodding his head toward Effie. "I beg your pardon, Effie. I shouldn't have raised my voice." He sits back down and puts his napkin in his lap. "Maybe a better way for Stonefield to show his appreciation would be to put his hand to some work."

"Yes, that's an excellent idea," Effie says. "But not yet. He really should be in bed." As she returns to her seat she says, "Stonefield, your body seems to be recovering quickly, but you need more time to mend, don't you agree?"

Stonefield doesn't answer—he's turning her words over in his head in a quiet way.

But I can tell his silence makes Henry want to hit the table with his fist. I say, "I don't know, Effie, he looks as healthy as you and he looks thousands stronger than Henry."

Henry glares at me.

"Well." Effie speaks up to keep me and Henry from fighting. "It's best if he rests longer to give his body a chance to heal itself completely." She raises her chin, proud-like, to show me she knows what she's talking about.

I decide not to argue with her, because if Stonefield doesn't have to be out working on the farm, it means he can be with me.

Papa takes the last frog leg off the platter. "Well, I'm sure Stonefield will be in perfect health before too long. His help will be the most useful at harvest, anyhow—it's going to be a big one, what with all this rain, eh, Henry?"

Henry's face brightens, and for the first time tonight, he smiles at Papa. The thought of a good harvest cools him off a bit. He nods at Papa. "Biggest one in years, I'd say."

Effie's voice is animated. "That reminds me—you know my father's been talking about having a church built in Roubidoux before harvest—part of his dream to make the Roubidoux area into a bona fide township, now that he's retired from missionary work? Well, it looks as if his dream will come true after all. His friend Reverend Preston, a traveling preacher, has agreed to help us build it and a small parsonage. He arrives tomorrow, and the building should be done by the end of September. And he's staying on as minister when it's finished. A real church!"

Papa leans forward. His eyes light up. "Will there be hymn shouting? I always thought it'd be nice to hear a big group of people singing out the same song at the same time, loud enough so God can hear it through the rafters."

"Yes! Father says Reverend Preston knows lots of hymns—he

has a whole book of them. He even writes his own when he gets the inspiration."

Henry sits up straighter in his chair. "A church." He nods. "That's exactly what we need to start transforming Roubidoux into a real town, Effie."

She leans toward him. "It's a shame we've been without one for so long. And the building could be used as a school during the week, if we can convince enough people that we need one and get them to spare their children from their chores for just a few hours a day." She turns to me. "Don't you think having a real church with a real preacher is exciting, Catrina?"

The thought of sitting still, all cooped up with a load of people, and having to listen to somebody shout about God for hours doesn't suit me, but I like the spark in Effie's eyes, so I smile back at her. "Maybe you could be the schoolteacher, Effie."

She turns quiet and stares at the table.

Oh Hell. Folks wouldn't want her to be the one teaching their children. Sometimes I forget. Effie says that's because I'm self-centered and don't pay attention to what's happening around me, but I say it's because I'm just good at minding my own business and maybe she should try it. But I'm not stupid. Most people think Effie's papa's wrong for marrying a black woman in the Congo and for bringing his black babies back to America to live with him as daughters. Effie and her sister are the only black people that folks in Roubidoux have ever seen, but everybody knows that a person with dark skin isn't supposed to teach things to people with pale skin, even if she is the smartest person in Roubidoux. I bet God doesn't agree with that, because if He did, Effie would never have crossed Him by teaching me to read.

She sits up straight, her head held high. "Teaching is important, but it's not my particular vocation. Perhaps Reverend Preston could be persuaded to teach as well as preach." She smiles. "We'll find out soon enough."

Henry's been hanging on her words, and when she pushes her plate away with the frog leg untouched, he puts his knife and fork down. "It's getting late. I better take Effie home," he says, standing. "We don't want Mr. Lenox to worry."

I haven't even had a chance to play the fiddle for her or serve the shoofly pie, but she must have forgotten because she stands up from the table, too. "Yes, thank you, Henry. And thank you, Mr. Dickinson, for having me. And, Catrina, thank you for supper. It was . . . interesting."

Papa rises from his chair as Henry offers Effie his arm and leads her to the door like he's courting her. I raise my eyebrows at Stonefield and he raises his at me. I want to laugh, but I swallow it and cough instead.

"Good night," Effie says. "I'll come by tomorrow morning right after breakfast to visit and see how Stonefield's doing." What she really means is she'll come by tomorrow to make sure I'm behaving proper with Stonefield and to keep me away from him.

Lord, let her try.

As if Henry can read my thoughts, he turns to me and says, "Now, Cat, remember that Father's to be chaperone while I'm out, and you're not to run off." He nods at Papa before he turns to take Effie's arm.

Oh Lord.

After they leave and supper's cleared, I go to the mantel and take down my fiddle. Tonight I feel like music is just what we need. Mother's father, Grandpa Wells, gave me the fiddle when he was still alive. He taught me his songs back when I was little. But I don't like to play for the spring and harvest dances where people come to show off like peacocks. I like to play for people who let the music dig under their skin and cut into their soul. The sharp achy notes pull up the weeds growing inside and shake off the dirt to make room for new things. Tonight I want to feel the music shake me again.

As soon as I start playing "The Cuckoo," I can tell Stonefield's just like me. The music takes hold of him right off. His eyes slide shut and his body rocks from the good kind of pain. I swear I can hear his heart beating the same as mine. I feel so happy now, I switch to "Little Liza Jane," and Stonefield taps his heel and slaps his thigh to the rhythm. He looks at me like he wants to swing me around the room. I wish I could play the fiddle and dance with him at the same time.

Next is "Black River." Near the end, Papa puts his pipe down and opens his desk drawer. I hold my breath as he feels for the secret catch way in the back. When it releases, he opens the hidden compartment and pulls out his harmonica, which he stuffed in there after my mother died. He hasn't played it since. The surprise of seeing it in his hands makes my bow stop with a screech.

He blows the dust out of the harmonica with a loud burst of notes. "Play a lively one, Cat."

Stonefield grins. "High diddle diddle, the Cat played the fiddle."

Seeing both of them smiling at me that way flips my heart inside out so all the happiness in there shows. I laugh as I call the next tune. " 'Devil's Dream'!" Henry hates it because of the name, but it's one of my favorites. As soon as I start playing, and Papa's harmonica joins in, the leaping music takes hold of my feet and I can't keep still. I spin and twirl around the room as I play the fiddle, imagining I'm blazing circles in the floorboards like the circles Stonefield made in the cane.

Stonefield's face blurs past me as I turn around and around the room. Then he's out of his chair and behind me, his hands on my waist, his feet following mine as I play, and we dance. I've never seen partners dance a jig this way before, but Lordy, I like it. His hands are hot coals resting right above my hips, making my insides start to boil. When he laughs in my ear, it sounds low and deep, like Roubidoux Spring bubbling up from under the ground, and it makes me want to jump right in.

Papa's face is red and sweaty. He's huffing away on the harmonica so fast I'm afraid he'll lose his breath. Almost as soon as I think it, it happens. Papa starts to cough, clutching his left shoulder like he's in pain. The harmonica slips from his hand and clanks onto the floorboards. I toss the fiddle into a chair and run to his side at the same time Stonefield reaches him. Good thing, too, because Papa stumbles backward and we have to catch him.

"Papa!"

We pull him onto the cot in the study. The stiffness in his arms relaxes a little and he stops coughing.

"I'm all right, Cat." He pats my hand and nods at Stonefield as he tries to catch his breath. "I'm just getting too old for this."

My heart's racing. I squeeze his hand hard. "Please don't play anymore, then, Papa. I like to hear it, but it's not worth the risk of making you ill."

"Oh, I'm all right." He pats my hand again, firmer this time. "What's the use of living if a man can't enjoy himself every once and again?" He runs his big hand over my hair like he used to when I was little and Henry and I would sit by the fire while Mother spun yarn and Papa spun tales about selkies, giants, and fairies.

His smile reassures me and slowly makes my heartbeat go back to normal. By the time I help him to his bed and blow out his candle, Henry's already come home, earlier than I expected. He's usually in a good mood after visiting with Effie and her family because he loves to hear Mr. Lenox tell about his days as a missionary and how he wants to help make a civilized town out of Roubidoux, but tonight Henry comes storming into the house like a thundercloud and flings his coat into the corner.

"What happened?" I ask.

"It's nothing."

There's nothing that makes me madder than *nothing*. "It's something," I say. "Damn it, Henry, what the Hell is it?"

"Stop talking like a man, Cat. Where's Father? You know you

can't be with *him* without a chaperone." He jerks his head toward Stonefield.

"Papa wasn't feeling well—"

Henry scowls at us and takes large strides to the kitchen.

"Was Mr. Lenox mad we kept Effie so late?" I ask.

"No!" Henry's voice is full of heat. "And I don't want to hear about Effie," he yells, flinging open the cellar door and stomping down the steps. When he comes back up, he's got the last jug of ale we brewed at harvest hooked on his finger. Henry hardly ever drinks. "What are you gaping at?" He glares at Stonefield. "Have you finally run out of other people's words and can't come up with any of your own?"

Stonefield's expression doesn't change. He stares cold at Henry for a moment, then turns without a sound, walks into the study, and shuts the door.

"You go to your room, too, Cat." Henry's face darkens. "Or I'll throw your little stone back out into the field where you found it." He carries the jug to his room and slams the door.

7

IN THE MORNING, AFTER BREAKFAST, EFFIE DOESN'T COME. She always does what she says she'll do, so something's wrong. Henry knows what it is, but he won't talk to me. He just lies in his room like an old dog and only stumbles out of bed to fetch water or to use the outhouse. If he was the old Henry, I'd go in and make him tell me, and he would. I'd make him talk till all the poison seeped out of him and I could make him grin again. Then he'd toss my hair, which meant the same thing as a hug. But none of that will happen now.

I'm so tired. I didn't sleep well. I woke with an empty feeling in my belly that I tried filling with biscuits and gravy, but nothing takes it away. A crow caws outside. The sound sends a shiver down my back. I wish Stonefield and Papa would get up. When I checked on Papa earlier, he was sleeping easy, so I didn't have the heart to wake him. I keep imagining Effie wagging her finger, saying, *Let them rest so they can mend.*

I feel alone even though I'm not the only one here. That's the way it was when visitors filled the house after Mother's funeral—everyone walked around quiet as ghosts. The thought brings my darkness with it. My darkness stays away when Stonefield's near, but when he's not, it comes creeping back in.

Stonefield. I call to him in my head. *Stonefield, please come to me.* But the door to the study doesn't open. This house feels like a chicken coop. I walk out the front door and don't stop. I climb Hudgens Hill, skirt the cemetery, and head down into Hudgens Hollow where Roubidoux Creek branches off into a little stream.

The air's cooler here. I breathe in the fresh green scent of river water and ferns and the sweet smell of rotting leaves turning into dirt. Nobody comes here anymore. All the Hudgenses died years ago and people think the hollow's haunted. That's why no one's bought the land. It's not really haunted, though, except by me. This is where I do most of my wild work.

One day when I was little, I sat in a meadow by myself picking wildflowers and carried them in my apron to the creek branch where the holes in the large smooth rocks were full of water, making little pools. I filled each pool with flowers—one with sun-colored dandelion heads, another with flaming red jewelweed, one with larkspur as blue as the sky, and another with purple violets. It took ages, but when I stood back and saw the water rushing between the gray stones that held those perfect circles of bright color, I thought my heart might stop beating at the beauty of it.

I've been making things ever since with vines, thorns, leaves, stones, clay, sticks, flowers, water—I've got all the things I need right here. Once I worked all day piling flat round rocks like stacks of flapjacks through the woods. When I finished, the hollow was full of tall stone pillars standing like silent guardians among the oak trees. They're still here.

Most of my work fades if the wind and rain don't scatter it, or it falls apart and rots back into the ground, becoming something new and different. I like watching it change and slip away, but I wish I could share with someone the beauty of that fragile in-between moment when it's not quite mine and not quite nature's—the magical time before it disappears. I should have shown Mother my wild work. She would have understood.

My work from several days ago is still here. Hundreds of curling tendril vines dangle from tree branches, each with a little feather pinned to its end with a thorn. I collected the feathers all year. Red, brown, black, blue, white, gray, yellow. I walk under the trees with my hands in the air and let the soft slips of shimmering color brush against my fingers as I pass. I wish Stonefield were here. I run my finger over the pebble necklace he gave me.

When I think of him, I know what I'll make next. But the thunder rumbling in the distance means I have to hurry or it will wash away before I'm finished. I run to the woods. All the cold night rains and sunny days have started to turn the color of some trees early. The sassafras has gone from green to gold with a tinge of red creeping in. I fill my pockets with leaves and carry them to the stream. I already know which rock I'll use before I get there—the smooth flat one the size of a wagon wheel.

The thunder gets louder as I sit on the bank near the boulder. The smell of approaching rain fills the air. I work fast, cutting away pieces of the leaves with my fingernails and wetting them so they'll stick to the rock. I use the golden strips and red slivers to make a flaming version of Stonefield's circle design. The image has been burning in my thoughts ever since I first saw it in the cane field.

I stand and gaze at the swirling lines of bright gold. For a moment, I think the dark rock's cracking and light's shining out from its insides. It blinds me like a flash of white lightning. I feel dizzy, but I don't want to rest—I want to make more wild work as this one gets washed away. The rain will be here in a whipstitch. If I hurry, I can do some rain work. I turn and climb up onto my rain stone, a huge smooth rock bigger than me, and lie down on my back, my arms and legs spread out, my face to the sky. The rain will help me form the image I want to make on the rock.

Now. The drops hit me like little fists. Sometimes, rain can beat the bad thoughts far away from me. Its soft wet blows almost make me forget that Stonefield's not here beside me and that Effie didn't come like she said and that Henry's hiding drunk in his room. I try to imagine instead the raindrops turning from little fists into a thousand little kisses. If I can, they might make me forget that Mother's gone and will never come back. And that it's my fault.

The moment I am able to imagine the little fists turning into kisses on my skin, Stonefield's laugh rumbles deep in my head. But it's so clear, I can't tell if I'm hearing it with my ears or my mind. I open my eyes. He's standing by my rain stone, smiling like the sun.

"Catrina."

My heart comes alive every time he says my name. I smile back at him, blinking through the rain. He holds out a hand to help me up, but I wave it away. "I'm not finished yet."

He doesn't ask what I mean, but nods and waits like he already knows. I stay still until the gray surface of my rain stone turns completely black except for where I'm lying, then I reach for his hand, and he pulls me to my feet. His warmth courses through my cold fingers as I jump down beside him. We laugh at the silhouetted image I left behind on the wet rock. The strange, skinny rock girl looks surprised, with her arms, legs, and hair all spread out that way. Slowly, the girl disappears as the blackness of the rain swallows her up. But this time, I'm not alone when she goes. Stonefield's hand is large and firm around mine. I feel the hot blood flowing under his skin. I'm not a cold stone girl. I'm full of something bright and burning.

He walks to my circle design and squats beside it, tracing what's left of it with his finger. We watch as the rain pushes the last of the leaves from the rock into the creek. As they float away, the golden strips look like little flames flickering on the surface of the water.

Catrina, he says, silent, as he looks up at me. *Show me more.*

I think a flock of tiny thistle birds lives under my breastbone and they're all beating their wings at once. No one's ever asked to see what I do in the woods. No one's ever looked so hungry and thirsty for more of me like Stonefield does. I take his hand and pull him to his feet.

He follows me over the stones, into the woods. Rain pelts our faces and soaks our clothes. We weave between the stone guardians toward my feather vines. When he sees them, Stonefield stops and stares, slowly turning to take everything in. Raindrops hit the feathers, making them twirl and spin.

I spin, too. I turn around and around until the whole world blurs. Stonefield, the sky, the woods, the dirt, the rain—we all melt together. It reminds me of the thaumatrope Henry bought for me at the county fair when I was little—when I twisted the strings in my fingers, the spinning pictures turned into one magical image that took my breath away.

Spinning makes me feel weightless, like my soul's coming loose from my body. The dizziness turns my legs weak, and I slip to the thick carpet of brown leaves below. Hudgens Hollow keeps spinning around me. Stonefield lies down, too, his hair touching mine and his body stretched out in the opposite direction. We must look like paper dolls connected at our heads, cut from the same piece and opened up. We lie quiet under the twirling feathers until the rain stops and the thunder rolls off to some other land. Water drips from weighted tree limbs.

"Catrina, your art—the fire leaves, the rain girl, the stone pillars, the feather vines—it's beautiful." His voice is so low, I'm not sure I heard him right.

"Art?" The word makes me think of expensive pictures in fancy gold frames. Henry says a man in St. Louis paid the price of two Thoroughbred horses for a painting of the Mississippi River just so he could look at it in his parlor whenever he pleased.

I twist around to see Stonefield. "You think my wild work is art?"

He nods. "The most beautiful I've ever seen."

I grin back. "You mean the most beautiful that you can remember."

He rolls over on his stomach to face me. His features are sharp and fierce, but his words turn so tender, I want to touch the softness of his lips with my fingertips. "Some things are beautiful because they're pleasing, and some things are beautiful because they're true. If pleasure and truth come together—that's the kind of beauty no one can forget." When he looks at me that way, it seems like his words have two meanings—his mouth talks about my work and his eyes talk about me.

My heart beats faster. "I don't know anything about art. My wild work comes from my head. And from somewhere behind my rib cage where it gnaws at me until I have to let it go. I don't know what else to do but bring it here and set it free."

"That's what makes it true—it comes from straight inside you. That's why it's so beautiful." His steady stare turns my skin warm. "And it belongs here in the hills and the hollows, near the plants and stones. It belongs in the creek and the air."

He's saying things I've felt but never had the right person to tell them to. His words stir me up like a spoon in a bubbling pot.

"Everything here in the wild lives without being told how it should be done. Maybe you and I belong here, too." He glances up at the feathers fluttering above us.

It's true, isn't it? I say in the way only he can hear.

He rests his forehead against mine. *Yes, it's true.*

I smile. *True and beautiful.*

8

WE WORK SIDE BY SIDE ALL AFTERNOON, ONLY stopping to eat the biscuits and cheese I stuffed in my pockets. Having Stonefield help with my wild work fills me up with light like I swallowed all the stars in the sky. I can't stop laughing for the joy of it. Sometimes he stops what he's doing and grins at me, the breeze ruffling his hair and flapping the ends of his white linen shirt. He looks so alive, I want to step into his body and live inside him. I think maybe our souls are connected and always have been, but somehow our bodies got separated and lost to each other. Until now.

Stonefield helps me build a sled from tree limbs to pull loads of rocks through the woods. He understands what I want almost before I do and helps me move more stones and gather more blooms than I ever could on my own. By early afternoon, we've built a small, round, roofless house of creek stones under the hanging feathers. Our door is a curtain of ivy and our floor is a thick bed of posy petals—wild roses, bright butterfly weed, soft blue aster—and scattered leaves of mint.

As we dust off our hands and admire our finished work, a shot rings out from the direction of Roubidoux Hollow, followed by a second.

"It's Papa," I whisper.

Stonefield's eyebrows knot up in concern.

"No, it's all right—that's how he calls for me when he wants me to come home—if something was wrong, he'd only shoot once. Still, I better go before he gets worried. And you need to get back to the study soon." I swallow the disappointment that swells in my throat.

"We can come back tonight when everyone's sleeping."

"I don't want to wait that long."

Stonefield grins. He picks up a tiny yellow-gray feather that's fallen to the ground. " 'We'll quickly dream away the time; and then the moon, like to a silver bow new-bent in heaven, shall behold the night of our solemnities.' "

He twirls the yellowthroat's feather in his fingers as he talks. Words I've only read on paper come alive when he says them. I smile and glance at our work one more time before I turn to go.

Stonefield takes hold of my hair and pulls me back against him. His fingers find my neck. "Catrina." His words are warm breaths on my skin. "I'll come back tonight and meet you here after supper." He unbuttons the top button of my shirt and slides the yellow feather through the buttonhole, then pins it down by buttoning it again. "Don't forget."

I lift my face and laugh at the sky. Nothing could ever make me forget him, not in a thousand years. I shake loose his fingers, even though I want them to tighten around me, and run toward home. Lord, I wish it was night.

When I get home, Henry's not there, but Papa's humming "Camptown Races" in the smokehouse, where he's fixing the floorboards.

"Papa, are you all right? I'm sorry it's so late in the afternoon and I wasn't here for dinner—"

"Cat." When he sees me, his face lights up. Since Stonefield arrived at the farm, Papa seems to have found a taste of new life. He smiles. "Don't worry, Henry doesn't know you weren't here—he's been gone, too." He doesn't ask me where I've been, he just puts his hammer down to take hold of my arm.

A clanking noise sounds from outside.

"Look at this!" He leads me out the back door of the smokehouse and beams.

I yelp. "Holy Moses!"

Napoleon is running on some kind of contraption that moves under his feet as he runs, but the dog stays in one place. The contraption's hooked to a wheel that moves the handle on the butter churn up and down. The clanking is the sound of the butter being churned by Napoleon the dog.

"Papa—"

"Isn't it amazing? After you went to bed last night, I guess Stonefield couldn't sleep. First he fixed the broken swing in the oak tree, but then Henry and I heard him tinkering out here and came out to find him working. I stayed up most the night watching him. He said he made this for you so you wouldn't have to bother staying at home churning the butter, because he imagined you had better things to do. He said he can make one that will even toss the laundry around in a tub till it's clean. Can you believe it?"

Warmth spreads through my body, starting behind my ribs and reaching all the way to my toes and fingertips. Nobody's ever done a thing like that for me. No wonder they slept so late! A laugh bubbles up in my chest, and when it comes out, I can hardly stop.

Papa laughs, too. "Cat, the dogs love it. I let them take turns. Just look at Napoleon wag his tail."

"It's the best present I ever got! I bet Henry thought it was something! Now maybe he'll leave off bothering Stonefield after seeing how helpful and hardworking he is."

Papa's face falls. "I reckon Henry didn't care for it. He says you have too much time on your hands as it is or you wouldn't keep running off to the woods."

My skin turns hot. Oh Hell. "Henry knows I'd plow the fields as good as a man if he'd let me, but he just wants me to stay at home."

Papa shakes his head, puzzled. "I don't know what's ailing him. Must be the start of this war—he's worried Missouri will be lost to the Confederates. I tried easing his mind off it. I told him Stonefield was probably the brightest fellow I'd ever met and that I'd given the boy my pocket watch for a present because I want him to think of us as family since he's without any, but Henry didn't seem pleased."

Something sharp scratches at my throat and I can hardly get the words out. "You gave Stonefield the gold watch that your father gave to you?"

"Yes!"

Henry was already mad—now he must be steaming not to inherit his own grandfather's watch and see it go to a near stranger. My heart turns heavy. If Henry gets too fired up about Stonefield, he could ruin everything. "Papa, where did Henry go?"

He scratches his head. "It's the damnedest thing, Cat."

"What?"

"Henry went a-courtin'."

Courting? I feel like Lot's wife in the Bible, when God turned her into a pillar of salt. The slightest breeze could make me crumble into a thousand little grains. "You mean he went to see Effie?"

"Nope." Papa shakes his head. "Henry's gone to propose to Miss Dora Hoss."

"Damnation!" I kick a stone, barely missing Napoleon and the butter churn contraption.

"Cat—"

"He wouldn't do such a fool thing."

"Lots of young men marry their sweethearts before they go off to war."

"Dora's not his sweetheart. Henry loves Effie like she's God's own cousin. What's he doing with Dora Hoss?" I kick the side of the smokehouse. "And Henry isn't joining the army." The thought sends a shiver up my spine. He wouldn't leave us alone on the farm, especially with Papa so frail. "You must've got it wrong."

"I don't know, Cat." A line of worry creeps across his forehead, and I hate Henry for being the cause of it. "A lot of the young men are talking about joining the army, and Henry has strong opinions about keeping Missouri in the Union. And he's always been outspoken about slavery and how it's tearing the country apart. He isn't the type to sit by idle. You know that, Cat. And before he left this morning he told me himself that he was going to propose to Dora."

"No!" My voice turns loud, and Napoleon starts barking and his legs go faster.

My legs start moving, too.

"Cat, where're you going? You already missed dinner, and it's almost suppertime."

"I'm going to Effie's," I yell.

"But you never go to the Lenox place. You said you'd rather climb a thorn tree with an armload of snakes."

It's true. But I don't care. I have to see Effie.

9

I'M ALL HOT AND SWEATY BY THE TIME I RUN THE THREE miles to Effie's. It's a good thing for me that Effie's father has never thought to get himself some watchdogs, because peering through windows to find Effie is thousands better than knocking on the door. I quit coming to Effie's house long ago so I wouldn't accidentally slap her sister, Lu. Lu Lenox talks like buttered sugar, but her eyes say puckered sour things.

She's been mad at me for ages for something that wasn't even my fault. Once, when I was swimming in the creek, Frank Louis was spying on me from behind a tree on the bank. Lu was always sweet on Frank and thought he was the handsomest boy in Roubidoux, but when she caught him looking, he called her a "nosy nigger" and grabbed her and bent her over, saying, "I'll teach you a lesson." He pulled up her dress and spanked her on the seat of her bloomers. I heard Lu screaming for him to stop, so I snuck out of the creek and grabbed a handful of rocks. But Frank saw me, and he knows full well I have good aim, so he let her go. She ran off crying, but Frank just laughed as he walked away.

I thought sure and certain Mr. Lenox would find Frank and make him pay for what he did to his daughter, but Mr. Lenox never did a thing. Lu must've been too ashamed to tell him. I never mentioned it either, but Lu still hates me even though it wasn't my fault. Frank is mean as spit. He thinks the people of Roubidoux are too soft on Mr. Lenox for treating his black daughters the same as if they were white.

I think Mr. Lenox is right to demand his daughters be treated with respect, but my trouble with him is that he's determined to pull God into every conversation. Maybe God took it personally when Mr. Lenox quit the missionary business after his wife died, and now Mr. Lenox is afraid the Almighty will feel snubbed if he doesn't dote on Him. God and I have never been on friendly terms, so it's probably best if I stay out of it.

I scoop a handful of pebbles into my pocket and throw some at Effie's window on the second floor, but nothing happens. I come closer and stand on my toes to look through the first floor windows, which are large and high just like the mirrors inside—Mr. Lenox put in a special order to St. Louis for them and they were brought in on the train to Rolla, where he has a general store. I remember the day Mr. Lenox brought the mirrors home on his wagon. As Henry helped him carry them inside, the glass reflected the blue heavens and white clouds above, so it looked like they were bringing great pieces of sky into the Lenox house. Everything they own is store-bought, even the soap. I shade my eyes against the glare and squint into the dark parlor.

I jump when I catch sight of a young woman with wild hair and large eyes staring at me through the opposite window across the parlor. She looks like a roving mad girl from a book . . . But then, sucking in my breath, I realize it's just my own self, reflected in the hanging mirror.

"People say you're witchy." The voice behind me is creamy-sweet.

I whirl around so fast, I almost lose my balance.

Lu's laughter sounds flat, like a broken little bell.

"Did Effie tell you I'm witchy?" My face turns warm. I don't want Lu to see how much that would hurt me. I remember the wild-eyed mad girl reflected in the mirror. Is that how people see me?

She rolls her eyes. "Effie never tells me anything." Lu glances at Stonefield's pebble necklace around my neck and his feather in my button before gazing past my shoulder to her own reflection in the window. She smooths her black wavy hair that she's put up in a bun like a grown-up woman, even though she's only fifteen. "But Dora Hoss is full of interesting information."

I snort. "Dora Hoss is full of bullshit."

Lu blinks at me like she's testing her eyelids to see if they work right. "Catrina Dickinson!" She says my name like Effie does, but with a cup less honey and a pinch more salt. "What an awful thing to say about the girl who's going to be your sister-in-law. I'm astonished."

My arms shake from wanting to slap her. "Does Effie know?"

"How could she? It just happened—I've only had time to tell a handful of people on my walk home. Your brother arrived at the Hoss place as I was leaving from a visit with Dora, and I heard the whole thing through the window of the front porch. Goodness, Catrina, you don't need to scowl at me that way— it's not like I was eavesdropping. Anyone would have heard what was going on. I'm not deaf, you know."

"Where's Effie?"

Lu sighs. "Effie, Effie, Effie. Heavens. How dull conversations can be when people keep harping on the same topic." But as soon as she says it, she smiles, and I'm struck by the beauty of her perfect teeth and smooth dark skin. If her smile were real, she'd be as pretty as Effie. Lu's voice turns thick with sweetness. "Catrina, I've been dying to hear about your mysterious Devil man. Do tell, before the curiosity kills me."

"I didn't come to rescue you from your curiosity, I came to see Effie."

"You could tell me about him, and I'll tell you all about the handsome preacher my papa picked up from the train depot in Rolla this morning. They've already put up signs over there for his tent meetings here in Roubidoux. The first one's tomorrow. He sure is a powerful speaker. He talks so familiar-like about Hell, you'd think he was born and raised there."

My hands tighten into fists. "Tell me where Effie is or I'll—"

"Goodness gracious!" Her smile vanishes. "No need to be rude." She fingers the locket at her neck.

Maybe her dead mother's tintype is in there. The thought twists my heart and makes my fists loosen up. "I'm sorry," I mumble. "But I need to see her about something important."

"Oh!" Lu's face brightens with interest. She glances up at the attic window. "I believe my sister's locked herself in her lair, reading her horrid books. She's been dull as dishwater since—"

"Thanks." I turn and run to the back door of their house.

"Well!" she calls after me. "Why don't you just go right in and make yourself at home!"

It's been ages since I stepped inside the Lenox place. I'd forgotten how it smells of furniture polish and fresh-washed linens. Mirrors hang on all the walls, so as I run through the rooms, it looks like I'm racing a wild girl through the house. I run up the stairs to the little door leading to the attic steps, but my hand stops, frozen in the air above the doorknob. I want to rush right up and demand that Effie explain why she didn't come when she said she would and ask what happened with Henry, but I know I shouldn't because people always think it's rude when I say things straight and plain.

I knock.

"Come in."

I walk slowly up the steps and look around at the exposed rafters and the newsprint pasted on the walls for insulation. It's warm up here and has the comforting smell of wood and dust. The light shining through the attic window falls on Effie, who's sitting on a pile of pillows in a corner. She doesn't turn to look at me, but keeps staring out the window at the sky.

I step closer. A thick book lies open on her lap, but it's slipped to the side as if she's forgotten all about it. Both pages show a diagram of a heart that's been cut open, one half on each page, so the reader can see how it works inside. Every part is neatly labeled to explain its function.

"Effie." I wish she'd look at me. "Why didn't you come?" I didn't mean to ask her that. I was going to wait and let her talk first, but I can't help it—if I don't speak, my heart might crack open like the diagram in Effie's book, and all the little parts will stop working. "What's wrong with Henry? Effie, why didn't you come?"

She finally turns to me. She slides the book to the floor. "I couldn't come over. It would have been unkind to Henry."

"But he's the one being an ass. He's the one—"

"Henry asked me to marry him and I said no."

"Oh, Effie." My knees turn tired and I drop down next to her. "Why? You like Henry better than anybody. And when you're around, he forgets to look at the clock or open the newspaper. After you leave, he always whistles the same song."

Effie stares at the floorboards. Her voice turns so quiet, I can hardly hear her.

"What song?"

"'Her Bright Smile Haunts Me Still.'"

Effie stands up and walks to the window so I can't see her face when she talks. "I want to practice medicine, Catrina."

"Like a doctor? But how? I thought doctor schools won't allow you—"

"In the Congo, in my mother's village. Father's missionary friends say they can use my help and they've offered to take me with them next year. I'll be finished tutoring Lu by then. This is my chance."

I can't imagine life without Effie. "I don't want you to leave."

"Catrina—"

"And what about Henry?" I'm grasping for a hold, but pebbles keep slipping through my fingers. "What if he joins the Union Army and goes off and gets himself killed? If you marry him, you could make him stay. He wouldn't leave if you asked him not to—I just know it. You can't go, Effie."

She takes a deep breath and turns to me. "I love Henry," she whispers. "More than I can say."

My heart beats faster. "You do?" I never heard Effie talk about love. The thought that she could feel the same way about Henry as I feel about Stonefield makes something inside me flip over: my desire for her to stay here flips to the bottom of my heart and the desire for her to be happy and with the person she loves flips to the top.

She shakes her head. "But I don't think I should marry him."

"Why? Because your skin's black and his isn't?" I pick at a piece of brown newsprint curling off the wall. "Nobody gave your father much trouble for marrying your mother. Of course, he was in the Congo where they didn't care so much as here. Well, I mean, certain, there was some damned fool talk here, Papa said, when they heard about it, but it always came to nothing." I don't say it always came to nothing because Mr. Lenox was so rich and a missionary to boot. No one dared cross a servant of the Lord who'd inherited his family's money along with the mill and the general store off in Rolla. "You and Henry can just stay right here, safe in Roubidoux, and you'll be fine."

Not only had people in Roubidoux never even seen a person with black skin until Effie and Lu came back with Mr. Lenox from the mission field, we never saw much of anybody from anywhere. Still don't, unless a person goes to Rolla, and the railroad line only stretched out that far last year. Papa said that when Mr. Lenox came back with his two motherless babies to collect his inheritance and build a fine house here in the hills and turn Roubidoux into a real town, everyone fell all over themselves to pretend they weren't shocked at the color of his babies' skin.

But sometimes people talk. Frank Louis is the loudest. His kin come from down south in Kentucky where he says Mr. Lenox would have been tarred and feathered for such a thing.

I rip the shred of newsprint off the wall and crumple it in my fist. "Well, who cares what people think anyway. If they say it's not proper, they can all go to H—"

"We can't get married here, Catrina. It's impossible. You just don't realize. You don't even notice how people wrinkle up their noses when Henry talks so kindly to me or how they spit in the dirt at my feet when he turns to open the door for me. And if you heard about Frank Louis's efforts to raise a boycott of my father's store among the folks in Rolla last week, you've never said a word to me about it."

"I'm sorry. I didn't know—"

"You hide over in your woods and never see. You don't care

and you don't pay attention to what's going on all around you. There's a war brewing about such things—the fate of people with skin like mine—ripping the country apart, for Heaven's sake. And Lu and I are the lucky ones. Others have it so much worse. Sometimes I think you live in another world altogether. But Henry knows. He says we can take a trip somewhere to get married—out of the country if we have to, like my papa and mama were married. But if we came back to the States, there are plenty of people who would make it hard on us. Henry says he doesn't care, but it would be dangerous."

"Well, I'm with Henry."

"But that's not even the reason, Catrina." Effie traces the veins of the heart in her book. "I think marrying Henry would be unfair to him. I'd always be longing for that part of me I gave away."

"Effie, if he really loves you, he'll go with you to the Congo— you won't have to give anything away."

"No, I'd never ask him to do that. He loves the farm and the life he's worked so hard to make here. And I won't stand in the way of him joining the Union Army. He told me he plans to enlist as soon as he solidifies arrangements for you and your father's security."

It's true, then. My heart sinks.

"And, Cat, you must know how passionate he feels about the slavery problem and how he wants to be involved in the changes he hopes will come about because of this war. How could I stop him from fighting for the things he cares about and believes in? I—I love him for that. It would be as difficult for Henry to give any of that up as it would be for me to give up my own dream."

Effie lays her hand over the picture of the heart and looks at me. "And, Catrina, I can't give it up—it's what makes me feel alive. Have you ever had something that burns inside you like a fire, or calls to you like a voice you can't ignore or you'll lose one of the most important parts of yourself?"

Her words take hold of me tight and shake me. I swallow hard. "Yes." It comes out in a whisper. "I know what that feels like."

She kneels down beside me. "Truly?" She takes my hand like she did at the supper table when she stood up for me and Stonefield.

It makes my whole body feel warm. I nod, wondering if I should say more. She'd never laugh or repeat what I say to anyone—I know it in my bones. I squeeze her hand. "Effie, I feel that way about being with Stonefield. Like my soul and his are twins. He helps me see who I am because he and I are like the same person. When we're apart, it's as if a piece of me is lost—just like you said."

She tilts her head to one side. "What do you mean? You've only just met him."

"But it's as if we've known each other for ages. We're the same, him and me. There's something drawing us together. I can feel him pulling at me right now like I'm a compass needle being tugged north."

"But, Catrina—"

"When we're together, I sometimes hear his voice in my head, talking to me. And he can hear mine."

Effie's eyebrows wrinkle up. She bites her lip.

Oh Lord. My face turns hot and I yank my hand away. "I thought you'd understand. I shouldn't have told you."

"Catrina, it's just that—"

A floorboard creaks on the steps.

Effie and I freeze and hold our breath.

Lu steps into the attic. She's beaming like she just struck gold.

10

EFFIE AND I STAND AT THE SAME TIME. EFFIE PICKS UP
the book with the drawings of the open heart and carefully
closes it. "How long have you been listening on the steps, Lu?"

"Listening?" Her eyes widen and her voice rises. "I just came
up to tell you about the dance at the Hoss place, that's all."

"Damn." I cross my arms and stare bullets into Lu.

Lu gasps at the word *damn*.

I wish I could climb out the attic window and fly away with
Effie so she won't have to hear what Lu's about to say.

Effie hugs the book to her chest. "What dance?"

"Father says everyone's invited to the Hoss place tonight.
Preacher Preston's already there, visiting. I'd say he's probably
the handsomest man in Missouri, wouldn't you, Effie?"

Effie isn't following Lu's chatter and just stares at her with a
blank face like she's speaking another language.

Lu teeters up and down on her toes as she talks and clasps
her hands together like she might burst apart. "There'll be

music and dancing!" She glances at me. "You can ride over with us, Catrina."

"I'm not going. I want to go home." To Stonefield. I think of our little round house of rocks with the floor of petals.

"You have to come to the dance, Catrina. Your papa and Henry will meet us there. Maybe they'll bring your Devil man, too! You all have to attend on account of your family being the guests of honor."

Effie looks up, puzzled. "Why are the Dickinsons the guests of honor at the Hosses' dance?"

"Oh, didn't Catrina tell you?" Lu does the blinking thing again. "Henry just got engaged to Dora Hoss!"

Effie keeps staring straight ahead, but her eyes stop focusing. It's like she's looking at something that we can't see. "Oh." Her voice sounds far away. She frowns at the floor. "Lu, go on and get ready. We'll be along in a minute."

"But what about Catrina?" Lu stares at my shirt and my pants. "Shouldn't I find her one of your dresses to wear?"

Effie doesn't even glance up.

I wave Lu away. "Leave us alone."

Lu wrinkles her nose. "You can't wear a shirt and pants to a dance! And certainly not men's boots."

"I guess I'll go naked, then. And barefoot." I pull off a boot and fling it at her.

Lu yelps as it grazes her skirts.

I take off the other boot and rear back, ready to throw it, but Lu squeaks, turns, and clops down the steps.

I drop the boot and look at Effie. I want to wrap my arms

78

around her and push away Lu's words. I reach for her, but she walks quietly to the window and sets her book on the sill.

"Henry and Dora." She says it firm, like she's certain it must be the correct answer to a question. Effie likes there to be a right answer for everything. I imagine her trying to make it true in her mind that Henry and Dora belong together.

She stands up straighter. "It's good that Henry has someone by his side." She nods to herself. "He needs a helpmate, a partner, and he deserves to be happy."

"How can you say that, Effie? You're the one he loves, and you love him."

But Effie just crosses her arms over her chest. I wish she'd swear or throw something, but she just stands there quiet and still.

I push my boot away with my foot. "Effie, you don't have to go to that stupid dance, you know. Just stay here in the attic where it's nice and quiet and read your book. That's what I'd do."

"No." She shakes her head. "I'm going."

"Well, you can leave the Hoss place whenever you want. No one can tell you what to do. You're a strong person. You don't need those people, Effie."

She lifts her chin, and I can tell she's going to say that I'm wrong and she's right. "Of course I need them. We all need each other. Even you, Catrina. You may ignore people and run away when it suits you, but I won't." She stares at me steady. "*I'm no coward.*"

Lord, Lord, Lord. I've never wanted to strike Effie as much as I do right now. She's not just talking about how I've never been good at being around other people; she's talking about how I can't abide being around *those* people. Our neighbors in Roubidoux who all saw me kill Mother at the molasses make.

I kick the boot hard and it goes flying across the attic and hits the wall. "Well, you can have the whole damn lot. I don't need any of them." My face burns hot as fever. "And if I want to leave with Stonefield, we'll go whenever the Hell we please. *I'm* not afraid to be with the one I love!"

Effie flinches. Her eyes fill with a fire I've never seen before. But she doesn't shout or storm away. She presses her lips tight together and touches her locket the way Lu did, holding it between her fingers as she glares at me. She takes slow, deep breaths until the fire subsides and she is calm again. She nods. Her eyes and her voice soften just a little. "I know, Catrina. I don't want us to be harsh with each other." She takes my hand. "I do hope that you'll come to the party. For my sake."

I try to keep my arm stiff because I'm right about not needing other people and she's wrong and I want her to know it, but I can't because she's too warm for me to stay frozen all the way. My rightness starts to melt into hers and I can't tell the difference anymore.

She squeezes my hand until it's not a fist. "You're the only one who knows how I feel about Henry. I know how hard this is for you, Catrina, but I'm always doing things for you—can't you do this for me?"

Her words fall heavy on me, tilting me. And I'm like a book

sliding off a windowsill with the pages flying open. Both halves of my heart—the half that knows what I want and the half that knows what is right—slip to the floor and the little parts break loose. They're all mixed up, and I can't figure out where they belong.

As we ride to the party in the back of Mr. Lenox's wagon, Lu goes on and on about Dora and Henry and how they make a sweet couple and won't they look fine on their wedding day, and all the most mush-minded things I ever heard. Effie sits up straight and tall, staring off into the valley as if Lu's words are light as feathers and she can't feel them. But I know she does. Lord. I'd like to thump Lu's head. I imagine it'd make a dull, hollow sound, like thumping a watermelon.

I lean back against the side of the wagon, longing for a pipe to smoke. It's dusk. The in-between time is my favorite part of the day, when the world hovers betwixt the light and the dark. The bats and fireflies wake up, frogs and crickets start singing together, and the trees melt into one jagged, sawtooth line against the purple sky. I wish I could linger here forever inside this hazy in-between.

We cross Wolf Creek onto the Hosses' property, and I shut my eyes. I take a deep breath and let it out slow like I'm blowing smoke rings. They make me think of Stonefield. I conjure up the image of him smiling at me, his eyes crinkling in the corners, his teeth perfect white stones set all in a row. I keep a tight hold on the memory, but Stonefield's smile starts slipping away as we head up the steep road on Hoss Hill.

People's laughter and the happy sound of a banjo ring out from the hilltop. I shouldn't have come. I grope for the remnants of Stonefield's image, but everything's clouded over. The wagon crests the top of the hill. Bright light pours out all the windows of the house, but I can't feel it. My darkness is coming to get me. Feels like I'm headed backward in time, to the blackest moment of all, when my mother died.

We were making molasses, and all the folks along Roubidoux Creek and in the hills gathered to the farm to help bring in the cane from the field and cook up the sugar juice with us like we do every year. Henry hooked up the mule to the sorghum press and put me in charge of it. He said all I had to do was keep the mule going round and round it while Mother fed sorghum stalks into the press, and I was to mind that no one got knocked in the head by the bar as it went by.

It was a long day, and I was mad that I was stuck in one place with a tiresome task. Even after all the other young people had finished cutting the cane and were just gossiping and flirting under the crab apple trees, I had to stay put. After a while, I took up Henry's gun and started aiming at the rabbits hopping around in the bare cane field. Shooting a dozen would have been easy as pie. I took a bead on one, and without thinking, I pulled the trigger. The old mule startled at the gunshot and took off when Mother wasn't ready. She was standing up from the press when the bar came around full speed.

I saw her fall and ran to her, but she was already dead by the time I got there.

The wagon stops in front of the Hoss place.

The world's slipping from its foundations, pressing down and smothering me. I grip the side of the wagon. How can I bear all their eyes on me again? I can't go inside that house. All those voices, all those people. It will take me straight back to when they rushed over after Mother fell and crowded around so thick and loud I couldn't move, couldn't breathe. How many of them did I strike before I broke free? Everything turned so dark, I can't remember. And now I'm supposed to just walk inside and join them like nothing happened.

Gentle fingers pry my hands from the side of the wagon. I open my eyes slow. Effie peers at me, studying my face like I'm a drawing in one of her books. She's expecting me to get out, but my arms and legs are nailed to the wagon; my head's full of rocks.

"Catrina, let's go inside."

Lu and Mr. Lenox have already walked to the porch. The front door opens for them and yellow light and laughter trickle out. I climb out of the wagon. Effie winds her arm in mine and steps forward, taking me with her. "We can stay near the back of the room and talk with Jane Dillard if you want. She asks about you all the time."

I like Jane—she's kind and talks about interesting things— but she was at the molasses make that day, too, and saw what I did. We're almost to the door.

"Catrina, I know this is hard for you, coming here. I just

want you to know I appreciate you being by my side because—"
She glances at the door. "It's hard for me to be here tonight, too."

I gaze toward the ridge that overlooks our sorghum field, wishing I could see Stonefield's circle design from where I'm standing. A whippoorwill cries in the distance. I can hardly bear to enter the house, but Effie needs me.

I nod and open the door.

Walking into the house is like climbing out of a dark cave into the midday sun. I just stand there blinking for a moment, dazed. Lu's already laughing and clapping her hands to the music and Effie's glancing around the room for Jane.

Dora Hoss's twangy voice rings out above the rest. "Well broom me out! Look who's here."

Before I can get my bearings, Dora comes sweeping past Effie as if she's not even there and clamps hold of my sleeve like a crawdad. "Cat!"

My whole body turns stiff as the dead. Cat was Mother's name for me. Only Papa and Henry call me that now.

Dora's breathless. Her pasty cheeks have turned into red candy apples. Her polka dot dress with the long bell sleeves looks like it's two sizes too tight. Lord. She better not eat a single slice of custard pie or her corset might bust loose and her brooch might go flying off and put someone's eye out.

She glances at my men's pants and boots. "Didn't you have time to change out of your work clothes? What a shame!" Her laugh sounds like a squealing piglet. "But I'm glad you came."

"I'm not."

Dora laughs like it's a joke. "You're always so funny, Cat."

She's too close. I can barely breathe. "Don't—" I step backward toward the door, but Lu's in the way. "Don't call me that."

Dora's lips purse up and she glances around.

Oh Hell. I need air. I need to get free. I reach out for Effie, but Dora has wedged herself between us till she's pushed Effie outside of her little huddle, and now I'm stuck between Dora and Lu.

Dora lowers her voice. "Why must you ruin everything, Catrina Dickinson? I was right. You *are* witchy."

A lump swells in my throat and I can hardly swallow. It's not true. I push the darkness down so I can find something to say to her that isn't cold and sharp, but I can't find anything good or proper inside me. Maybe they're right—maybe there's something wrong with me. I don't know how to be with other people. I can't even be a good friend to Effie when she needs me. When God made me, He must have left out an important part that's meant to be connected to everyone else.

Effie parts the wall Dora has made and moves to my side. I grope for her arm and pull her close.

She steps forward, strong and sure. "Hello, Dora. You look well." Effie's warm hand steadies me. "We're so happy for you and Henry." She plucks the sweet words and gives them to Dora as easy as picking wildflowers, even though it must be killing her.

Dora's face turns smug, like she's been waiting for this moment all her life. "Why, thank you, Effie. Henry and I are happy as larks, like it was always meant to be. And to think he was pining for me all these years, working up the nerve to declare his love!"

Lord.

"Henry's already asked Preacher Preston to perform the ceremony next month before Henry enlists! Everything's been such a glorious whirlwind—"

"Where's my father?"

Dora frowns at me for interrupting.

The music stops, and I look around the room. I hope that wasn't Papa playing the harmonica.

Lu's dark eyes are bright. "Yes, where is he?"

Effie squeezes my elbow. "Let's go look for him."

But Dora grabs my arm and scowls at Effie. "Oh no, you don't steal my soon-to-be sister-in-law from me as soon as she gets here, you dark little thief! Who do you think you are, girl?" She turns to me and laughs as if we're sharing a joke. "Effie, go along and find Mr. Dickinson for Cat."

Effie lifts her chin, and I think she's going to refuse, but then she tells me in a quiet voice, "I'm going to look for your father. I'll be right back." She turns, walking away into the crowd of laughing people. I fling Dora's hand from my arm and start after Effie, but Dora grabs me back.

Lu squints at me. "I want to see your Devil man. Why did he make that awful sign in your field, Catrina? And how could your papa take in such a peculiar stranger?"

I clench my fists at my sides and force myself to swallow the words stinging my tongue.

Dora joins in. "I hear his skin is brown as the dirt—is he Indian? Nobody would make such a wicked-looking sign in a field for no reason. And if it's from the Devil, well!"

Lu nods. She glances at my top button and her eyes sharpen. "Heavens! Is that a yellowthroat's feather?"

Dora gasps.

I touch Stonefield's tiny gift.

Lu's eyes are round as saucers. Her voice turns shrill. "Everybody knows yellowthroats are *witches'* birds."

"Broom me out!" Dora shakes her head, still looking at the feather. "I'm concerned for you, Cat. After all, we're going to be sisters. Your brother expects me to help guide you in the right direction, and I can see now the reason for his concern."

My breath's coming too fast. "Where's Papa?" The music starts again, ringing in my ears. I think it's Papa playing the harmonica, but the room's too crowded to see him. He shouldn't be playing. It's too hard on him—he said so himself. The house feels like it's tipping from the weight of all the people.

Lu keeps talking like I'm not there. "Dora, you have your work cut out for you, helping Catrina—you should have heard what she said about that Devil man. She said she can hear his voice just like a demon in her head, telling her what to say and what to do—"

"My granny says to get rid of a witch's spell, you need to get yourself some mistletoe at midnight and open your Bible without looking. Read the first verse you see seven times, tuck the mistletoe in, and sleep with the Bible under your pillow." Dora glances at me. "I'd bet you've never read a word of the Bible." She pats my wrist. "But don't worry, Cat—as soon as we're sisters, I can help change that."

Dora's too close. Her voice makes my head ache. I can smell

the cider on her breath and the sweat of too many bodies in the room.

"You'd lose that bet." I edge away from her.

Dora folds her arms across her chest and turns to Lu. "Granny says a witch can't touch the Bible without it feeling like a swarm of bees."

"That's bull." And I've read heaps more of the Bible than Dora has and some parts more than once, but I don't waste my words on her. I push away from Dora and Lu to find Effie. I can't breathe.

"Papa?" I move toward the sound of the harmonica, but as soon as I break through the crowd I see it's not him, after all. Lord, everything's topsy-turvy. Dancers brush against me as they twirl and clap. Laughter bursts in my ears. People's eyes widen when they see me. Is it because they're remembering that day at the molasses make?

I turn away from their eyes. This is how drowning must feel. I can't hold myself up much longer. I wish Stonefield were here. I call to him in my silent voice, *Stonefield, where are you?*

"Catrina. I was looking for you."

But the heavy hand on my shoulder isn't Stonefield's, it's Henry's.

"Henry." I'm surprised at how relieved I am to see him. I lean against him for support. I feel so dizzy.

"Are you all right, Cat?" He takes my shoulders gentle, like he's afraid of hurting me.

I cling to his solid, familiar frame and breathe in the smell of his clean homespun shirt. "I—I was looking for Papa. I was afraid he was playing the harmonica."

Henry lets me rest my head on his chest for a moment, and I can hear his heart beating under his ribs. I think about how it's the same heart he's always had, the same heart that beat before the accident, back when he loved me more.

He pushes me away a little bit so he can look me in the eyes. He lowers his voice. "Cat, I wanted to tell you first, about me and Dora, but things are happening so fast. The war's practically on our doorstep and I can't just sit here idle. I want to make sure you and Father are taken care of before I—"

He frowns at my shirt and pants. "I thought the Lenox girls might help you get fixed up nice. It's been a long time since people had a chance to visit with you, and this is a special occasion."

I want to plead with Henry to hold me like he did a moment ago, just until I can clear my head. But at that moment, a young man I've never seen before joins us at Henry's side.

Henry stands up straighter and smiles at the man. "Reverend Preston! I'd like you to meet my sister, Catrina."

Reverend Preston looks barely older than me, but he already has a neatly trimmed beard of white and yellow gold. His eyes are sky colored and his pale blond hair's the soft wild down of a thistle—his looks are at odds with his stern outfit, a pressed black suit, starched white shirt, and a tightly knotted black ribbon tie.

He clasps my hands in his like I'm his long-lost friend.

I nod. "How do you do." I try to pull away, but he presses tighter.

"Miss Dickinson." His drawl is warm and strong, like apple cider mixed with Kentucky bourbon. His voice is full of some kind of power—the kind that must have made Andrew and Peter drop their nets and follow Jesus. "Miss Dickinson, the moment your name fell from Miss Effie Lenox's lips, God's own Holy Spirit spoke to me concerning you."

I want to pull away, but a question jumps out of my mouth. "What did He say?"

"He told me there are wondrous things in store for you."

"Why didn't He tell me?"

"I'm His messenger. Sometimes people can't hear His words until they're spoken by another." He pulls my hands closer to his chest. A sweet, cloying smell hangs about him from the sprig of lavender he wears in his buttonhole. He lowers his voice. "God's Spirit is speaking to me right this moment, Miss Catrina. He says you are in the midst of spiritual turmoil—caught betwixt the light and the dark."

The words jolt me from the inside. I yank my hands away. Hell. God had no right to tell a stranger such things. God's a worse gossip than Lu.

Preacher Preston's hands stay open in front of him. He looks as if he's waiting for God to drop a new set of ten commandments into his arms. His smooth, lilting words seem to roll off his tongue and melt into the air. "The Spirit bids me say, 'Take care,' Miss Catrina. 'Satan disguises himself as a beautiful angel of light. Be not deceived by his brightness.'"

The preacher's eyes are blue as forget-me-nots and look at me so earnest that I nod. But the nod's a lie because I'd give a thousand heaps of treasure just to see a beautiful angel of light in my darkness right this second, even if it was Satan.

Reverend Preston starts to say more, but Lu appears at his side and takes hold of his sleeve. She giggles, even though nothing's funny.

"Oh, Reverend Preston, my friends are just dying to meet you!" She pulls on his sleeve to turn him away, and I take my chance and step back from the preacher to search for Papa. Before I can get free, Henry takes hold of my arm.

"Where are you going, Cat? You should stay and visit more with Reverend Preston and the young ladies. After all, you're part of their circle now that Dora will become your sister-in-law next month." He smiles down at me as if he's done me a great favor by getting engaged.

"Why are you marrying Dora?" I know my question will make him mad, but I don't care.

Henry glances around to see if anyone is listening. "Cat, I should have mentioned it to you earlier, that's true, but sometimes these sorts of things are hard to explai—"

"And you should have told me you were enlisting. Or is that one of those things that's hard to explain, too?"

Henry takes a deep breath. "Most matters of importance are hard to explain to you, Cat. Sometimes it seems like you don't even want to try to understand what's going on around you—all you want to do is run away to the woods or that cave where you never have to deal with other people or what's happening in the real world."

My fingers curl into fists. I wanted to make Henry angry, but his voice is calm and I'm so enraged I can't speak.

"It's a good thing you have me to think about your future and help establish you so you won't be completely on your own. After we're married, Dora will live in the house with you and Father while I'm away. She'll be better able than I have been to help you form connections—"

"What about Stonefield?" My voice cracks. The dam cracks, too.

Henry's nostrils flare like a bull's. "That's not important," he says under his breath. He glances nervously toward Reverend Preston, but the preacher's nodding at Lu and her friends, who keep squealing and bouncing like they've got briars in their bloomers.

Henry slides the feather from my button and tries to make his voice sound gentle. "Stonefield doesn't belong here, Cat."

I reach for the feather, but Henry's already snapped it between his fingers, breaking it in two.

I slap his hand, and the pieces fall to the floor. "Where is he?" My words come out louder than the voices around us. "Why didn't you bring him here with you—he's our guest!"

Henry pulls me to the corner, farther away from people. His brow wrinkles like a row of homespun poorly woven. His breath smells of ale and something stronger—moonshine. "At supper, I told him he should stay at the house so he wouldn't embarrass you."

My heart sinks.

"He wouldn't even speak back to me. Your play actor just glared and pulled out Father's watch, pretending to check the time, taunting me, the little Devil. It was all I could do to keep from smacking his arrogant face."

No, I don't believe him anymore. I turn to the pieces of the feather on the floor and drop to my knees to pick them up and stick them back in my buttonhole.

Henry's voice is low. "But you're doing a fine job embarrassing yourself without his help." He glances over his shoulder. "People are looking at you."

"I don't care."

His face hardens. I can tell he's picking out his next words like arrows that he'll shoot straight into my heart.

"Mother would be disappointed in you, Cat."

I shove him as hard as I can. My darkness is a flood now, pouring over me, swallowing me up. I'm drowning like one of the heathens God wouldn't let on the ark. If I don't get out of here, I'll sink to the bottom of the sea.

"Catrina." All at once, Effie's by my side. "It's me. I've been looking for you. Catrina, come with me." The lines of her face are drawn tight. "Jane has some cider for us. Let's listen to the music. Dance with me."

Effie never dances with anyone but Henry.

She puts her hand on my arm. "Please."

"I can't."

"Stay with me, Catrina."

If I stay, I know I'll pull her down with me when I go under, and I love her too much to do that. I push away and stumble through my darkness to the door. I step outside. The world's quiet out here. The fresh night air fills my lungs and pulls me out and away. I don't look back because I can't bear to see the disappointment in Effie's eyes.

I run. The wind kisses my face and tosses my hair. It moves its fingers over my skin, reminding me I'm alive. I can finally breathe. I run to the ridge behind the Hoss place and gaze down into our valley. I pull the seeing stone out from where it hangs over my heart and peer through it. Even in the falling dark, what's left of Stonefield's circles in the cane are easy to see. Just looking at them calms me. I squint into the distance, looking for the lit-up windows of our house, but I don't see a thing. Stonefield's gone.

Behind me, someone opens the front door and loud noises pour out.

"Cat!"

Henry. Let him try to stop me.

I bolt down the road under the trees. I know where Stonefield is. He's at Hudgens Hollow, waiting for me like he said. I can feel it.

11

I'M OUT OF BREATH WHEN I REACH HUDGENS CEMETERY.
It's darker now and harder to see, but the swollen moon
keeps the night from swallowing me up. As I walk, I catch
glimpses in the woods of tiny fairy lights that disappear just as I
turn to look at them. The closer I get, the surer I am that I'm
not imagining them. By the time I reach the creek, I see them—
little lamps made from small tins of grease with a lit rag in
each, perched on stones in the water. The flickering lights cast
a golden glow on the rushing current.

My heart races as I run along the bank, following the path
of lamp stones down the stream. Soon the trail of lights is on
dry land and the lamps burn from the tops of my high stone
pillars. I weave between them, feeling the rush of cool valley
air flowing through me like new blood. My footsteps, breath,
and heartbeat all chant *Stone-field, Stone-field* as I run.

Catrina.

His silent voice reaches me before I even see him. It makes
my heart beat faster. I walk slow toward the entrance of our

round stone house and stand five paces from it, watching him through the ivy curtain hanging over the doorway. He's lighting the last of the lamps along the top of the wall, making a ring of light around him. His body is taut and muscular like a wild colt's, moving with the kind of ease and sureness that animals own. And just like them, he's not aware of the beauty and power it gives him.

The mix of gold and shadow dancing across his features gives him an otherworldly look, as if he's part god and part human—like those giants in the Bible whose fathers were sons of God and mothers were daughters of men. The sight of him steals all my words away.

"Catrina." His voice is like a strong hand curving around the nape of my neck. He gazes steady at me through the vines as he blows out the flame from the end of his stick. A slender gray ribbon of smoke unfurls into the darkness. "You didn't forget."

I shake my head.

He takes a step toward the doorway. "I started to think that I'd only dreamed you up and you weren't real after all." His serious features soften into a grin.

Lordy—his smile.

I step up to the entrance, where only the ivy curtain hangs between us and watch him through the gaps. Silence hangs like a spell, and we don't break it by speaking. When he looks into my eyes, I know he sees the wanting I have for him there. But I'm not ashamed, because when I look at him, I see the wanting in his eyes, too.

Maybe inside every person's head there's a little world of their own in a secret stone house where their true self lives, and if a person's brave enough, they can open someone else's door and walk inside. Stonefield's already crossed my threshold. No one else has tried—not even Effie, and certainly not Henry. But Stonefield did it so easy. When I'm with him, I don't care that God left out the part of me connected to everyone else, and I pray a *thank you* to Him for connecting me to Stonefield.

Come in with me. Stonefield's eyes pull me closer.

I push past the ivy vines. They part and slide away from me as I walk through the doorway. I stand in the center of our circle house and look up at the feathers dangling from the branches above us. The light glints off each one as it sways and turns, flashing its colors.

Stonefield reaches toward me and takes the broken feather pieces from my button. He strokes them with his thumb as if by touching them, he can find out what happened. He presses them deep into his pocket and reaches up to pick a new yellow feather from a dangling vine and slides it into its place.

I smile and sit down on the carpet of posies beside a flat rock with a small grease light and a pile of books on it. "These are Papa's." I run my finger over the spines.

Stonefield sits down next to me. "He gave them to me. And this, too." He pulls Papa's watch out of his other pocket. "I think he wants me to have things to call my own."

I squint at the titles of the books and see Shakespeare's *Hamlet* and *Romeo and Juliet*; a brand-new book by a Mr. Walt Whitman; and Papa's old weathered copy of the Holy Bible.

"Which one have you been reading?"

Stonefield lifts a book off the top of the stack. "This one's full of beautiful things. Have you read it?"

I laugh. "The Bible? Parts of it. I never thought of it as beautiful."

"Ah, but it is." He opens it to the middle. "Sometimes the words come alive, and I mark them so I can hunt them down later and read them again." He turns the pages until he finds the ones he's looking for. "I marked a lot of words in this part—a song by a man named Solomon. Have you read it?"

I shake my head. "Hunt them down and read them to me."

Stonefield lies down near the grease lamp and props himself up with his elbow. He draws his finger over the verse as he reads it in his rumbly voice. "'Let him kiss me with the kisses of his mouth: for thy love is better than wine.'"

Lord. I grab the book from his hands and peer at the words. "Are you sure this is the Bible?"

He nods.

"I didn't know God could write this way."

"Read it."

I find the next place he marked and read the words out slow to make sure I get them right. "'A bundle of myrrh is my well-beloved unto me; he shall lie all night betwixt my breasts.'" Lord, Lord. My heart starts pounding between my own breasts. I glance up at Stonefield.

He takes the Bible from my hands and continues reading. "'Behold, thou art fair, my love; behold, thou art fair; thou hast doves' eyes.'" He keeps reading, but looks at me, like he's stored the words up in his memory. " 'O my dove, that art in the clefts of the rock, in the secret places, let me see thy countenance, let me hear thy voice.' "

Stonefield. You saw me in the cleft of the rock, in my secret place. You're the only one who really sees me. I lie back on the soft bed of petals and stare up at the dancing feathers as I listen to him read the beautiful words.

" 'For sweet is thy voice, and thy countenance is comely.' "

Stonefield, you hear my voice even when I'm not speaking. No one's ever been this close to me, been a part of me, like you are. The warm scent of roses mixes with the cool smell of mint leaves and fills me up, making me light-headed.

He puts down the Bible and reaches out to cradle my cheek in his hand. His skin smells of soap and coffee and sweat and earth. I bring his hand to my lips and kiss his palm and the tips of his fingers.

Catrina. " 'Set me as a seal upon thine heart.' "

I slide his hand down my neck, between my breasts, and press it to my chest.

He leans toward me. " 'For love is strong as death.' " His gravelly voice is deep and low, sending shivers up my back. When he kisses me, my body dies and comes to life as something new, like snow melting into a rushing river. I didn't know his lips touching mine had the power to draw my soul to the surface. I feel it quivering just beneath my skin. When he lifts his head, I reach for him and pull him back to me. Will my spirit escape my body when I kiss him this time?

But the shot from a distant gun rings out through the hollow, making us jump and pull away. It comes from the direction of home.

Papa.

A second shot rings out.

We stare at each other for a moment without moving. My heart feels like it's being ripped in half.

"I know you have to go." Stonefield strokes my cheek. "But we'll always have this secret place." His words are like fingers— their caress sends rippling waves spreading out inside me. He closes his eyes and lowers his forehead gently onto mine. *And we also have this place right here inside us that's all our own.*

I can hear his unspoken words more clearly than I ever have before.

I'll be as close as your own thoughts, Catrina. Just come to me and I'll be here. Stonefield kisses my forehead and stands up, reaching out his hand to take me home. We run all the way. Henry's wagon's in the yard and lights burn in the windows. Henry's pacing the front porch with Papa's gun.

"What's wrong?" I call as we get near. "Is it Papa?"

As soon as Henry sees us, he lifts the gun like he's going to shoot, then he sets it against the porch railing and walks toward us so fast and steady, it looks like he's going to barrel us over. "Father's asleep." His face is hard and wild and fixed in one expression like Mr. Lenox's masks from the Congo that hang in his study.

I stop walking and step backward as he comes closer. "What's happened?"

But he doesn't answer and comes straight at Stonefield like a locomotive on a track. Henry's fist slams into Stonefield's face, knocking him backward and spinning him to the side.

"I knew it. How dare you take her into the woods alone?"

He hauls back to strike him again, but I grab his fist and twist his arm down. "Stop it, Henry!"

"Somebody has to mind your reputation if you won't, Cat."

The smell of liquor on his breath is stronger than earlier. He pushes me away and stands glaring at Stonefield, who stares back at him, his chest rising and falling. Stonefield's hands become fists and I know he's thinking how good it would feel to hit Henry back. A dark red mark covers his face and his eye's already started to swell. If he and Henry were dogs, they'd have their teeth bared, growling, and their fur on end.

Henry raises his finger inches from Stonefield and points right into his face. "If it weren't for my father, I'd send you off tonight the same way you came to us—with nothing."

I think Stonefield will push Henry's hand away, or shove him backward, but he stands firm, with a steady look in his eyes like a copperhead staring into the barrel of a rifle.

It unnerves Henry. I can tell by the way his mouth twitches. He takes his hand away and wipes his chin.

"Get to the house, Cat."

I don't move.

"From now on, he'll sleep in the barn. And you're to stay indoors after supper each night." He turns to me. "I said get!"

"No!" I shout. "You're not Papa. You can't tell us what to do."

Henry's laugh is sad and makes the hair on my arms rise.

"You're right—I'm not Father." His features twist into a painful grin. "But I appear to be the only one in the world who gives a damn about what becomes of you, Cat. And I say"—he points his gun to the sky—"get to the house!" The shot cracks the night.

I open my mouth to shout something back to him, but Stonefield speaks. His voice is low and calm. Almost icy.

"Catrina, your brother's right."

"What?" Henry and I both turn to him.

I shake my head. *But, Stonefield, there's nothing wrong with wanting to be together. It's wrong of him to keep us apart.*

"You should go with him, Catrina." Stonefield's cold eyes are still on Henry, but I can hear him add in a warm voice to me, *I'll help your father with the farmwork and if you appease Henry, he'll shut up and leave us alone. Don't worry—we'll find a way to be together. He can't keep us apart. Nothing can.*

I stare at him.

"Your brother loves you—he's just doing his duty." But *"forty thousand brothers could not, with all their quantity of love, make up my sum."*

Hamlet said that about Ophelia. I turn my face away so Henry can't see me smile at Stonefield's words. I nod. "All right. I'll go." I imagine Henry's mouth hanging open as he watches me obey him and walk toward the house.

As I open the door, I say, "Good night, Henry. Good night, Stonefield."

Henry says nothing, but Stonefield says, quiet, "Good night, Catrina," *my dove.* He walks away, toward the barn. *"Parting is such sweet sorrow, that I shall say good night till it be morrow."*

12

I THOUGHT THE HARD PART WOULD BE FIGURING OUT how to skip Reverend Preston's all-day tent meetings so Stonefield and I could be together while everyone's away, but Henry sent Stonefield out to the field at dawn to repair the stalks, and Papa woke up with one of his throat sicknesses that keeps him in bed all day. So I pretend to have one, too. Papa and I have got them almost every year of our lives. They hurt like the Devil and leave our throats feeling like they've been rubbed inside with sanding paper.

Henry doesn't like that I'm staying home, but he can't make me go to the tent meeting or to the Hosses' for supper afterward with him if I'm sick, so he flips through Papa's Bible until he finds the passage he wants and walks over to my bed, setting the Bible in front of me on the blanket. He squints at me like he's trying to see through my throat to find out if it's really sore or not. He taps the page.

"I want you to read and ponder on that this morning, Cat. And don't forget to pray."

"I will." I whisper it in a crackly voice so it sounds like it hurts to talk, and pull the book up close as Henry leaves to go pick up Dora and take her to the tent meeting.

Hebrews 10:25: "Not forsaking the assembling of ourselves together, as the manner of some is; but exhorting one another: and so much the more, as ye see the day approaching." I read the verse over and over again until Henry's wagon finally disappears around the bend, then I close the book and run all the way to the field.

It's like Stonefield and I are wooden jigsaw puzzles and we're the only ones who know how to assemble ourselves together. When I'm with him, it's easier to find my missing pieces—the pieces that prove I can be known and understood by someone. The pieces that prove I'm not a mistake God made. If God wants me to be exhorted, then He should preach at me to not forsake Stonefield.

Napoleon and the other dogs follow me to the field, racing along beside me with their big dog grins as if they can tell how happy I am. But I don't go find Stonefield right away. I want him to make good progress on his task first, so Henry won't be suspicious. Besides, I have a surprise in mind for Stonefield. While he works in the northeast corner of the field, I begin my wild work.

I use wet red and yellow leaves—sassafras, sumac, and Virginia creeper—to outline the giant black rock in Stone Field. The colors seem to melt into each other as I form a ring of bright rays around it. If we could see the rock from the sky, I bet it would look like it's on fire. By the time I'm done, I hear Stonefield moving through the stalks, nearing the center of the field. The flaming stone gives me an idea.

I duck down quick as I see him through the cane. Did he see me? *Stonefield.*

Catrina, where are you?

Come find me.

I hear him step into the clearing by the rock. I laugh and bolt, running toward Roubidoux Spring.

Where are you going?

I laugh and keep running out of the field. I hear the crunch of his footsteps in the dried leaves behind me.

Catrina.

Come to me.

I've almost got you. His silent voice is closer now—it seems to flow over the rushing current.

I go upstream along the bank of Roubidoux Creek, duck past the willow tree, the spring, and go around the bend and into the meadow.

Catrina. Stonefield sees me the same time I see him. He smiles and runs to catch me. I'm crossing the hay meadow ahead of him. The wild wheat grass is almost as high as my hips. It's the dark golden color of Stonefield's eyes. He takes hold of my hair and pulls me around, gentle but firm. The world spins blue and gold, even after we stop running.

Caught you.

The meadow spreads out between the two hills with the creek behind us flashing silver through the trees. Only the sun sees us. I skim my open palms over the tips of the swaying grass, mimicking the wind that caresses the field in rippling waves.

Stonefield draws me in by my hair like it's a net. He lifts his hands to breathe in the scent of my hair still tangled in his fingers.

I say, "I have an idea for new wild work, but I need your help."

"What do you want me to do?"

"I want you to be the art." I pull the bottom of his shirt up over his head as he lifts his arms. It billows in my hands, a white flag in the breeze. His body is sun-gold. The muscles in his arms slope like distant hills, like the steep and rounded land I love.

"Stonefield." I savor the sweetness of the name on my tongue and the strength of its simple sound.

"Catrina." His voice is soft and warm and low. Like a bed of hay.

"Lie down," I whisper.

He lies back in the golden grass and crosses his arms behind his head. I squat beside him, clearing a space free of hay, and pick up a fallen walnut, still in its green hull and large as a ball of yarn. When I cut it open with a stone, the air fills with its sweet, sharp, earthy scent. Inside it, the black substance surrounding the hard nut looks like dark molasses, but it's thick as butter. I set the open hull on the ground, careful—once the stuff touches the skin, it will stain for weeks or even months.

"Are you going to feed me that?" Stonefield squints at me, stern. "First frog legs and now walnut mush—are they witchy love potions?"

I ball up his shirt and throw it at him, but it flies past his head. Keeping one arm behind his head, he reaches back for the shirt and hurls it at me. Laughing, I catch it and toss it as hard as I can over the hay fortress surrounding us. The shirt flutters away like a white dove. Stonefield's serious expression breaks into a grin. I straddle him at the waist, my knees on the ground. He watches me, his arms still crossed behind his head.

I take the green walnut and slip a turkey feather from my deep pocket. "This will bind your heart to mine."

"It's already bound."

"I've thought of a charm—I'll say it over the ink."

Stonefield brings his arms down and rests his hands on my thighs.

I hold the walnut hull beneath my lips and speak. "Into his skin, over his heart. Take me with you, never to part."

He slides his hands to my hips. "It's already so. The day you came to me in the cane field, you owned my heart."

I smile as I dip the quill tip into the thick black ink. "This is for always."

"Then I want it."

"Lie still as a dead man." I start drawing the circle design from the field on Stonefield's chest. I dip the quill back in the hull before sliding it over his skin, re-creating the paths and swirls from memory. Saving the fire rock for last, I paint it carefully over his heart.

I stop for a moment.

"Stonefield, one time when Effie and I were little, she read me a story where the last line said that the characters lived 'happily ever after,' and Effie said it was an untruth. She said feelings are fleeting and that trying to hold on to happiness is folly—like chasing after the wind. What do you think?"

Stonefield lifts his chin and closes his eyes. He doesn't say anything for several moments. When a breeze tousles his hair, he grins. "Maybe Effie is right about the chasing." The breeze lifts the hair off his forehead, and Stonefield opens his eyes. "We shouldn't chase after the wind. Or happiness. But it's folly to run away from them, too. They come to us in their own time—we should pay attention and enjoy them while they're here."

I love that Stonefield thinks the way I do. We should just keep living in the here and now. The past is too painful and the future is too uncertain. I almost wish I had amnesia like him, but just being with him here in the present is like a wonderful, beautiful amnesia. I laugh and tilt my head back, letting the breeze and the happiness flit over my face and through my hair. "I'll have to tell Effie you agree. But I'm afraid she might think that if I don't know where you came from or what you've been, then I shouldn't love you."

He raises his eyebrows. *What do you think?*

I dip the feather in the ink and carefully draw the last flame on the rock with a flourish. "Effie is smarter than anyone I ever met, but she doesn't know what my heart knows. And even if she could count off a thousand reasons why I shouldn't be with you, it wouldn't stop my heart from wanting what it wants."

"What if I do find out where I came from and what I've been?" His eyes never leave mine, but I can see something different there that makes my heart skip a beat.

"Is your memory coming back?" I let the quill drop to the grass.

"At the beginning, right after the fever, it seemed like my life was a book with blank pages until I got to the part where you found me. But now it's like the lost words are appearing on the pages." He looks away from me to stare at the shadowy woods in the distance as he lies beneath me in the grass, and I feel him shifting his focus from the present to the past. It sends a cold shiver through me.

"What do you remember?"

"I remember the day I learned to read—I was maybe four or five. A woman with skin white as paper leaned over my shoulder and pointed at the letters. She smelled like cake and tea. She didn't know my language and didn't try to learn it, but she wanted to teach me hers. English—what I speak now."

"What was your other language?"

Stonefield shakes his head, still gazing into the dark woods. "I don't know its name." His eyes narrow. "The teacher woman called it a savage tongue and washed my mouth out with lye soap every time I spoke it." He turns his gaze to the sky. "I remember, but it was so long ago."

I take a deep breath. "Yes, it was long ago." His past seems so far away from me, I want to pull him back from it. "It doesn't matter now. If you spoke that other language, I wouldn't know it and we wouldn't understand each other. See? The past doesn't matter. The future, either. Just now. Here."

He pulls in a deep breath. He's still staring past me. "It was a mission school—an orphanage. A stranger left me there when my family died of scarlet fever and the mission took me in." He licks his lips and talks fast, as if he's trying to catch every single memory that fires at him like bullets. "My mother—when she was alive, she told us stories. I missed them when I was in school, but after I learned to read the stories in the books at the mission, I didn't feel so alone anymore."

I squeeze his hand to bring him back to me, but he pulls his hand away and props himself onto his elbows, staring into the woods.

"When I graduated, the white woman gave me three volumes of Shakespeare." His eyes light up with a new memory. "I was a teacher at the mission—I taught children how to read! I remember the smell of chalk as the students wrote on their slates."

I squeeze his shoulder. "But now you're on your own. You don't need the mission school anymore or those missionaries. You—"

His brow wrinkles up. "But who am I? How did I get here?"

"Stonefield." I find it hard to swallow. "You're Stonefield. You're here now, with me."

He blinks at me, as if just realizing where he is.

"And whatever memories are hiding in that head of yours, they can't keep me from loving you."

His eyes sharpen their focus, and he is finally looking at me again. "Promise?" He sits all the way up with me in his lap, and leans forward to kiss me.

"I promise!" I laugh and push him back down. "You'll smear my work! It needs to dry a little before we wash it off."

"Let me paint you, too."

"Your circle design?"

He nods.

I hand him the feather and watch his reaction as I take off my shirt. I laugh at the way his eyes widen. I turn and lie on my stomach so he can paint my back.

He kneels beside me.

I move my hair out of the way and turn to look at him over my shoulder. "I'm ready."

"Wait," he whispers. "First I want to paint you in my mind so I'll never forget how you look lying here in the hay. Nymph. Are you human or are you a spirit of the meadow?"

I smile and close my eyes. "A spirit born from dirt and stones and grass? Maybe I am. And if I lie still long enough, the earth will take me back."

When it takes you, tell it to take me, too. He moves onto me, his knees on each side supporting his weight, and brushes the soft part of the feather lightly up my back.

Lord.

He turns the feather around and dips the quill in the walnut ink. When he starts drawing the circle design, the smooth slow feel of it makes me want to cry out and arch my back, but I do my best to hold still. When he's finished painting, I lie there, waiting for it to dry. After a few moments, I glance over my shoulder.

"How does it look?"

He smiles. *Beautiful.*

I laugh and roll over, shaking him off.

"Don't smudge it!" he mimics me.

"I think it's ready—let's wash the ink off so we can see the stain."

The springwater's a deep bluish green where it bubbles up from under the hill, creating a pool below the overhanging bluff. Cool air rushes to meet us as we run toward it. We both already have our shirts off, and Stonefield gets his pants off first. He runs to the edge of the swirling spring and leaps in, hollering like a wild man. I get mine off as he comes back to the surface. When he sees me, he yells, "Jump!"

The water's winter cold and swallows me up like a grave. It turns my skin into a thousand cracking icicles. I open my eyes under the water and see Stonefield swimming toward me. We rise together, breaking through the surface at the same time.

I holler from the icy jolt, but it's a good kind of shock—like when Jesus was baptized and came up out of the river knowing he was a God who had the power to rise from the dead.

Stonefield swims in place, grinning. His wet, tangled hair hangs in his eyes, and his skin catches the light and glistens. We're both naked at the same time for the first time, and close enough to touch. The thought makes me light-headed.

I tread water, breathless. "It worked." My teeth chatter as I stare at the dark circle design on Stonefield's chest. It looks clean and perfect after the thick walnut ink's been washed away.

He studies the art on his chest. "The rock—it looks like it's on fire." When he moves, his naked body glows like burnished copper in the swirling water. Like a beautiful angel of light.

"Stonefield, I want to show you something I made."

13

"I WANT TO SEE IT." STONEFIELD'S EYES SHINE LIKE AMBER held up to the light.

"We can see it best from my secret place. If we swim under the bluff, we can climb a tunnel up to it instead of walking around and up the hill."

"Under the bluff?"

"Roubidoux Spring starts from under the bluff and flows out here through a space in the rock wall. The opening's not far from the surface, so we'll have some daylight shining on the water through the hole, and once we get into the cavern, I know the way through the tunnel in the dark."

"You've done this before?"

I pause, glancing at the stone face of the bluff where it meets the water. "Well . . . no. I usually get to my secret place through a cave opening in the woods. But I've seen turtles swim under this bluff. And I've explored the inside with a candle, coming from the other entrance, and found the cavern and the source of the spring—there's a little pool right inside. I've watched turtles swim through the hole and climb up onto the cave ledge, so I know how to do it."

"Well, I've watched hawks soar in the sky, so you should let me hold you while I fly off a cliff, since I know how to do it." He splashes water in my face.

I laugh and grab his head and shoulders, dunking him under. When he pushes back up, he's grinning like the sun. If he were to hold me, I would leap anywhere with him and never look back.

With a shake of his head, he flings the wet hair away from his face. *I feel the same way, Catrina.* "I'll go wherever you take me." *The deeper the better.*

Then come with me. I draw in a great breath and dive under the roiling surface, pushing water past me like a bird pushes wind past her wings. I shoot into the bottomless spring until I feel the water throbbing from a hole in the stone wall.

I'm a minnow swimming through the gap. I glance behind me. Patches of light and shade dance over Stonefield as he follows me into the darkness. As soon as I clear the rim, I stretch my arms out in front of me and rise to the surface slow, so I won't scrape against the rock wall of the cave pool. I break the surface and take a breath. I can barely see now.

I hear Stonefield surface.

"I'm here," he calls. He makes splashing noises as he pulls himself out of the water and I see the outline of his body as he moves into the cave and disappears into the darkness.

We made it. I reach for the edge of the pool and drag myself up onto the muddy floor of the cave. A little sunlight travels through the water, lighting up the pool, but the cave is so dark, I can only see vague shapes near the water.

I call, "Where are you?" My voice sounds strange bouncing off the stone walls.

"Here," he calls from a little farther ahead. I feel with my hands in front of me as I creep toward his voice. Thick cold mud squeezes between my toes and fingers. The smell of damp rock tickles my nose. Stonefield's naked body is slick and wet when I reach him. Lord, it makes something deep inside me flutter like it wants loose.

His arms slide under mine, steadying me. I smile at the strangeness of grasping hold of him without seeing what I'm doing. His arms are strong enough to carry me. Or crush me. I feel the unspent power in his tight muscles, like an unbroken mustang waiting for the chute gate to open. I start pulling him closer, but make myself let go. I want to take him deeper and higher. "Follow me." The cave's blacker than my worst darkness, but a thousand candles are burning inside me.

Stonefield rests his palm between my shoulder blades so he won't lose me as I turn to search out the tunnel entrance. I move forward slow with one hand stretched out and one pawing the air above me.

"Here it is. The ceiling's low—duck down."

The tunnel floor slopes uphill. Stonefield lets go of me to feel along the wall. His hand slides smooth down my back. The caress sends shivers up my spine. Lordy, I want him in my arms. Our way turns steep, and we have to walk hunched over as the ceiling lowers. Soon we're crawling on our hands and knees in the mud. After ages and ages of climbing, I slow down.

"Let's rest."

Stonefield's wet skin touches mine and gives me goose bumps. The sound of our breathing fills the tunnel.

Catrina.

I feel his presence inside me like the Holy Ghost speaking in a still, small voice. He moves toward me, and the slightest touch brushes against my hair. He leans closer, and I feel the warmth of his breath on my cheek. When he whispers, his words tickle my ear.

"Even when I can't look at you, I still see you, Catrina. I paint you in my mind with colors that come alive in the dark."

"Maybe you're an artist, too."

"I make my own wild work by thinking of you."

I lean toward his words. Stonefield's cheek brushes against mine as he lowers his head. His lips are hot on my neck as he tastes my skin.

Oh Lord. My heart forgets its rhythm and bangs against my chest like a mad thing. Stonefield must hear how loud he makes my breath come in and out. But I don't want to stop here. I want to take him to my secret place on the edge of the cliff, the edge of the sky.

Stonefield. "Let's keep going." *We're almost there.*

We start again, crawling until the ceiling rises, then walking bent forward when the floor levels. Finally, we reach the spot where the branch splits and connects to the main tunnel.

"This way." I walk faster, running my hands along the familiar walls. A snatch of light shines in the distance.

Stonefield rushes to catch up and bumps into me. He tries grabbing me around the waist, but I slip out of his hands into the mud. Our laughter fills the tunnel as I get up and we race toward the piece of sky. Almost there. I glance over my shoulder to look at him and stumble to the ground. Stonefield trips over my feet. We land on the mud floor of my secret place and I crawl to the ledge. He catches hold of me, laughing, and we collapse again, our bare arms and legs tangled together. When I look up, all I see is blue.

In the distance, the sound of voices singing in four-part harmony rises from Reverend Preston's tent meeting:

"Sweet rivers of redeeming love,
Lie just before mine eyes,
Had I the pinions of a dove,
I'd to those rivers fly."

Our bodies slide over each other like water. He folds me into his arms, and I draw him closer until there's no space left between us. His heart pulses against mine.

"I'd rise superior to my pain,
With joy outstrip the wind;
I'd cross o'er Jordan's stormy waves,
And leave the world behind."

"Catrina." He breathes my name like a secret. *I caught you.*

"Stonefield." I run my hands over the hills and hollows of him, exploring the strange new land of his body. *I let you.*

"I view the monster death, and smile,
Now he has lost his sting;
Though darkness rages all the while,
I still in triumph sing."

His breaths turn into kisses, waking my skin everywhere his mouth touches as if it's been sleeping until this second. I don't want him to stop until he wakes up every part of me.

My dove, in the cleft of the rock, the secret place. He kisses me a thousand times, until the world slips off its hinges, and I can't tell which way's up or down—everything is sky.

"I hold my Saviour in my arms,
And will not let Him go;
I'm so delighted with His charms,
No other god I'll know."

When our bodies come together, we cry out at the shock of it, and the sound echoes across the valley. My head tilts back, and my hair tumbles over the edge of the cliff. The world's upside-down. We see the black rock in the middle of Stone Field—a circle of darkness, set ablaze. And as I melt into the warmth of his arms, nothing else matters.

14

I<small>T'S ALMOST TWILIGHT BY THE TIME WE SWIM BACK</small>
through the spring and put our clothes on, shivering from
the cold water and the evening air flowing into the valley. In
Stone Field, the sorghum stalks are silhouetted against the dark
blue sky. They've grown thicker and are filling with sweet sugar
juice—these September stalks are no longer the thin grassy
shoots from the summer, but they're not quite ripe enough for
the press. I don't want this moment to move into the future. I
want to linger in Stone Field where it's sweet and peaceful.

But I need to go see how Papa's doing, and Henry will be back
soon. As we approach the house, I give Stonefield one last kiss.
He heads toward the barn and I start walking to the quiet house.

Lordy, just in time—the sound of Henry's wagon rounding
the bend sends me galloping to the back door and tearing
through the house toward my room. I hope Papa can't hear the
ruckus I'm making as I throw open my door and start peeling
off my wet clothes. I wad them up in a ball and stuff them under
my bed, then grab the nightgown I took off this morning and

shove it over my head. I jump into bed right as I hear Henry walk through the front door. He builds a fire and then walks to my room.

"You all right?"

I nod, but don't say anything. He keeps talking, thinking my throat hurts too much to speak.

"Effie and Dora send you their well wishes and say to tell you they'll miss you this week at the meetings."

I nod again, wishing he'd leave me be. Maybe it's my quietness, but Henry seems antsy to talk.

"I'm worried about your safety, Cat."

I wait for him to go on.

"I've been thinking about our little farmhand who acts like he doesn't remember where he came from or why he's here."

I bite my tongue, I want so bad to say something.

"I wouldn't be surprised if he's one of those Creek Indians who've joined up with the Confederates. Some of them want to stay neutral and be let alone. But there's just no place for middle ground anymore. If Stonefield's Creek, then what side is he on?"

"He doesn't have a side." I whisper the words as if my throat hurts too much to speak loud. "He lost his memory about all that."

"That's what he says. But what's he doing up here, alone, away from his people?"

I shake my head. "I don't know, Henry."

"Well, the fact is, we don't know anything about him, Cat. I'd hate to think we're harboring a traitor in our own house." He sighs and runs a hand through his hair. "I don't know. I'm trying to take care of you and Father, but everything is changing. Roubidoux's not safe anymore. There's a lot of hotheaded talk going around. Frank Louis left the Hosses' in a huff earlier, claiming that if anyone with Federalist leanings steps within a hundred feet of his property, he'll shoot." Henry's laugh sounds sad. "Frank Louis! We used to shoot rabbits together when we were boys and now he wants to shoot me."

He rubs his chin. "I need to protect you, Cat, but I'll be gone sooner than I planned. I don't think it's proper under the circumstances that I wait till next month to enlist. I talked with Mr. Hoss today and we've agreed that Dora and I will be married in Rolla tomorrow morning by the justice of the peace and spend about a week in St. Louis for our honeymoon."

What?

"I'll give Stonefield detailed instructions about what work I want done each day that I can't be here to work the farm myself. He needs to be constantly employed. If he hopes to remain here, he'll have to account for every minute of his time while I'm away and complete every work order I give to the exact detail. And if he doesn't, he's gone the moment I return—Father will just have to deal with it."

He looks at me, his eyes lined with worry. "Do you understand?"

Dora living here in a week? Henry off to war! It's like the world's gone mad. The only thing that keeps me from crying out in anger is the thought of having Stonefield all to myself while they're on their honeymoon. I nod, staring at the floor. I wish Henry would leave the doorway.

He waits, as if he expects me to say something like "Congratulations," or maybe he wants me to tell him how grateful I am for all he's done for me. But when I don't, he sighs. "I'll tell Father about tomorrow. Don't worry—you sleep in and rest. You don't have to attend—it will be a simple ceremony, just Dora, me, and the justice of the peace. It's for the best."

I just nod again and slide down under the covers, pulling them over my head to block out the image of my brother, who looks at me with disappointment on his face. I hate him for rushing to marry a fool woman he doesn't love just so he'll have someone to hold before he goes to war, someone to write him letters while he's away, and someone to make sure I stay penned in and proper while he's gone. I know he's marrying Dora because he can't have the woman he loves. Lord, how could he do such a thing.

It's been four days since Henry left, and every one a dream. In the mornings, I work side by side with Stonefield, helping him finish the work Henry assigned to him for the day, and then we eat supper with Papa. When my father retires to his study, we have the evenings to ourselves to do whatever we want.

Tonight it's almost dusk. We sneak into the pantry and pinch some oil to fill the grease lights in our little stone house. We didn't eat much at supper with Papa tonight because we want to have a picnic at night, just the two of us. I grab some salted pork and a jar of mustard pickles I made last summer, and

Stonefield fills a sack with biscuits and hooks a half-full jug of cider on his thumb. I pat Napoleon on the head as I close the door, and we're off to the woods.

We lie on the ground in our roofless house, with the food set out over the blanket, the little lamps burning, and the big starry sky hanging above us. For a while, we eat and talk about the wild work we want to make, but then we just lie quiet, our bodies tangled up together on the ground, staring up through the dangling feathers to the stars.

"Lookit." I point straight up. "Pegasus."

"What's Pegasus?"

"If you connect those stars"—I trace them in the air with my finger—"you can draw the flying horse, Pegasus. Papa's read all about the ancient Greeks and their stories about gods and creatures that are even more cockeyed than the stories in the Bible."

"I think I see your flying horse."

"Part horse and part bird. These Greek folks loved the creatures who weren't quite one thing nor the other, but something in-between. See?" I point to the southern part of the sky. "There's old Capricornus. He's part goat and part fish. I bet he's much more comfortable in the sky than trying to live on land with the normal goats or in the water with the fish, don't you?"

Stonefield gives a little snort-laugh. "I know how he feels, not being quite one thing nor the other. I wish I could have known these Greek people."

"Me too. Look—there's you and me." I smile up at Pisces.

"Where?"

"To the right of Pegasus. Papa says that's Aphrodite and Eros, the goddess and god of love. They escaped from the monster Typhon by leaping into the sea and turning themselves into fish."

"Looks like they're connected."

"They tied themselves together with a rope so they'd never lose each other."

Stonefield takes my hand and locks his fingers into mine. "And they've managed to stay together all this time."

"Maybe they escaped from time, too. I don't think there's time up there, do you?"

"Nor distance." Stonefield sits up and reaches for *Leaves of Grass*. "Mr. Whitman writes about that. Listen to this." He opens the book near the light of the grease lamp. I close my eyes and listen to the soft whisper of the pages as they turn. When Stonefield stops, it's as if the book is holding its breath.

" 'What is it, then, between us?' " he reads. " 'What is the count of the scores or hundreds of years between us? Whatever it is, it avails not—distance avails not, and place avails not . . . I am with you.' "

The pages let out their breath as Stonefield closes the covers. "He's right, this Mr. Whitman. These thoughts he's speaking to us now through this book—he wrote them days and days ago and miles away from us, but we hear them as if he's whispering in our ears right now. He may be dead, for all we know, but it doesn't matter. He's right here, speaking to us."

"Haunting us?"

"Maybe . . . yes. Catrina, that's the way it will be with us. Love is stronger than even death."

"Yes. I hope you haunt me when you die." I imagine the smile on his lips.

"And you must haunt me, too. We'll live here, together, like Aphrodite and Eros live in the sky." The lid of the small chest that we made from oak wood creaks open and Stonefield fumbles around for something inside it. I hear the scratch of a graphite pencil on paper and then he closes the book again, setting it inside the chest. "Nothing can come between us, Catrina." His skin brushes mine. *We'll always have this invisible rope tying us together.*

He leans over and when he kisses me, my soul rises and wants free as it always does when his lips touch mine. My mouth, my neck, my shoulders—every part of me he kisses feels my aching spirit beneath the skin. It wants to be with his soul and hold it in the same way our bodies are touching each other. I can feel our souls slipping free of us, to cleave together and become one. And then I let Stonefield come inside me, again, closer to me than anyone else. He's deep inside me, part of me. He *is* me. He looks into my eyes as we move together, and I can tell he's thinking the same thing. My heart's beating faster as it gets ready for that moment our souls leap from our bodies. When mine leaves me I see white light, and my body trembles with the pleasure of releasing it. I'm light as air. Stonefield feels it, too—he's shaking in my arms.

We hold on till all is still. Our bodies have died a little while our souls are hovering in an embrace over our heads. Our breath, coming fast, is the only thing that tells me we're both alive. Slow, our spirits let go of each other and slip back into our bodies, making us heavy again. We stare at each other in wonder. Each time we come together it's like a miracle from the Bible. Like God flies us up to Heaven for a peek, and then lets us go back down to earth. We lie there, stunned. Soon, sleep washes over me slow and easy like Stonefield's voice in my head. *Always.*

15

THE GREASE LIGHTS HAVE GONE OUT WHEN I WAKE
in the night to Stonefield's moans. He's tossing on the
ground like a new-caught fish. I fumble in the dark and shake
him awake.

"Stonefield, are you all right?"

He gasps, and I feel him jolt, like he's just fallen out of his
dream. He's breathing hard. I hold on to him and wait till his
breath slows down. His skin is cool, but damp with sweat.

"Was it a nightmare?"

He turns onto his side, facing me. I can barely see him in the
dark. "Memories. Dreams about things that happened to me."

Lord. I sit up. "What do you remember?"

"How I got here."

I wait.

He's quiet, like he wants my permission to continue.

I don't want to hear about his past, but I say, "Go ahead.
Tell it."

"I was teaching my primary class at the Mission School for

Orphaned Children. It was in Lanesville, Missouri." His voice sounds distant, as if he's far away inside the story he's telling.

"That's not far from here." But Stonefield doesn't hear me, he's so lost in his memory.

"My students called me Mr. Hanson. Thomas Hanson. Half of the children were absent with a fever going around, but the group that remained was excited. We were finishing up the last part of their first reader, each student taking a turn reading aloud. They were so proud to be finishing their first real book, and we had a celebration planned afterward—with games and shadow pantomimes—they could hardly contain themselves."

I wait, quiet, to let him tell the rest.

"But we didn't finish." Stonefield's voice is so low I can barely hear him. "The door burst open right when Tommy Williams started reading. He dropped the book. I remember watching it fall to the floor—it seemed to fall so slowly, like time wasn't paying attention to the rules anymore. Then all at once, time sped up. Men in gray uniforms rushed into our classroom. Papers flew from my desk, and the children screamed."

I feel his body tense up as if the soldiers might burst through our secret house right this instant.

"The men took hold of me by the arm and fired questions at me."

"What kind of questions?"

"They yelled, 'Which are you for, the North or the South?' I said I wasn't for either one. They said everyone had to pick sides, but I just wanted them to leave without hurting any of my students. So I told them I didn't want to be a part of the war, and just wanted to be left in peace, but they wouldn't have it."

"What did they do?"

"They said I must be a nigger or an Indian savage or I'd know better. They wanted to know if I was mostly white, or mostly some other thing, like Mexican, Negro, or Muscogee Creek Indian. When they said Muscogee Creek, I recognized it as the name of my people. I knew nothing about them, but I knew they were mine. I hadn't heard the term in so many years. I was so stunned, I didn't say anything and just shook my head, so the men laughed at me for not knowing who I was or where I came from." His body's trembling now.

"What happened?"

"First they said they'd shoot me in front of the children if I didn't tell them what I was and which side I was on." His fingers tighten around mine. "But then they decided I was probably part Indian and part Negro—they called me a mutt. And since I refused to join the Confederacy, they decided to sell me into slavery down in Oklahoma Territory, where they were headed."

"How did you get away?"

"I bolted." He slips his hand from mine. "I jumped out the second-story window." He shakes his head. "How could I do that? How could I just abandon my students?" He runs his hand through his hair. "By the time they made it down the stairs and out the door, I'd already hopped into the back of a wagon of supplies on the road, headed northeast toward St. Louis. I didn't care where I was going as long as it was in the opposite direction of those men and Oklahoma Territory, where they wanted to sell me. But the children's fever sickness caught hold of me on the way and I fell out of the wagon somewhere near Roubidoux."

I take hold of his hand again. "And ended up in a cane field."

"Not just any cane field." He locks his fingers around mine and pulls me close. Finally, he's coming back to the here and now.

"Stonefield," I whisper. "Now that you remember it, you can forget all about it again. You can just be you, here with me."

His hand loosens just a bit in mine, and I can feel his arm stiffen. "I can't, Catrina. Not if I don't know who I am."

"But you do know who you are. You remembered."

"I remembered that someone took things away from me when I was young. They took me away from the Creek Indians and took my name—I don't even remember it—and they called me Thomas Hanson instead. They took my language and forced me to speak theirs until I forgot my own. I won't know who I am until I find out more about that part of me they stole away."

"Maybe the less you find out the better—you know how people feel about Creek Indians."

"People?" He pulls his hand from mine. "You mean people like you?"

"I didn't mean me." I reach for his fingers again in the dark and can't find them. "I mean those men who came to your school and the writers in the newspapers who make Henry worried about the Creeks who joined the Confederates." I tell him what Henry said, and how no one in Roubidoux would like that he was a Creek Indian.

Stonefield stays quiet for a long time. Finally, he says in a low voice, "I need to know more about who I am."

"Stonefield—"

"That's not my name. Neither is Thomas Hanson."

"But that's the past." I find his arm and hold on tight, wishing I could squeeze away the stiffness and draw him back to me. "None of it matters now."

He pulls away and turns onto his side. His voice sounds distant. "It matters to me."

I wake up to the smell of the decaying roses and mint leaves, and I feel his warm body rise and fall in sleep beside me. It's already late in the morning. Maybe we're just dreaming. I stare up at the swaying feathers and wait for them to turn into wooden ceiling beams. I expect at any moment to hear Henry's voice calling from the kitchen, but Henry's still away, and I am in the woods with Stonefield. All I hear are morning birds and the bubbling creek. I close my eyes.

I want the dream to keep going.

I wonder if Joseph in the Bible felt this way when he dreamed about the sun, moon, and stars bowing down to him. But his brothers found out about it and threw him in a pit and sold him into slavery to keep the beautiful vision from coming true. He should have just lain still and kept on dreaming. It reminds me of the memory that Stonefield recalled last night, of the men who came to the mission and tried to sell him into slavery for not joining the army.

What will happen to Stonefield? If Creek Indians are considered Confederates and most folks around here are for the Union, will they turn him in as a traitor? I remember what Henry said before he left for St. Louis: exactly what those men at the mission school said, "There's just no place for middle ground."

Lord, Henry. Won't he be worse than ever if he finds out Stonefield's Creek like he thought. It makes me all-overish. I wish Stonefield would let his past alone and not go chasing after the missing pieces.

I want this dream to last, but our time is running out just like it did for Joseph. Henry and Dora are coming back tomorrow. I turn and lie on my stomach. My restlessness wakes Stonefield, and he stirs beside me. Mr. Whitman's *Leaves of Grass* lies open on the ground beside him.

"What is it, then, between us?" The memory of the lines he read last night floats back to me. *"What is the count of the scores or hundreds of years between us? Whatever it is, it avails not— distance avails not, and place avails not . . . I am with you."*

Stonefield sits up and yawns. He traces the dark circles of walnut ink on my back, gentle.

I breathe in the gingery smell of wet cedar trees. *Go slow,* I say to him, silent. I ration my breaths, stretching and measuring them to make each one last longer. *Make time slow down. I want to stay here with you for scores or hundreds of years. Always.*

Even as I think the words, a darkness moves over me like the shadow of a storm cloud. I want to stop it before it swallows us. "Stonefield," I whisper, "please don't tell Henry your memory's returned. If he finds out you're a Creek Indian like those Confederates, he'll—"

A twig snaps outside.

I stop. The darkness rolls in thick. Something's not right. We're not alone.

Stonefield's finger stops.

All the little hairs on my arms rise.

Please, no.

I don't open my eyes—I screw them shut tighter.

Keep going. I hold my breath. *It's no one. Please, let's keep dreaming.*

Catrina—

But it's too late. Someone gasps from our doorway.

I know that when I open my eyes, I'll be wide-awake. I turn to look.

It's Lu.

My heart sinks.

The words *you're a Creek Indian like those Confederates* still hang in the air—I know she heard them. She stares through the ivy curtain at the circle designs on our naked bodies.

Oh Hell.

I never saw her look so stunned. She grasps an envelope tight in her hands like she's trying to wring blood from it. I want to shut my eyes and make her disappear, but all I can do is stare back at her.

Lu blinks as if she's trying to decide if we're real or not. Her look of surprise turns to disgust. "Heavens," she whispers in a shaky voice, "you really do belong to the Devil." The crumpled letter slips from her fingers to the ground.

My heart turns cold as December as I watch her run away.

16

My NAME ON THE ENVELOPE IS WRITTEN IN EFFIE'S steady, graceful hand. I imagine her across the hollow, up in the corner of her attic, channeling steady, graceful thoughts onto the paper—thoughts for me. I am unsteady and graceless—my hands are shaking as I smooth out the creases Lu made when she crushed the letter in her fist. I read it out loud to Stonefield, whose eyes are still lit with angry fire sparked by Lu trespassing on our secret place. My voice shakes worse than my hands.

Dear Catrina,

Please excuse my use of a messenger, but I am host to visitors who have come to hear Reverend Preston preach this evening, and Lu kindly offered to deliver this to you at your father's house for me. I trust Mr. Dickinson is well. I have heard the happy news that your brother and Mrs. Dickinson are expected to arrive home soon. Please express to them our congratulations on their recent nuptials.

As you know, my father's houseguest, Reverend Preston, was holding tent meetings in the evenings as we finished building our new church. Now that it is finished, the reverend particularly requested that I invite you to the first meeting early this evening. We have a beautiful new bell in the roof of the building, and I will be ringing it myself. When you hear it, I hope you will come join us.

The hymn sings are lovely, and Reverend Preston is truly a passionate speaker. I've observed that the sentiments of the people of Roubidoux have been heightened by his stirring sermons to a fever pitch of religious excitement. The spiritual fervor seems contagious, drawing people from as far as two counties away to our ever-growing tent meetings.

But such a diagnosis worries me slightly. Although I am happy to see our friends and neighbors so eager to obey the scriptures, I fear that sometimes the good preacher's sermons lead them to overzealousness in some matters, including harshly judging those who choose not to attend the meetings. Perhaps a cure to this problem may be found in the simple act of you accepting Reverend Preston's invitation to join us this evening. He seems to have a particular interest in your spiritual well-being and is eager to be a friend to you, as he says that God has put you on his heart. Stonefield's presence would also be highly desired. I believe the townspeople's fears and suspicions about him might be allayed by his presence, and the congregation and Reverend Preston might come to know and understand you both better, bringing a healthy peace to all concerned.

Please do come, Catrina. My mind would be eased by your presence. Please give my kind regards to your father as well as my wish for his continued health. I remain always:

Your faithful friend,
Effie Lenox

I wait to hear what Stonefield will say. He searches my face to know my feelings, but I scarcely know them myself. I take hold of the page and tear out, careful, a phrase from the letter and read it aloud.

" 'Your brother and Mrs. Dickinson are expected to arrive home soon.' "

I smooth the strip of paper through my fingers. "Effie doesn't want Henry to find us together—she knows he'd be a hothead about it. It's a warning—she's trying to help us." I take the little strip of Effie's words and pin it to one of the dangling feathers with a thorn. It waves and spins through the air.

"There's another message in the letter." Stonefield points to the middle of the page. "Look. This preacher person is saying bad things about us in his sermons." He frowns at the paper in my hands.

I imagine the forget-me-not blue of Reverend Preston's eyes and the earnest sound of his voice when he said God had wondrous things in store for me. "Effie didn't say that."

"It's there between her words." He points to that part of the letter:

"I fear that sometimes the good preacher's sermons lead them to overzealousness in some matters, including harshly judging those who choose not to attend the meetings."

My heart beats faster. "You think Reverend Preston is saying slanderous things about us from the pulpit? Why would he do that? Effie says he wants to be my friend."

"She says he's particularly interested in your spiritual well-being—maybe he thinks you need to repent before you can be his special friend." Stonefield makes a face and rolls his eyes. "Something's going on at his meetings that makes Effie uncomfortable. I aim to go tonight and find out what it is."

My nose wrinkles up. "You mean you want to get cleaned up and wear a shirt and sit through a long-winded sermon?"

Stonefield shakes his head. "I don't plan on doing any of those things. No, I mean I want to spy on this preacher man and find out what he says about people when he doesn't know they're around."

I tear out Effie's second warning and pin it to another feather. Her words twirl round and round in one direction until the slip of paper can't twist any more, then it spins back the other way. I wish I could twist the words until Effie's meaning is wrung clear from them. "When Effie rings the bell tonight, I'll go with you."

Before I fold the ragged letter back into the envelope and place it in the oak chest, I tear one more strip of words free from the rest and pin it to a yellowthroat's feather. It flutters back and forth like a banner over me:

I remain always:

Your faithful friend,
Effie Lenox

Even from the road, as we round the bend in the twilight, I smell the whitewash and fresh lumber of the new church. At first we hear nothing but crickets and cicadas, and if it weren't for the horses and wagons out front, I'd think no one was inside.

A sharp "Amen!" cuts through the silence, then the noise seems to pour out all at once—a waterfall of *amens*, *hallelujahs*, and *praise the Lords*. Stonefield takes my hand, and we run toward a small grove of hawthorn trees near the door while the noise covers the sound of our feet. A flock of thrushes takes flight, shaking the thorny branches and rattling red berries as we hurry behind the trees for cover and watch through the half-opened windows.

The church is packed as tight as Dora's corsets, with the bulging congregation overflowing up in front onto the platform where Reverend Preston strides back and forth, clutching a leather Bible. The shouts and murmurs fade again to silence.

The ribbons of Reverend Preston's black tie flutter over his shoulder as his boots click across the new wood planks. His tousled blond hair stands on end, as if he climbed out of bed that morning with more important things on his mind than grooming. His eyes are closed so he can pay better attention to the voice of the Holy Spirit talking to him, but he doesn't falter in his pace—he walks strong and sure like he knows God will catch him if he stumbles.

He stops in the center of the platform and opens his eyes. Even from far away, they shine bluer than the September sky above me. The congregation takes in their breath and holds it, waiting to hear the words of the Lord fall from the preacher's lips.

"Beloved, listen to my voice." It's like asking thirsty people to drink. His voice flows, rich and mellow, carrying God's words all the way to the back of the church without a speck of effort. "You are here tonight because you hunger after truth." He squeezes the Bible harder till it trembles in his hand.

"Yes!" People in the congregation nod their heads.

"But the truth you seek isn't found among the hills and hollows of this dark earth." He sweeps the Bible toward the opposite window to indicate Roubidoux and all the land beyond.

"No, it's not!" someone calls out.

He points with the Bible toward the congregation. "Nor is it found in the hills and hollows of your hearts."

"No?" they cry.

Reverend Preston shakes his head. "No!" His handsome features tighten into a frown. "The truth doesn't dwell in these dark, lowly places. Heavenly wisdom can never be found in earthly knowledge."

"Tell us!" someone shouts.

"Say on!" Others join in.

Reverend Preston raises his Bible. "This truth that you seek comes from up above." He points the Good Book toward Heaven. "The righteous pursue things of the spirit while the wicked ignore the words of the Lord. We should not waste our time reading earthly books written by sinful men." He shakes his head. "This is the only book we will ever need!" He pounds the Bible with his fist.

He wipes the sweat from his forehead with his sleeve. "The wicked follow their savage hearts and seek pleasure in earthly wiles—charms of the flesh." He gazes off into the distance, and a grave look settles over his features as if he is imagining what horrible things the wicked people might be doing with each other right this minute. "But the earth shall pass away, Beloved! It will perish along with the wicked heathens who cling to it."

"Amen!" Lu's voice catches my attention, and I notice her sitting at Reverend Preston's feet on the crowded steps of the platform with a look of rapture on her face. I want to slap it off. I know she's thinking of me and Stonefield and how we must be wicked for seeking pleasure in earthly things like being alone together, naked in the woods. I know she talks about us to people. Maybe even Reverend Preston.

Stonefield's just as angry as I am—I feel his body turn stiff beside me.

I search for Effie and find her standing calm by the wall near the back, her hands folded neatly together in front of her as she listens. Only the tight way her lips are pressed together lets me know that she's concerned.

Reverend Preston lowers his Bible. "The wicked belong to the Devil."

Lu nods. "Yes!"

"They worship the created instead of the Creator, loving the natural realm instead of storing up spiritual treasures in Heaven."

Stonefield makes a noise like a low growl in his throat. "You scullion!" he says under his breath.

At the Shakespeare insult, I turn to look at him, but Stonefield's not smiling. His jaw clenches, his eyes are on fire. "Lu's talked bad about us to people, Catrina. He's preaching about you and me because we don't come to his church and we want to be left alone together. Didn't you hear him? He said I have a savage heart. Just like those soldiers who came to my classroom and called me savage. And my teacher saying I spoke a savage tongue. He's saying you and I are the wicked heathens."

"He didn't say it was us."

"He didn't have to."

"You've seen them," Reverend Preston goes on, "the ones who give in to the temptation of the Devil and this world."

"Yes, I've seen them!" Lu cries.

Stonefield's arms are taut, as if he wants to strangle the preacher with one hand and Lu with the other.

Reverend Preston turns to Lu, his blue eyes burning like the

142

hottest part of a flame. "The wicked live in sin and refuse the fellowship of the godly, ignoring the goodness of God's truth."

"Yes!" Lu stands up. Her body's rigid, shaking. "I've seen them with my own eyes!"

My hands tighten around the hawthorn branch, its thorns cut into my skin.

People in the congregation are hungry to hear more, and they call out for Lu to "Say on, say on!"

Effie is the only one who seems to want her sister to stop. She shakes her head at Lu, but Lu doesn't pay attention.

"They live like filthy animals, sinning for all the whole world to see! They're wicked, wicked!"

Hawthorn berries burst in my clenched fists, red juice squeezes between my fingers like blood. I feel Stonefield separating from me, moving through the trees, toward the doors.

No, Stonefield, wait. I follow, trying to catch hold of his arm, but he's out of my reach.

Reverend Preston's eyes close again and he doesn't see us through the windows. He keeps preaching. "Beloved, such souls are in grave danger. Spiritual danger." His voice grows deeper, stronger. "There is a spiritual battle—a war—waging in their savage hearts, and they must choose a side. They must choose between this earthly kingdom, which brings only death, and the Kingdom of Heaven, which brings eternal life. Such a soul can still be saved. It must be saved. For on the Day of Atonement, if it has not repented, God will throw it into the very pit of *Hell*!"

As Reverend Preston shouts *Hell*, Stonefield opens the door. The new hinges squeak. People turn and cry out, surprised to see Stonefield standing all quiet with his fists clenched, glaring at Reverend Preston.

Lu clutches the preacher's arm. "It's him—the Indian heathen! He's a Creek Confederate, too. And look at the mark of the Devil on his chest—it's the same as the one in Dickinson's field!"

The whole church comes alive with voices.

"Look!"

"It's true!"

"Lord help us!"

I run to him. "It's not true!"

"Look at her," Lu gasps.

Everyone speaks at once, crowding in.

"It's the Dickinson girl."

"Is that blood all over her hands?"

"What's she done?"

I wipe my hands on my pants, but the hawthorn berry stains won't go away.

"What happened?"

I shrink, pressing back into Stonefield for support. They're all staring and shouting and crowding in on me. Like the day I killed Mother, they're trying to suffocate and crush me. My darkness comes rolling back.

Stonefield's strong arm reaches to slide around my waist, but it's too late. My darkness takes me. I go limp and slip from him, falling against cold hands that reach out to grab me.

"Look—the Devil's sign is on her, too—you can see it through the back of her shirt!"

"Mercy, it's a man's shirt, too—and pants!"

They're closing in and I'm a coon stuck in a trap, wishing I had the strength to claw and bite my way free of them. *Stonefield!*

Growling like a bear, he grabs their hands, tearing them away from me. "Leave her alone!"

Now they're grasping for him, seizing him. The whole room shifts back and forth as I'm jostled and thrust forward. I fall, and my head slams the edge of an oak bench. My knee cracks against the floor.

Pain shoots up my leg and down my skull.

Catrina—

Everything disappears.

17

I THINK I'M IN A DARK CAVE. SOMETIMES I HEAR PEOPLE murmuring my name. They seem so far away.

"How can a body sleep for so long? It's been a whole night and almost another day!"

"She's had a concussion, Lu. I'm thankful her wound wasn't too deep. My stitches are small, but I'm afraid there'll still be a scar."

"Goodness gracious! And right across her forehead where everyone can see. It's a shame—some folks have said she'd be the prettiest girl in Roubidoux if she weren't so wild, but she'll never be thought pretty now. Scars are so ugly. Don't you agree, Reverend Preston?"

"Miss Lu, our Savior's scars are a thing of beauty, for by His stripes we are healed."

"Effie, my dear, you did an excellent job. We should thank the Lord for sparing her and for putting you there at the ready to mend her up so fast and able."

"But, Father, there would be no need for mending if people hadn't treated her so roughly."

"Miss Effie, what happened that night was no accident. The Holy Ghost works in mysterious ways. I've been praying for Miss Catrina from the day I first met her. The Lord put her on my heart in a special way. I see her image in my dreams most every night. I am meant to help her. The Lord's Spirit called out to her spirit and drew her to the house of the Lord. It was out of deep love for her that He allowed her to be bruised and broken. Not for her destruction, but that she might come to know spiritual healing."

"Heavens! I hope so. But I doubt she even wants to have her spirit healed. I think she likes being wicked."

"Hush, Lu. We can't know the condition of a person's heart, but what we can do is help heal the body. Now, take those linens out to wash like I asked. Excuse me, Reverend Preston, we need to tidy things up before I go let Mr. Dickinson know what's happened. I'm not sure if Henry and Dora have returned yet."

"Yes, of course. Your father has given me leave to stand prayer vigil in a guest room down the hall through the night. I will be nearby if needed."

"You can help Lu care for Catrina."

The cave grows darker, and the voices trickle away like a stream. I drift back to sleep. When I wake again, things seem quieter. I open my eyes real slow against the painful throbbing in my temples and find I'm not in a cave after all. I'm lying on a soft feather bed, alone in one of the Lenoxes' guest rooms.

Thunder rumbles outside, and my hungry stomach echoes the noise. Rain pelts against the house.

I struggle to sit up. So weak. Bandages are wrapped around my aching head. My throat is sore and swollen. I wait while the memories of what happened slide into place.

The congregation pressing in. Reverend Preston preaching about wicked heathens and savages. *Stonefield*. He tried to save me from them. What happened to him? I remember his eyes, wide and fierce. Did the people bind him like a dangerous animal and drag him away, or is he back home with Henry? Henry *and Dora*, I remind myself. They will be back from their honeymoon and living in the house.

I throw the covers off, but I still feel tangled up. Oh Hell. Somebody's taken off my pants and shirt and put a damned nightdress on me, complete with damned underclothes. I pull off the twisty dress but leave on the camisole and bloomers. I stretch my leg and bend it. Good. My knee's black and purple and powerful sore, but I think I can walk. I slide my feet to the floor and rise. The room tips to one side and my body turns to water. I fall backward against the bed for a moment, but push right back up. Holding on to the bedpost, I wait for my balance to return as I stare at one of Mr. Lenox's wooden masks from the Congo, hanging on the opposite wall. It stares back at me, appalled, its eyes large, its mouth round.

I hobble across the room, find my boots in the corner, and struggle to pull them on. It looks to be early morning—still a little dark. The house is quiet but for the low rumble of thunder and the drum of rain on the roof. I walk quiet as I can past the other guest room, where Reverend Preston must be praying, and limp down the stairs. The steps creak louder than the thunder, but it doesn't take me long to get to the front door. The moment I step outside, I'm soaked through.

An upstairs window creaks open.

I run.

Pain shoots down my leg.

The gray sky brightens in a sudden burst of lightning, and every leaf on every tree stands out clear and sharp for just a moment.

Run.

Thunder crashes and rolls over the hills, echoing through the hollow. Feels like it's booming inside my ribs and rolling through my heart.

Run.

The pain is almost unbearable. Rain slides down my face, into my eyes.

"Catrina!"

I stop, glancing through the trees. At first I think it's Stonefield calling to me from a distance, but it's coming from behind me, from the Lenox house.

"Miss Catrina!"

Reverend Preston.

"You're not well!"

My head's swimming, eyelids heavy like iron hinges.

"It's too far to be running to your house in this weather. Come back to the Lenoxes'—we'll get you warm and dry. I'll ride over to fetch your brother for you."

No, not Henry.

"I'm fine!" I shout. I run, forcing my sore leg to move faster. The pain shoots up into my skull.

So dizzy.

I feel faint.

And then the preacher is right behind me. "I only want to help you," he says.

He's probably telling the truth, but his sort of help means taking away the things about me he thinks are wicked, and I don't want any part of me to be taken away. The gray world spins. It's a child's top, spinning on the edge of a table. Spinning, spinning. It falls and hits my forehead, knocking me down into the wet grass. My darkness throbs against my eyes, my temples. The rain beats against my face.

His hands take hold of me. I try pushing them away, but they're the sort of hands that don't argue or fight—they just hold firm.

"Miss Catrina, you're not in your right mind."

"Which mind am I in—I've only got the one." I lunge away from him, but he's still got ahold of me. I moan, twisting and writhing to get free. He won't let go.

"The Devil's tricked your mind. He tells us wrong is right—he's the great deceiver. He makes darkness look like light and evil look like goodness." He slides his arms all the way around my waist and lifts me from the ground.

I hate that he's stronger than me.

I slap him. He winces but doesn't loosen his grip. I stare at the red mark in the shape of my hand on his face. I expect him to turn that cheek and give me the other one to slap, too, like Jesus says, but he only swallows hard and looks at me with those grave eyes.

"The Lord sent me to help you, Miss Catrina, and I won't disobey Him." He pulls me closer and I can smell the lavender on his clothes, even though we're both soaking wet. My darkness throbs so heavy in my head, I can hardly see. Fear coils and releases inside me. I kick my legs. His arms only tighten around me.

"Let me go!" I bash my head into his chin. He walks faster, taking me back to the Lenox house, farther away from home. I scratch the skin of his arms. It bleeds under my nails. He walks on, every step putting more distance between me and the hollow, where Stonefield might be waiting for me.

I shake my head, thrashing my wet hair like stinging whips across his eyes. His fingers are wrapped around my wrists like manacles. I bite them, hard. But he tastes like skin, not steel.

"Damn you, damn you, damn you!" My voice turns scratchy and hoarse from screaming, till I sound like an old hag. A witch. I can't tell if I'm crying or if it's only the rain streaming down my face.

He prays under his breath while I curse him all the way back to the house.

18

THINGS ONLY TURN WORSE WHEN WE GET TO THE house.

I must be having a nightmare. If I thrash and jerk my body hard enough, I'll wake up. But no matter how hard I fight them, Reverend Preston still holds me down on the bed in the Lenox guest room, his chest on mine, his knee over my thighs, while Lu attempts to tie my wrists and ankles to the bedposts with ropes of twisted linen.

"Effie!" I cry. "Papa! Where are you?"

Why aren't they here?

"Stonefield, speak to me!"

"Goodness!" Lu cries. "I told you she hears the Indian's voice in her head!"

Maybe if I relax my muscles, the dream will change—I can dream that I'll fall asleep on this bed and wake up in my own bed, or in the secret house with Stonefield.

"Miss Lu, she's quieted down. Hurry and tie the last bind. Gently, now—don't bruise her. We don't want to make things worse for her; we just need to keep her from hurting herself. Here's the sleeping powder your sister left for her. Just mix it in the warm milk."

I turn my mind to the rhythmic sound of rain dripping from the roof and the distant barking of a dog until the voices in the room become nothing more than a low hum. I breathe in the fresh earthy smell of mud on the damp camisole I'm wearing and imagine I'm running through the rain again, toward Stonefield, with no one to stop me.

"Reverend Preston, I hardly think these binds are necessary!"

It's Effie's strong, clear voice, the next morning.

I struggle to wake, but sleep hangs on me like a thick mountain fog. "Effie?" The word sounds like the croaking of a bullfrog. My throat's so sore, I must have finally caught the sickness from Papa like I pretended to Henry.

"Listen to that horrible voice—I told you, Effie!"

"Hush, Lu. Rest, Catrina." Slender fingers tug at the knots tied near my wrists and then my ankles, releasing me. I can't open my eyes.

"Stonefield?" I moan as bullets shoot through my stiff limbs. My whole body's turned numb—they must have left me to sleep in this position with my arms tied up. I cry out in pain and shake my limbs to force some feeling into them. The bed shudders and bangs against the wall.

"See, Effie—she's possessed!" Lu screeches. "Preacher Preston's right—it's a demon inside her!"

I shake my head hard against the pillow.

"No!" My voice is so hoarse and rough—it scares even me.

Effie's warm hand slides into mine. "Catrina's had a concussion and been treated very roughly, Lu. She's not feeling herself. It's important that she relax—she needs rest. Henry, we'll let you have some time with your sister. Come, Lu, Reverend Preston."

"Miss Effie, since you've taken the binds off, perhaps I should stay—"

"I'm sure Henry can handle everything."

"Yes . . . yes, of course."

"Thank you both," Henry says as he sits down beside my bed. "My sister and I will be fine."

When they're gone, I use all my strength to push the sleep away. I drag my eyes open to look at him.

"Catrina. Dora and I were so worried about you. Imagine coming home from St. Louis to such a mess. When we got back late last night we found Effie with Father, who'd taken a turn for the worse with his throat sickness. Dora's with him now. When Effie told us about what happened at the church, I came here with her right away."

"Papa?" I force the word out.

"It started out with the throat sickness you both had before we left, but Effie's worried his is turning into rheumatic fever like he had when he was young. He's very weak."

"I want to go see him."

"You're not strong enough yet. We don't want your own throat sicknesses to turn into rheumatic fever like Father's. You need to stay put until you're well, and Reverend Preston has expressed his hope that you will do so. He seems quite concerned for y—"

"I want to see Stonefield."

Henry pushes the chair away as he stands up. It screeches across the floorboards. "That savage almost got you killed. I know you're feeling poorly, Catrina, but I won't stand for it." He starts pacing in front of the bed. "Cat." His voice turns softer, pleading. "Don't trouble yourself about him. It will only make your illness worse."

"Being away from him is making me worse."

"Don't be ridiculous." Henry's voice takes a sharp turn upward, where his anger lies. "I don't know how the fool's managed to charm you and Father, but it's clear to me he's mad as a bat out in daylight. I found some more of his nonsense in the hollow—huge rock pillars all over the woods—almost as ridiculous as the circles he cut in the cane field. When I told him I'd tear them down, he almost went mad with shaking— he looked like he was going to bust. He cussed up and down for me to leave the art alone. Ha! Art, he called it!" Henry shakes his head. He pulls the chair back to the bed and sits down again.

"He said that?" Warmth fills me at hearing Stonefield's fierce protection of my wild work.

"Yep, he called it art—I swear he did. He said if I knocked them down, I'd be knocking down 'beauty and truth.' He's as batty as they come, Cat. He doesn't belong here—it's obvious to me now."

Henry clears his throat. "Lu told us he's a Creek Indian. I think he's one of those Indians where the effort of acting civilized makes him go insane. He spouts nothing but nonsense and he could turn violent again at the drop of a hat. For God's sake, now listen, Cat. While we were in St. Louis, I met with Dr. Rueben from the St. Louis Asylum—"

"Stonefield's as sane as I am."

"Well." Henry's eyes shift away from me. "To tell the truth, it was *your* mental state Dora and I were concerned about. Dr. Rueben thinks this boy may have been a bad influence on you and made things worse than they already were for your fragile mental condition. You haven't been yourself ever since Mother died. Now, Reverend Preston feels—"

"Where is he?" I struggle to push myself up.

"Reverend Preston? He just went downstairs so we could talk. Catrina, he practically saved your life! Effie can hardly get him to leave your side. He wants to help you, and Dora and I agree with the measures he's proposed."

"Stonefield. Where is he?"

"Damn it, Cat. Lie down. He's gone." Henry swipes his hand through the air as if he's waving Stonefield out of existence. "After we came home last night, he left. I didn't even have to tell him to—he did it on his own. He's gone, Cat. It's for your own good."

For my own good? "You don't know what's good for me!" The words tear out of my sore throat. "You never have."

Stonefield, gone? It's not true. He would never leave me.

A faint sound stirs inside me. A voice saying my name?

"Stonefield!" My heart comes alive. I throw the covers to the floor and push myself from the bed. My legs forget how to stand. They tremble as I move toward the window.

"Lie down, Cat!"

The sky's still a dull gray. Rain has soaked the bark of the trees, turning them black.

Stonefield? My legs buckle and Henry catches me.

Did I only imagine Stonefield's faint voice?

Through the window I see a yellow leaf separate from a nearby limb.

People say if you catch a falling leaf before it hits the ground, it means you'll get a long stretch of happiness. I watch it float, slow, all the way down to the grass. Coldness seeps through the panes.

Oh God. *Stonefield, where are you? I'll meet you in Hudgens Hollow.* "I'm coming." The words are a painful growl from my raw throat.

"Who are you talking to? Come back to the bed and lie down, Cat."

"I won't!" My throat's on fire. I shove him away from me.

Henry's eyes widen at my strange, terrible voice. He's afraid of me, afraid of the demon that Reverend Preston thinks is inside me.

I push past him.

"Stop!" Henry moves between me and the door. "Stonefield's gone, Cat." The mixture of anger and fear on his face makes my breath tighten in my chest. "You're unwell, damn it! That heathen is the last thing you should be concerned about. If you try to run after him, I will contact authorities of the Union Army faster than you can blink and tell them to come get that traitor. I know exactly where he is. Birds of a feather flock together."

"He's not a traitor! He's nothing—not for the South or the North. He's—"

"Being neither one nor the other's the same thing as being a traitor."

"No, it's not!"

"Tell that to the Federalist soldiers. Any one of them would be happy as a dog with two tails to catch a Confederate Creek Indian and find an interesting way to kill him."

Lord. I clench my fists so hard, my nails cut into my palms. "Henry, you can't keep us apart. If you know where he's gone you have to tell me."

Henry steps toward me and takes hold of my shoulders. "You need Reverend Preston's help, Cat. At first I thought the doctor in St. Louis might help you, but Reverend Preston's assured me you don't need to go to that hospital. He says your wild ways and the voices you hear are a spiritual problem—the work of Satan. He's experienced in these things, Cat. He'll cast out the spirits that plague you, so you don't have to hear their voices anymore telling you to dress like a man and do all these sorts of wild things that come into your head."

He draws me closer. "After the reverend casts the demon out of you, you won't even want to spend your time with heathens anymore. You'll finally find some peace. Don't you want to change your ways, Cat?"

"No!" The word is a howl. It rips my sore throat on its way out of my mouth.

At my shouting, Reverend Preston opens the door and glances from me to Henry. Henry nods to him.

I bolt past them, but my legs get tangled in the damned nightdress. Henry grabs hold of the ends of the skirt.

The preacher calls. "Lu, bring the bindings!"

I rip at the dress to tear myself free of Henry's hold.

"Oh my Heavens!" Lu cries. She clutches the locket holding her mother's tintype as if it's an amulet. "She's taking her clothes off again."

As soon as I've torn the gown into pieces to get it off me and have on only the undergarments, I rush toward the open door, but Reverend Preston catches me and drags me back into my nightmare.

Henry helps him, holding my arms down on the bed.

Lu cries, "Reverend, where's Effie?"

"She went to check on Mr. Dickinson." Reverend Preston's hands are on my thigh and hip, pressing me to the mattress. Only Stonefield has ever touched me in those private places.

"Get off me!" I kick my legs and twist away from him.

When Lu finishes tying the binds, she backs away from the bed, her eyes wide. I glare at her. I want to shake her so hard that all the little pieces of her heart break and jumble together like mine.

I croak, "'You starvelling, you eel-skin, you dried

neat's-tongue, you bull's-pizzle, you stock-fish . . . you vile standing tuck!' " I spit at her.

Reverend Preston licks his lips and stares into my eyes, searching. "In the name of Jesus Christ, demon, who are you?"

No matter how clear and earnest Reverend Preston's eyes are, they don't see me. They're looking right into me, but they're searching for someone else.

A lump swells in my throat. " 'Sanguine coward, thou bed-presser, thou horseback-breaker, thou huge hill of flesh!' " A deep sob rises and heaves against my ribs, wanting release.

"In the name of Jesus, I demand to know whose words these are."

My sob bursts out as a laugh. A witch's laugh. "Shakespeare's."

Reverend Preston's triumphant voice rolls like thunder through the room. "Shakespeare, you foul spirit, in the name of Jesus Christ, I bind you."

Lord.

Henry glances from me to the preacher and back, not know-ing what the Hell to think.

My arms and legs are weak from struggling. I can't fight anymore. I want to be free of them all. I want to go home to the hollow. I want to feel the wind on my face, and the grass under my feet. I want to sink into the earth like Ophelia until my body turns into water, moss, and stone.

Reverend Preston presses his palm against my forehead. "Shakespeare, I command you in the name of Jesus Christ to leave this girl." He pushes down hard. "Out, demon!"

I'm too tired to fight him anymore. I don't care what Henry

or the preacher do or think. I let myself go limp. My body shudders as I release the tension in my muscles.

The room turns quiet as Mother's grave.

When Reverend Preston lifts his hand from me, my head feels light, like I might float up to the ceiling. But my body's bound to the bed.

I turn my face to the wall so they can't see my tears. I'm racked with pain, but not from the throat sickness and the bindings around my wrists. They think they've pried the wicked parts of me loose and forced them from me. But all my parts are still here. My body shakes and my veins throb from the effort of keeping myself intact. I'm still me.

19

Lu's quiet as she sets a cup of water on the bedside table. It's been almost two weeks since she tied me to the bedposts and she hasn't spoken a word to me since. For Lu, that's rare as snake feathers. I'm keeping just as mum. I never speak when anyone's in the room, even if it's Effie. It's partly because my sore throat's full of knives and hurts thousands more than any of my other throat sicknesses, but partly because I don't want to give them any reason to think that the demon changed its mind and moved back into my body.

I want to go home and see Papa, but it's not truly home anymore with Dora living there. And I can't bear it with Stonefield gone.

Lu adds a log to the fire. The days have an autumn chill to them now that seems to have settled into my bones. What I wouldn't give for a pipe to smoke. Lord, how I hate Lu. I turn to look as she sweeps the hearth, and glare at her back as I remember how she told people about me and Stonefield and turned them against us in the church.

It's like she can feel the hot hate on her back, because she turns around all of a sudden. She sees the look on my face and her eyes grow wide. I keep staring at her so she'll say something. But she doesn't say a thing.

Damn, I want to yell at her so bad. I want to demand that she tell why she did such a hateful thing, but I can't speak. I slide the covers off and sit up. It's hard to do—my arms feel like they've never been used before and my head's full of rocks. The floorboards are cold. It takes a moment for me to make my legs work, but I rise and step to the window. Mist coats the inside of the panes. I slide my finger down the cool wet glass, speaking my angry question to Lu without using my voice.

Why?

The letters are dark against the mist. Droplets of water trickle from them like tears.

Lu comes closer to read my writing. "Why has this happened? It wasn't your fault." She brushes the dirt from the logs off her skirt. "Your demon made you do it."

All the anger I have for her grows thousands heavier and I write, quick and mad, on the window.

No demon! Just me.

The line on her forehead grows deeper. Her mouth hardens into a frown. "If it wasn't the Devil making you so wicked, then what in Heaven's name is wrong with you, Catrina Dickinson?"

Fuming, I sweep my hand across the words and fling the water from my fingers at Lu.

She flinches and backs away from me. "Why are you so bad, Catrina?" She glances at the rag basket by the fireplace where Effie stuffed the remnants of the nightdress. "That was my mama's nightdress you tore up." Her eyes are wet.

Even if I had a voice, I wouldn't know what to say to that.

"When Effie told me to get you something clean to wear, I thought of it right away and ran to get it out of my trunk. When I put it on you, Effie said you looked comfortable. I said you looked pretty as a picture, when you weren't awake causing trouble."

I wonder if she's making a joke, but she doesn't smile. Is she trying to make up with me? It doesn't sound like an apology.

"When I was little, I wore it wrapped around my shoulders like a shawl or wound it around my hair the way Papa says the women in the Congo wear their headdresses. At night, I used to lay it over me like a blanket when I went to sleep. The sleeves covered my arms, and the skirt covered my feet."

I stare at a knot in the floorboards that looks like an accusing eye staring back at me. But I should be staring at Lu for how she treated me and Stonefield. I didn't know it was her mama's nightdress.

"The first time you took it off, when you ran out into the rain in your unmentionables, just one button was lost, and I fixed it right away so you could wear it again, but the last time—" A tight line forms across her forehead.

The last time, I tore her mama's nightdress into pieces. I

remember her wide eyes and the insults that I hurled at her that night when I wished I could break her heart like mine.

She spins away to leave, her skirts swishing, and almost runs into Reverend Preston as he walks through the door.

"Pardon me, Miss Lu." His eyes widen when he sees me shivering by the window. "Miss Lu, is there something wrong?"

Lu glances at the window where I wiped my angry words away. "Well, I—" She turns to Reverend Preston, blinking. "I don't rightly know. I was surprised as you are to see her get out of bed."

"The Lord has wrought a wondrous change in her." He smiles at me. "But complete healing of the body and soul will take time."

Lu doesn't meet my eyes, but nods at Reverend Preston before walking out of the room.

"I think you should lie back down." He puts his arm around me to lead me to the bed, pulls the chair closer, and sits down. "I'm glad you're feeling better, Miss Catrina. I've been looking forward to the day when you were well enough to endure some company. Miss Effie tells me you read books." He reaches into his jacket pocket and pulls out a small leather-bound volume.

"I'd like to read to you from *The Pilgrim's Progress* by John Bunyan."

I grimace.

"Now, I don't believe in reading for pleasure, and I am certain that the only education a person truly needs can be gleaned from the Word of the Lord, which has ever been my only textbook. But this little book is one my mother read to me when I was a child, and it was written for the express purpose of point-ing a person toward Heaven. Perhaps it might encourage you. It's about the journey of a man named Christian." His voice is liquid and golden like when he spoke the Words of the Lord. "I hope you'll find it inspiring, Miss Catrina."

But I've already read it. If my throat was well enough for me to speak, I'd be tempted to tell Reverend Preston that if he's hoping I'll be inspired to sacrifice myself and abandon the one I love like Christian does, to go searching for a city in the sky, he's going to be disappointed. But I can't speak, and Reverend Preston's already opening the book.

Henry enters the room right as Christian tumbles into a bog called the Slough of Despond. I can't remember the last time I was so happy to see my brother.

"Ah, a smile!" Reverend Preston stops reading to greet Henry and offer him his place beside the bed. "Your sister seems to be getting a little better. I believe the road to her improvement lies in edifying words and thinking on spiritual things." He closes *Pilgrim's Progress* and pats the cover.

Lord. I hardly heard a speck of the story. The whole time he was reading, I daydreamed that I found Stonefield and we ran far away together. We were living in the woods, making wild work that looked like a giant spider's web hanging between two oaks. We created it from delicate slender reeds and connected them together with thorns that couldn't be seen. Then my daydream switched to us wrestling in a field of bluebells and clover. Every time Reverend Preston read the word *suddenly*, I imagined pinning Stonefield down and kissing him.

Henry nods, approving. "Looks like your prescription's working."

"Well broom me out!" Dora appears in the doorway in a yellow dress that looks tight enough in the waist to squeeze her in half. "My sister-in-law! I came to visit you, but you were always asleep when I came by. And my goodness, you sleep sound as the dead—no one could wake you."

I managed to "fall asleep" whenever I heard Dora's loud voice carry through the hall and not wake up until she left.

She sweeps over to the bed. "But thank goodness, your demon's left you. I always said the Devil was the problem. Some people weren't sure about it, but I was. I said so, didn't I, Cat?"

My body turns into a fire, and I want to burn Dora up with it. Henry knows. He clasps my wrist. "Dora, I've told Catrina about our visit with Dr. Rueben in St. Louis." But he's not looking at Dora, he's staring at me. His eyes are saying, *Be proper, Cat. Don't cause a fuss. Be changed. Be fixed.*

"Oh my, yes, Cat, he was such an interesting man. I could listen to him go on and on about his lunatics for days!"

Oh Hell. I bristle. Henry's fingers tighten around my wrist.

"You should have heard what he said about you! And then how he went on about the stray Indian savage boy your father took in like a Good Samaritan! Mercy, it was like the man was reading from a book. I didn't understand the half of it."

Oh, if I had my voice! I turn away from them, to the wall. A hateful fire's scorching my insides.

Henry's grip doesn't lessen. "Dora and Reverend Preston, I think all the sudden company has exhausted Catrina. Would you mind if my sister and I had a moment alone before she rests?"

When they're gone, Henry speaks to the back of my head. "Next week I'll be enlisting and sent on assignment."

I turn and stare at him. How can he leave us right when Papa's so sick?

"Reverend Preston says he cast out your demon and it hasn't returned. You're healed from the evil spirit that was troubling you. This means a change for you—good things, Cat. A fresh start. But you have to be brave enough to do what's best. You have to be careful to keep the evil spirit from coming back." His fingers loosen and he pats my hand. "Reverend Preston wants to continue helping you find your way. And he's quite fond of you—he says he has always been especially interested in you ever since the Lord put it on his heart to guide you onto the right path. In fact, God told him that it is His will that he guide you toward the reverend's own path so that the two can merge. He . . . he's asked Father's permission to marry you, Cat."

I pull my hand away. My voice is gone, so I shake my head. I do it slow and serious, so he won't think I'm demon possessed.

"I talked to Father about it. I told him how good Reverend Preston has been to us and how he's helped you. Father agreed with me to give him permission."

I shake my head harder.

"Reverend Preston has forgiven the fact that you spent so much time unchaperoned with that heathen, because that was before your demon was cast from you. Not many men would be so willing to overlook such a thing. There's no reason for a girl not to accept such a good, respectable gentleman. And all the young ladies think he's the handsomest man in Missouri, to boot."

I shake my head so hard, it bangs against the wall.

Henry takes hold of my shoulders. "Listen to me, Cat." His words are a sharp whisper. "Listen. I'm joining the army. I've put it off because I was worried about you and Father being on your own. But now you have my Dora to help with the house and, when you marry in a month or two, Reverend Preston will take care of you and help Father manage the farm. You and he will live in the brand-new parsonage and he'll give you everything you could want or need. You'll be a respectable Christian woman."

I want to cry out in resistance, but it comes out as a moan.

"Cat, listen to me. I know you've lived in your own world for the past year or so since we lost Mother. But you can't ignore reality any longer. People in town are getting warm under the collar. Some folks in Roubidoux and Rolla are for the Confederacy now, like Dora's brother Bill—he's already run off to join the insurrectionists, the damned hothead. And there's some like Frank Louis, who don't respect either government, and demand to be left alone. Frank's been stirring things up, saying that if the Union Army demands anything from him, he'll use force to deny it. Things are getting dangerous, Cat."

Henry touches my cheek, and for a moment, it feels like he's the old Henry. But he's just trying to make me stay quiet and do what he wants.

"You'll appreciate having Reverend Preston here in my stead. He's well liked and has the support of most everyone in Roubidoux. And being a minister, he's one of the few who can afford to not be political, so he doesn't have enemies. He's a kind-hearted man, Cat, and I, for one, am grateful, especially as how Father's so weak, and Dora might be expecting a child within the year."

Henry squints at me as if he's trying to see my thoughts. He's nervous. He's waiting to see if my demon is truly gone. Maybe he thinks I will tear off my nightdress again and go running through the house.

I shake my head firm and make a groaning noise, the closest thing to a no that I can manage.

He's come to the end of his patience with me. He licks his lips and points a finger at me like I'm Napoleon the dog. "Cat, you will accept his visits and you will be proper and friendly."

I spit at his boots.

Henry leaps to his feet. "I've had enough of this ungrateful behavior. If you persist in being pigheaded about things, I'll just have to assume your demon has returned. Shall I go tell Reverend Preston that, or shall we calm down and do what's sensible?"

Lord, how I hate him! How can he do this to me? I fight the tears of anger that rise to my eyes. My whole body's shaking in rage, but I don't speak. I turn my glare to the floor.

When I am silent, he thinks it means I agree. He lets out a

sigh of relief and pats my knee. "This is the best thing for you, Cat. You'll see."

I pull my knee away from his hand. He does not hear the protest I am shouting in my head louder than a thousand steam engines. I am shouting that I will never marry Preacher Preston because Stonefield would never leave me.

Henry thinks he has me trapped under his thumb. But I'll be like one of those tiny gray lizards that he used to try to catch when he was little—when he caught one by the tail, the lizard just let it break off and left that tail behind. I'll figure out a way to escape him.

20

I'VE BEEN DEEMED WELL ENOUGH TO GO BACK HOME, BUT not well enough to do much else. I wanted so bad to see Papa, but when I finally do, I almost wish I hadn't. When Effie and I enter his study, the room is dark, but even in the low light, Papa looks altered. His face seems faded, like he hasn't been in the sun for a long time, and sitting in his old chair with his pipe, he seems smaller than I remember. I wrap my arms around him and bury my face in his shoulder. He lays his big hand on my head and strokes my hair slow, touching the scar on my forehead real gentle. I thought my tear ducts had all dried up and withered away, but suddenly they're filled.

"I'm all right, Cat." He pats my head. "Did you miss me?"

I nod but I don't say anything. I haven't spoken a word since my throat sickness took my voice away.

"I missed you reading to me." Papa's thin shoulders shake as he chuckles. "Dora tried, bless her, but she doesn't seem to know what the dickens a comma's for, and just races right past them."

I shake my head and thump my chest. Me. I should have been here with him.

Papa knows what I'm trying to say. He pats my knee. "No, no. Effie says you were sick, too."

I push my head into his shoulder again to wipe off the tears that come slipping out.

"Now, that's enough bellyaching." He pushes me away. "Remember that line Stonefield quoted to us—'What's gone and what's past help should be past grief.' It's true, Cat, so don't fret on it anymore."

When he mentions Stonefield, I feel an uneasy twinge in my stomach. How could he leave me when I was hurt? I have to find out where he went. I steal the pipe from Papa and take a long pull, hoping he says more about Stonefield. Maybe he'll explain what happened. But Effie clears her throat to change the subject.

"Mr. Dickinson." She's holding a small box. "Remember the instrument I told you about—the one that would help me hear your heart beat better?"

"The stetho-whatnot?"

"Yes, the stethoscope. It's here!" She opens the box and lifts out a small case. Coiled inside is a short hose with a flat wooden disc on one end and a wooden cone on the other. "May I?"

Papa nods, and Effie presses the flat part of the stethoscope against his chest and raises the other end to her ear. She holds still, listening, then gives us her big smile. "I can hear it perfectly!" She turns quiet again for several moments, as if Papa's heart is whispering a secret message to her that she's trying to make out.

"Oh," she whispers. Her eyebrows tighten up, slow, and her smile slips away.

"What's wrong, Miss Effie?" Papa asks. "What do you hear?"

"I'm not sure, but I—"

"Well broom me out!" Dora pops her head into the room. "I didn't know you all were having a little shindig in here. I think it's time we let our two invalids rest, don't you, Effie?"

Lord.

Over the days, my throat heals and my voice returns, but no one knows it—I don't want to say something that will make them doubt I'm fixed. I nod at Dora's fool chatter, my ears alert for mention of Stonefield. I know he'll come back to me. Why is he staying away so long? Sometimes when I'm alone, I whisper his name to my empty room over and over, imagining the words hanging in the air, filling up the space surrounding me. I write his name on the wet windowpane to see the tears drip from it.

When days pass and he still doesn't come, I carve his name into the skin of my arm with my angry fingernail until I bleed. I write it in the dust under the table, dragging my fingernail over the wooden floorboard, letting the splinters prick me. I pluck threads from the mattress to spell him into the bed beneath me and press myself into it, suffocating his name. But no one ever mentions him.

I've lost track of how long I've been away from him. Three

weeks? It must be only a month or so since I was first in Stone-field's arms and let him deep inside me, and now I've missed my cycle, something that never happens.

Dora, too, thinks she might have a child growing inside her. At least, she hopes so. She hints and giggles, never saying it plain and true—that wouldn't be proper.

I don't hint. I retch in a pan. I only eat dried toast. I've never needed rags in all the weeks I was in bed, still, no one suspects my secret. Not even Effie the doctor. I want to tell Stonefield. I need to know where he is. He should be here. Why isn't he here? Henry knows where he went.

Reverend Preston's always around. He hasn't even asked me to marry him yet, but everyone acts like I've already said yes. Won't they all be surprised one day when I run off to be with Stonefield. Our souls are already married.

Sometimes I head toward the door, to run away and find him, and then I remember how Reverend Preston caught me last time I ran away and pressed me to the bed while his eyes searched for the demon inside me. I stay where I am for now. When I run, it will be when Reverend Preston's not around to catch me and drag me back.

The preacher's finished reading *The Pilgrim's Progress* to me and lately he's taken to walking me from room to room, his arm bent so I can hold on at the crook of his elbow. As we walk through the house, passing our reflection in the windows, it looks like Reverend Preston has a pale ghost girl on his arm.

I *am* a ghost girl. Not using my voice is making me fade away into nothing. The shock of it hits me and shakes loose the tamped-down anger. It starts rising to the surface with each infuriating look of tenderness he gives me.

"Catrina." His blue eyes think they see me now, and his gaze has a cloying sweetness to it that overpowers even the scent of his lavender. "Shall we take our little evening walk?"

"No!" I can't be silent any longer.

But his eyes brighten. "Your voice! Praise the Lord—He's given it back to you."

"Reverend Preston—"

"Please, call me Samuel."

"Reverend Preston, my strength has returned. I need fresh air." I force my voice to sound calm and pleasant, but I'm set on getting as far away from him as possible. "When you see Effie and Mr. Lenox, ask them to take me with them on their trip to Rolla tomorrow." Once a week, the Lenox family drives to Rolla on the day the train arrives with shipments for the Lenox General Store.

Reverend Preston covers my hand with his. "Of course. I'll drive you and Miss Effie to Rolla myself. I bought my own horse and buggy and named the horse Faithful—she's a beauty."

Damn it all to Hell.

21

THE NEXT MORNING, AS WE GET READY TO LEAVE, Effie seems antsy. "Catrina, I'm relieved to see you looking so well." Her voice is different from normal—almost bubbly. "I'm looking forward to picking up my new shipment from Father's store. There's some soothing medicine for your father in it, too. It's so nice of your Reverend Preston to offer to drive us into town."

My Reverend Preston? Hell. She's as bad as the rest of them.

Effie smiles her middling smile at me. "But the buggy seat will be too crowded. I'll ride in the wagon with Lu and my father and meet you there."

"No!" I grab Effie's arm so she can't escape.

"Catrina, three's a crowd."

"I don't want to ride with him. Let Lu ride with him, and we can ride in the back of your father's wagon."

"Lu would talk Reverend Preston's ear off. Besides, you're the reason he offered his buggy."

At that moment, the preacher walks in. His face is red from

the effort of hitching up his horse. The color in his cheeks makes me think of the color of the columbines Henry once picked for Effie years ago. She pressed them in a book about blood's journey through the body. Right now she's so excited that if her skin was pale, Effie's cheeks would be that color, too.

Reverend Preston takes my coat and holds it up for me. I want to yank it away from him and throw it across the room, but I want to get out into the fresh air even more, so I slip my arms into the sleeves. As we leave, he starts to rest his hand on my back, to guide me out the door, but I pull away to walk my own stride.

When the preacher drives into Rolla and pulls the buggy up to the storefront, something isn't right. The townspeople are scurrying around like ants whose tiny hill has been stepped on. Dark blue uniforms dot the road and walkways, and a swarm of them congregates at the train depot under a brand-new stars-and-stripes flag that slaps and furls in the breeze.

As soon as we come to a stop, I hop out of the buggy without waiting for Reverend Preston to help me, because I don't wear fool skirts like Effie and Lu, who have to step down slow from the wagon with help from their father.

Mr. Lenox says, "You gals go on in with Reverend Preston. I'm going to see what the hubbub is about."

Effie frowns at the crowd, but obeys her father. Lu, Reverend Preston, and I follow her into the Lenox General Store. Her face lights up when the clerk recognizes her and pulls out a crate of new medicines, books, and tonics. Effie lifts a book out of the crate. She traces her fingers over the title, slow, like she's a blind person reading the words in Braille. *On the Origin of Species by Means of Natural Selection* by Charles Darwin. I never saw a person as hungry for knowledge as Effie.

"Will it help you with my father's illness?"

Effie stares at the cover for a minute. "No, it's Mr. Darwin's theory on how the world works. I've wanted to read it ever since it was published in January, but I've been too afraid."

"What's there to be afraid of?" I peer at the cover. It looks like a normal book.

"Mr. Darwin's ideas are new and strange. New ways of thinking can be powerful—stronger than guns or armies."

I think of the Union and Confederate armies, conscripting soldiers and growing larger every day.

Reverend Preston reaches for the book. "Miss Effie, nothing should make a Christian afraid." He turns it over in his hands lightly, as if it's just a toy or a trifle. "One need only read the Bible to have a firm foundation in this world."

Effie takes the book from him careful. "Truth has a way of pulling the foundation right out from under our feet. If our foundation is solid, then you're right—our fears are needless— but if it is faulty, then we had better be brave enough to find out."

Reverend Preston tilts his head to one side like Papa's dog Napoleon does when something puzzles him. "Miss Effie, I thought you said you're afraid to read this book."

Effie nods. "I am." She tucks the book into her satchel. "But I'll do it anyway."

The preacher shakes his head as if he doesn't understand.

"Well, at least your courage will serve you well when you venture to new lands this spring."

That doesn't make any sense. "What new lands? Effie's not going anywhere."

Effie takes my arm. "I meant to tell you in private, but I've only just learned for certain."

I wrench my arm away. "Learned what? Where are you going?"

But Effie doesn't even look upset. She seems happy about wherever it is she's being made to go.

"Africa, Catrina!" Her eyes light up.

Africa? Lord, she might as well go to the moon.

Effie's hands are clasped together as though if she didn't hold on to herself, she'd float away. "I'll finally be able to serve as a doctor to my mother's village in the Congo like I've always wanted. I'll be traveling there with Father's missionary friends in the spring."

I don't want her to go. Her wide smile makes me want to be able to smile, too, but I'm afraid that if I move my mouth even a little bit, then angry, cruel words will slip out and hurt her. So I pinch my lips up tight together and lock them shut.

Before Effie can say anything more, the noises from the crowd outside turn louder, and shouts rise up above the other voices. Reverend Preston takes Effie's crate and walks toward the door.

"You ladies wait here inside; I'll put this in the wagon and see what's happening out there."

But we don't stay inside. We follow him out the door and watch the crowd gathered under the flag. While Union soldiers pour from the train and fill the depot platform, the towns-people buzz around a man in the center of the group. It's Frank Louis.

Mr. Lenox breaks away from the group and joins Reverend Preston. When Frank spots the reverend, he yells out, "You—Preacher Preston! What do you think of this?" He gestures toward the soldiers. "These here government boys have took over the train line. No Southern newspapers will make it through. Ain't no cargo going in nor out but what they see fit!"

Reverend Preston doesn't seem to hear Frank, because he's looking beyond him, at something in the distance that makes his face turn serious. I don't see anything. Maybe he's listening to the Lord, who wants to give him some wisdom to share with Frank.

When Reverend Preston doesn't say anything, Frank's hand-some face turns red and splotchy.

Mr. Lenox calls out, "Let's stay calm now, Frank. You know the Rolla depot's the last stop on the line. With just a stretch of hilly wilderness between here and the Confederate troops, it's no wonder the Union Army decided to pay Rolla a little visit."

But Frank just frowns and spits tobacco in Mr. Lenox's di-rection as if he's not worth answering. He waves his arm toward the soldiers and shouts to the crowd, "I told y'all it would come to this with President Lincoln sticking his nose where it don't belong."

Reverend Preston sizes up the throng of soldiers watching Frank Louis. He leans toward Mr. Lenox and they say things too low for me to hear.

Frank has sweat patches under his arms. He wipes his forehead with his sleeve. "Ain't you heard they're a-marching through the county, conscripting people's horses and their sons?" He huffs and sputters. "These here boys are soldiers conscripted from up north who come down here to do the same to us. The government's got no right to come here and steal our property for their own use."

A tight-faced soldier in a spotless blue uniform and cap steps up to Frank. "Sir," he says in a deep voice, "say it plain, here and now—are you for the Union or against it?"

Frank looks like a kettle fit to blow steam. " 'Twas them fool government men that split the Union in the first place—drawing a line straight through the middle of it, thinkin' to shut everybody up with their Missouri Compromise. But it's just a line drawn in the dirt. And today you Union boys are crossin' it."

Several people in the crowd nod and murmur, but when they glance up at the soldiers, they get quiet.

"Ain't no Union if it's only run by the folks in the top half! I'm for my own self and don't want neither side telling me what to do." He shakes his head and calls out to Reverend Preston again. "You—Preacher! You have plenty to say on a Sunday—what do you have to say here and now?"

Reverend Preston doesn't look around or shuffle his feet. He steps right up onto the platform. With his shoulders back and his head lifted, he's almost taller than Frank. His strong, lilting voice carries easy over the crowd.

"I will not waste these people's time by speaking my own opinions, like some, but I will share with you the words of the

Holy Spirit. The Lord's Spirit says to me that the terror of this coming war is God's judgment on His people for their sins. But take heart, Beloved. One day this cycle of war will be broken. The Bible says, 'For out of Zion shall go forth the law, and the word of the Lord from Jerusalem. And he shall judge among the nations, and shall rebuke many people: and they shall beat their swords into plowshares, and their spears into pruning-hooks: nation shall not lift up sword against nation, neither shall they learn war any more.'"

A couple people call out "Amen!" but others grumble and spit in the dirt. Frank looks like he's about to explode. "That's damned fool talk! There's a war going on, Mister Preacher, and no amount of Bible words is going to change that. Y'all think these here Union soldiers won't force us to go against our will?"

He glares at the preacher and turns away, toward the rest of the crowd. "Some of y'all think the Confederates were wrong for swearing in a few savage Creek Indians and putting them under their protection."

I want to throw rocks at Frank like I did back when he saw me in the creek. I want to shout, "Stonefield's not a savage!"

Frank keeps going. "But them Indians who joined the Southern army did it freely, I heard. Looks like we ain't so lucky as to have a choice with these here Union soldiers. These Yankees claim to fight for freedom, but looks to me like they're aimin' to take ours."

Right then, while the men keep shouting, a pebble hits my boot and makes me jump. I look up and search for the person who threw it. That's when I see him. Stonefield. He's about twenty paces from the crowd, watching from the back of a wagon full of supplies. Frank's wagon. Stonefield's sitting on some bags of corn and sugar, his eyes on me. When he sees I've spotted him, he motions for me to come join him. I glance around—no one's looking at us; everyone's paying attention to Frank and the soldiers.

I run over to the wagon as Stonefield hops down. He takes me around the wagon bed and pulls me to the ground so that we're sitting behind the wheel.

"Stonefield!" I squeeze his hand.

"Did anyone see you?"

"No, no. They're all watching Frank."

He nods, but his eyes are full of anxious things. They're glassy like that first day. He looks like an animal being hunted. He reaches out gentle and touches the scar on my forehead, running his finger over it. "I tried to stop them from hurting you and taking you away—"

I stiffen. "But then you left." I touch a bruise on his cheek. "Why did you go, Stonefield?" The anger inside me makes me press down hard on his bruise.

He winces from the pain, but doesn't move away from me.

"Cat." He wraps his fingers around my hand and moves it to his lips. "I couldn't stay there with Henry. I'm at Frank's place." He kisses my fingertips. The feel of his soft lips eases away a little of my darkness that's seeped in. "Henry thinks that he can tell me who I am, who I can't love, who I can't be with, but he's wrong."

He leans in and his lips are hot against mine. His kiss is so hard, it pushes everything else in the world to the side, against the wall of my brain. His kiss is all I know.

We're both breathing fast as we pull away. Stonefield digs his fingers into my hair and holds on tight. "From now on, I'm the only one who can tell myself those things."

"Stonefield, what are you going to do? Why are you staying with Frank?"

"He's hired me on. I'm saving for traveling expenses and to buy a horse. I'll have enough soon, if these soldiers don't mess everything up." He glances under the wagon at the crowd.

I knew it. He's planning to run away with me. My heart beats out a dancing rhythm. We'll go to a place where we'll be free to be together and Henry will never find us. Warmth fills my body. I take his hand from my hair and slide my fingers between his so they're laced together.

He steals another look from under the wagon. "Even if they do mess things up, I'll find a way. No one can stop me from getting to Oklahoma Territory."

Oklahoma Territory? "But, Stonefield, there are better places— closer places—to hide, like the woods in Hudgens Hollow. Henry's enlisting this week—he'll be gone."

"I'm not planning on hiding. And I'm not afraid of Henry. I'm going to join the Muscogee Creek Indians in Oklahoma Territory."

His words hit me like rocks falling from the sky.

Stonefield keeps talking. "Henry thinks the Creeks are all just toys of the Confederates, but that's not true. There's a group that wants to be neither Confederate nor Union—they just want to be left alone. The papers say that President Lincoln received a letter from their chief, seeking asylum from joining the army because they want no part in this damned war. If he says yes, they'll travel to Fort Row in Kansas. If they do, I want to go with them. I belong with them." He ducks his head and glances under the wagon again at Frank and the crowd and the soldiers. "These aren't my people. This isn't my war."

The words tumble out of my mouth. "Stonefield, I'm your people. Your . . . your . . . person." My heart's rising up to my throat. "You can't leave! You belong here with me. Our house in the woods. We belong togeth—"

"I have to go find them." Stonefield's voice has changed— it's more solid than it used to be. Like dark molasses that's been cooked to a hardened brickle. I don't recognize it anymore. "Don't you see, Cat? I have to go find out what's been stolen from me. I have to find out where I come from."

"No, I don't see." I struggle to my feet. "I don't want to know where the Hell you came from. It doesn't matter. I want the past to stay in the past." I'm shaking. I've never told Stonefield about how I killed Mother. I never will. When I met him all I could see was the present, and that's how I want it to stay. "Forget the past." A lump swells in my throat. "Let's leave it behind. We belong together. Here. Now."

Stonefield pulls me back to the ground. "Cat, if you love me, you understand that I need to go."

I wrench my hands from him. "If you love *me*, you understand that you need to stay."

I wait for him to say, *You're right, Cat, we belong together, here.*

But he just looks at me with eyes that are full of hurt and full of other things I don't understand. I want his eyes to be empty again so they see only me.

I fling his hands away. "Go!"

My heart's on fire, burning up inside my rib cage. I want to slap him or hurt him somehow the way he's hurting me. "Just go, then, you . . . you *savage!*"

Stonefield's face goes dark like a storm of feelings all clouding together, but I tear the magic seeing stone from my neck and throw it at him before turning and bolting away.

22

MY ANGER AT STONEFIELD, INSTEAD OF COOLING, stews and bubbles all night, getting hotter and hotter until I can't think of anything else. When I remember how I plucked his name into the mattress that's pressed against my skin, I jump out of bed and rip the homespun to shreds. The torn strips of my bedding litter the floor, but his name is still there, in the pieces.

I shove the table aside and wipe away his name from where I had written it in the dust. But now he is on my dusty hands. I remember he's on the window, too. I run to it and breathe on the pane. His name reappears where I wrote it on the wet glass. I wipe it away, but his watery name is all over my fingers. No matter how hard I rub them, I still feel him on my skin. He's *in* my skin. His name is written in scabs on my flesh from when I scratched it there. I claw at the letters, gouging him from my body until he's gone, and my arm's a mess of blood. And still, his name hangs in the air where I whispered it over and over and over again.

I hate him for haunting me.

In the morning, I'm still sitting naked on the floor, reading his invisible name written all over my room. I'm not cold, because my anger has turned me scalding hot.

Reverend Preston calls on me to see if I'm in better spirits, but I pretend not to hear Dora when she calls from outside my door to tell me he's here. Yesterday, I didn't say one word to him on the ride home from Rolla and none of his words reached me, either. Maybe he thinks I lost my voice again. But it's thousands worse—I've lost Stonefield.

The dogs start barking like mad from the front of the house. At the sound of hoofbeats approaching and movement in the house, I wipe the blood from my hands with the pieces of torn bedding and make a bandage of them around my wound. I pull on my shirt and pants. Henry calls out something as the front door bangs open. I hear Papa leave his study and I peer out my door.

"Wait, Mr. Dickinson," Dora calls. "I think you should rest."

But Papa doesn't listen and struggles to walk on his own. I follow him down the hall and out onto the front porch where Reverend Preston and Henry are already standing. Two soldiers ride into the clearing on a pair of Frank Louis's best horses.

"What's this?" Papa asks Henry and the preacher.

Reverend Preston pulls at his ribbon tie, nervous. "It looks as though they've been to Frank's place and conscripted his horses. Yesterday he was giving the town quite an earful in front of the Union soldiers."

Henry shakes his head. "Probably jabbered like a fool. They must have gotten orders to enlist him into the Union Army."

If they have Frank's horses, what happened to Frank and Stonefield? Frank wouldn't have enlisted without a fight. As the dogs bark and growl, the men struggle to keep their new horses under control.

"Mr. Estlin Dickinson?" one shouts. The horses spin in circles, and the men fumble with the reins.

Papa calls Napoleon to his side and the dogs quiet down. "I'm Estlin Dickinson."

"We come on orders!"

Papa nods. "Say on."

"We're here to conscript a number of items and recruit qualifying men into the Union Army by orders of Major General John C. Frémont."

Henry speaks up. "My father is ill and over the age of enlistment. But I enlist on my own free will—no need for your conscription."

Dora clutches his arm like it's a surprise. The soldier dismounts and pulls out a small tablet and pencil. "Name and age?"

"Henry Wells Dickinson, nineteen."

"How many horses do you own?"

"Three."

"We'll be taking two."

The man looks up at Reverend Preston. "Name and age, sir?"

"Samuel Preston, twenty-one." His jaw's set tight and he stares back steady at the soldier. "I'm minister for the people of Roubidoux and must decline your enlistment."

"Ministers don't get to decline." The soldier keeps writing in his notebook.

Henry steps closer, and the man's pencil stops as he looks up, frowning.

"Reverend Preston is Roubidoux's schoolteacher as well. I believe that exempts him from your conscription."

"Yes, sir, it does."

The tightness in Reverend Preston's face relaxes.

The soldier looks at Henry. "Is the reverend your kin?"

"Yes, he is."

Reverend Preston smiles and rests his hand on my arm. "I'm engaged to be married to Miss Catrina Dickinson, Estlin's daughter."

I stiffen as he moves closer to me.

A voice shouts from behind us, jolting me like lightning.

"No!"

Stonefield. I turn and look over my shoulder. He's standing ten paces behind us at the corner of the house, glaring at Henry. Oh Hell.

"Liar!" Stonefield yells at the preacher as he starts walking toward the front of the house.

The soldier's hand moves toward his pistol and rests on the grip. "State your name and age, sir."

Stonefield turns to me. "Tell the man it isn't true." His eyes are wild like an animal's.

But I am wild, too, and I know how to hurt him now, how to tear his heart out like he did mine. I move closer to Reverend Preston, and he puts a protective arm around me as Stonefield watches.

Stonefield doesn't look at the soldier. He walks steady toward us, glaring at Reverend Preston with a look on his face like a mountain cat ready to strike. *It's not true, is it, Catrina? Say you are not his.*

But I don't speak back in our silent way. I say it loud. "It is true."

I never saw him look so fierce before; he looks like he could kill Reverend Preston and me several times over.

Henry knows. His voice booms out. "His name is Stonefield. He was the farmhand." His eyes glint like steel. "He's Creek Indian."

The soldier steps forward. "Muscogee Creek? They're the traitors causing trouble for us down in Indian Territory." He raises his voice and talks real slow, as if Stonefield's deaf or fool headed.

"Boy, is Stonefield your Indian name?"

Stonefield keeps glaring at Reverend Preston. His fingers tighten into fists. He wants to hit him. He steps closer. Lord, Lord, Lord.

Henry's face is blood red. His voice throbs with tied-down rage. "Sir," he calls to the soldier, "if the Union considers him a traitor, then arrest him—it's your duty!"

Lord.

"Mr. Stonefield, I hereby arrest you as a traitor to the nation. You shall—"

"I won't go with you." He's not even looking at them, but at me.

The soldier sets his notebook and pencil on his saddlebag and frowns hard at Stonefield. "Do you refuse to comply, boy?"

"I won't fight in your war." He's still staring at me.

The soldier nods at his companion on the horse, who draws a pistol. "If you resist and do not obey these orders, you will forfeit any right to a trial and will be considered a confirmed traitor and may be legally shot."

Stonefield's not looking at the men. His eyes are still hot on me. They're burning a hole through my heart. *Catrina.*

You said we would be together always. I say the words to him inside my head. *And now you plan to desert me. You* are *a traitor.*

I'm the traitor? His face hardens in a way I've never seen before. *May a curse fall upon us both.*

My body shudders at his silent voice. And I feel it—a curse falling on us, between us, like a heavy darkness, separating us from each other.

"Boy!" The soldier's hands are on Stonefield, turning him around.

Stonefield wrenches away from him and before the man can steady himself, Stonefield's fist is in his face. The soldier drops to the ground like a sack of flour. Reverend Preston grabs me out of the way.

The man on the horse lifts his gun.

Stonefield ducks, picks up a stone, and throws it at him. As it knocks the gun from the man's hand, Stonefield picks up another and hurls it at his head. The man falls from his horse, his leg still caught in the stirrup.

Dora screams. The first soldier scrambles on the ground for his dropped pistol, but Stonefield picks it up. Henry trips as he bolts toward the house for his rifle.

Stonefield looks at Reverend Preston clutching me, guarding me from him, and his face twists up in pain and anger. He turns away and mounts the soldier's horse.

By the time Henry's loaded the rifle, Stonefield, like a broken-off piece of my own heart, is gone.

23

I PACE THE PARLOR. MY HEART THROBS FROM THE PAIN of holding so much anger inside.

"Catrina, rest. There's nothing we can do at the moment." Effie's doctoring the soldier's head where Stonefield hit him right between the eyes with a rock, just like David walloped Goliath. Goliath had the bad fortune to die and then have his head cut off, but I think the soldier's wound is mostly to his pride. With his eyes closed, the round wound makes him look like an ugly Cyclops.

"Damned savage," he mutters as he plays with the threads unraveling from the sleeve of his blue uniform. He's impatient for his partner to return with the posse. "When I get my hands on him, he'll be begging for mercy. Just you wait and—"

Effie stuffs a pill into the man's mouth and hands him a cup of water. "Swallow. For the pain."

The soldiers gave Henry his orders—he's to join Union Infantry 85 tomorrow and ride with them to Springfield to help clear Major General Sterling Price's Confederates from Missouri.

Meanwhile, Stonefield's to be hunted down like a rabid coon. I wonder if he left Roubidoux.

"Effie, what happened to Frank? Did he join the army?"

The soldier lifts his head. "Frank Louis?" He scowls. "We gave him a good and proper warning, but he refused to comply. That damned resister had the nerve to shoot my hat off before he rode away. We started to chase him, but our orders were that if a resister escaped, we should burn down his house and barn and then report back, so we followed orders instead."

Effie shakes her head. "His house and barn have been destroyed? He'll be ruined."

"He'll be more than ruined. The posse will find him and the Indian both. Probably together, if you ask me. All the resisters in these parts have a way of finding each other—they like to join up, become bushwhackers. They think they're stronger together, but that just makes it easier for us to find them. And we will. Don't you worry about that, little lady!"

"Mr. Snodgrass, lie back." Effie presses on the soldier's chest, pushing him onto his pillow before he can protest.

Henry appears in the doorway. "Cat, I'd like to speak to you."

I follow him out to the hallway.

Henry's face is serious, but his eyes are lit up. "Look, Cat, I know my leaving is a little sooner than expected, but I've got everything in order as best I can. I shouldn't be gone long— this war will all be a distant memory in several months." His voice turns gentle, like he's soothing a child. "We'll quiet the rebels, and President Lincoln will help the country mend. Soon everything will be back to normal." He steps closer. "Now, I know you were unsure at first about marrying Reverend Preston, but I can see for myself the changes that have come about in you. You made it clear today that you want nothing to do with your old ways or . . . past acquaintances. I'm proud of you, Cat."

Acquaintances. Lord. We were never acquaintances. Our souls were knit together into one. And now Stonefield has ripped us apart by wanting to leave me. My hands become fists.

Henry rests his hand on my arm. "I only wish I could be here to see your wedding."

"You can."

Henry tilts his head. "But, Cat, I'm leaving tomorrow morning."

"I want to get married today."

"Broom me out!" Dora's beaming as she rushes into my room without knocking. "I'm so excited you're getting hitched to Samuel. Who would have thought it, him being a preacher and you being demon possessed only weeks ago!" She's been collecting things from her room to help get me "prettied up" for the hasty parlor wedding and take her mind off Henry leaving tomorrow.

"Dora, where's Effie?"

Her lips purse. "Effie insisted on going with Henry when he rode over to fetch Mr. Lenox. She claimed she had to get something for you from the house. I don't know why it couldn't wait.

It's not like you'll be moving out of Roubidoux. The parsonage is barely a mile from her house!" Dora's face is shiny and her hands are full of combs, tonics, soaps, and powders. I want to push her out of the room and slam the door. "Now, hurry up— I've heated the water Henry brought in. Get in the tub before it cools off!"

She follows me to the tub like a clucking hen. "You may have an ugly scar on your forehead, but at least we can make you *smell* pretty! You'll want the cream soap, I'm sure, and the lemon-perfumed powder—"

"Hell no." The last thing I want is to smell like a lemon pie. "I'll use my own soap." Mother taught me how to make it simple with grease, lye, and salt. I slip out of my pants and shirt and step into the hot water, hiding the inside of my arm so Dora doesn't see where I dug Stonefield's name from my skin.

She pouts for a moment, then brightens up. "Well, I distinctly heard Henry say you're to wear your very best outfit—'No ruffian clothes!' he said." She claps her hands. "Finally, you'll be seen in a proper dress. I'll find your best for you and lay it out on your bed. And I'll help you with your corset to make sure it's nice and tight for a pretty shape." She sucks in her breath, thrusts out her chest, and pats her own waistline.

"No." I slide deeper into the water.

"But I only want to help you."

Her words are the same ones Reverend Preston shouted in the rain, before he carried me to the house and tied me to the bed. I close my eyes so I don't have to look at her mopey expression.

"Henry says, and I agree, that you should—"

I slip down below the water till it covers my ears, my head. I want to stay here in this place where I am weightless. So warm, so fluid, so deep. It forgives the heaviness I carry. It takes it away and forgets—like a kind of mercy. I want to be a part of its nothingness, but I can't. My anger pulls me back to the surface. The cool air slaps me back into the world.

When I open my eyes, Dora's given up, and I'm left alone in the room. I finish my bath and rub my hair dry with the linen cloths. It's so long, I use up all the linen on the shelves. Henry expects me to pull it back and pin it up tight like a grown-up woman, now that I'm getting married and I've become a proper Christian. But I won't. I let it be the way it wants—thick and full like the wild lions in Effie's book about the Congo. It falls over my shoulders and down my back to my hips. The Bible says that Samson's long hair was magic, giving him strength. My hair may not be magic, but it will give me the power to stand up to Henry.

I open my trunk. Henry doesn't know that my corset is in the barn above the milking stool, where I've been using it to plug a drafty hole, and my dresses are in the rag box to be cut up for quilt patches. I'm not planning on taking them out, either. But I will wear the nicest clothes in my possession, just for him.

24

FFIE RAPS ON MY DOOR. I CAN TELL IT'S HER BECAUSE she's knocked that way since we were little—like a drummer playing a marching beat in front of an army.

"Come in."

"Oh!" she says when she sees me lying naked on the floor, gazing at the ceiling.

When I stare at the rafters long enough, I get mixed up. I start feeling like I'm actually stuck to the ceiling and staring down at the floor instead. I discovered it when I was little. One day Mother hung the chairs upside down from the rafters so their saggy woven seats would dry nice and tight after she'd soaked them—made the ceiling look just like a floor. I love the feeling of floating high above everything.

I sit up, and the world flips back to normal. But it's not, really—everything's topsy-turvy. I frown at the rafters.

Effie's voice sounds worried. "Dora wants to know what kind of flowers she should pick for your wedding bouquet. She's dying to see what you look like in your *dress*." Effie says the word *dress* like her mouth gets stuck on it.

"Tell her to break me off some sprigs of those pretty pale blossoms in the tiny trees by the spring."

Effie coughs, like she's choking. "The poison sumac?" She smiles and it changes her grave face into something bright and alive, like when a stone's thrown into the smooth surface of a pond. "I think not, Catrina."

One of her doctoring books is tucked under her arm. She walks over and sits down on the floor beside me. "Everyone knew Reverend Preston and you were courting and planned to marry, but I was surprised when I heard you wanted to get married today. I suppose with Henry leaving so soon, it seems right. War has a way of causing people to make big decisions quickly. I've heard there have been quite a few hasty parlor weddings throughout the county this month."

She runs her finger slow up and down the spine of her book. "I knew Reverend Preston was happy with the changes he's perceived in you lately, but I must admit I was surprised you returned his affection. From what you once told me, I thought you and Stonefield . . ."

"Things changed." I hug my knees, pressing the throbbing wound where I scratched out Stonefield's name. It burns.

She stares at the book in her lap and clears her throat. "Catrina, I know what it's like to have to find your own way without a mother's guidance." She clears her throat again, as if the words have gotten lodged there and she's having trouble getting them out. "I've had to figure out quite a few things on my own because my father doesn't feel comfortable talking about them. But books have helped me." She pulls the volume out from under her arm. "With you getting married so suddenly, and not having a mother's wisdom to advise you, I thought you might appreciate the knowledge in this book."

"*Fruits of Philosophy* by Anonymous," I read out loud. "Anonymous. That's a strange name. I've never heard of him."

"The writer is anonymous due to some people's squeamishness about the subject matter. But it's actually quite informative. The book is advanced scientific writing on women's anatomy and reproduction."

"Writing on women's *what*?" I open the book and flip through the pages.

"It explains how a woman's body works and how she can prevent herself from becoming pregnant unless she's ready."

Lordy. I didn't know such things were possible. "Effie, your Mr. Anonymous sounds like he wrote a good book, but I'm afraid he's a little too late to help me."

Effie turns quiet, letting my words sink in. As they do, her eyes get big. "Oh, Catrina!" She reaches for my hand. "You should have said something. I could have helped you before—" When she looks into my eyes, I know she can see what's behind them—me and Stonefield, and how we loved each other. But there's no disgust on her face like when Lu saw us in the secret house. The tight lines on Effie's face are from concern.

"Catrina, I should have been more observant when you were

sick. What kind of doctor would overlook such a symptom. I should have—"

"You were busy helping my papa when I couldn't." I try to keep my voice steady. "And making plans to go to Africa."

She squeezes my hand and gets up to wrap a blanket around me. "It's too cold in here to be sitting around undressed. You'll get sick!"

Dora's bubbly voice from the other side of the door calls out, "Reverend Preston is waiting—better heel it, girls!"

Effie calls, "We'll be ready soon, Dora." As we get up, she says, "Catrina, does Reverend Preston know about the baby?"

The wound on the inside of my arm throbs and I feel the hot blood beneath my skin, pulsing out Stonefield's name. I shake my head.

Effie frowns. "Well, it's understandable why you want to marry so quickly." Her eyes narrow. "But, Catrina, don't you think he deserves to be told before you marry?"

"No."

I press the wound harder. I remember how the preacher pushed me to the bed and tied my wrists. I don't care about the preacher. He should have pain, too. *That's* what he deserves.

"Why don't you want to tell him? Are you afraid he will change his mind? He seems to care for you very much."

"He only loves me because he wants to save me from myself." I squeeze my throbbing arm tight to my chest.

"And . . . Stonefield?"

I can't stay still. Hearing her say his name burns my ears.

My arm's inflamed with him. I rise to my feet and pace the floor, pressing his invisible name against my heart.

"Stonefield *is* my own self."

Effie tilts her head and squints at me like a puppy.

Her blank look infuriates me.

I beat Stonefield's name against my chest with my arm, my fist, hitting myself so I won't cry in front of her. "He tore me apart."

Deep lines of confusion form on Effie's forehead. I imagine her wondering if I still love Stonefield and how I can let Reverend Preston marry me if I do. And I want to shout, *Well, how could Henry marry dum-dum Dora when he loves you? And how could you let him when you love him back?*

Love's more rotten than stumbling into a bear trap. The iron jaws snap shut on you and you end up tearing off your own leg just to survive.

She watches me pacing, pounding my chest. She's real nervous now, glancing at the door. I should have kept quiet. She doesn't understand. I want to slap that look off her face.

"Damn it—stop staring at me like that, Effie! You've got all your fat books and your fancy words, but you don't know anything. Stop trying to fix me and mind your own business."

Effie's mouth puckers up into an angry frown. She shakes her head like she's deciding what to do, then she flings the book onto the floor and whips around so fast, I jump, startled. She opens the door and storms out, almost crashing into Dora.

"Need help, gals? The menfolk are waiting in the parlor."

I push Dora out of the way so I can see if Effie will turn

around and come back to me, to apologize, but she doesn't. She keeps walking all the way down the hall and into the front room.

"Goodness!" Dora gulps.

"I don't need your help, Dora. I'll be right out." I slam the door in her face.

The only help I need is someone to keep Henry from killing me when he sees what I'm going to wear to my damned wedding.

I've never worn the suit before. It's midnight black with a snowy linen shirt and fits me perfect. Mother gave it to Henry for his fourteenth birthday—his first grown-up man's suit. It still looks new because he grew out of it so quick. Effie and I helped Mother make it while she was teaching us to sew. When we were done, Effie slipped columbines in the pocket and wrapped it all up in fine tissue paper she got from Mr. Lenox's store. Henry was proud as a rooster strutting around in it.

Why should only men get to wear such simple, comfortable things? I take another puff on the pipe and blow a smoke ring. I hoped the pipe would calm me, but it's not working.

Henry's impatient knock rattles the door. "We're waiting. Come on out, Cat." He stomps away.

I open the door.

Dora rushes up to meet me with a bouquet of pale purple flowers. "Look, the lavender's in second bloom! Your bouquet will match Samuel's boutonniere—" She stops short when she sees what I'm wearing. For once in her life, she's speechless.

I pull a sprig of lavender from her bouquet and slip it into my breast pocket the way Reverend Preston wears it.

"But . . ." She looks as if her eyeballs might pop out of her head. "You can't wear that to your wedding. You're . . . you're a woman."

"I doubt wearing the suit or the lavender in my pocket will change that."

I walk past Dora into the parlor.

Papa, Mr. Lenox, Henry, and Reverend Preston all turn to me as I enter.

Lord.

Henry's eyebrows slide to the top of his head. Mr. Lenox starts blinking as if his eyelids are made of butterfly wings.

Reverend Preston's smile melts. When he sees my suit and the lavender in my pocket, his lips harden like cooled wax.

When Henry sees Reverend Preston's expression, his face turns red. "Cat, this isn't a game."

I agree. "Games are more fun."

Reverend Preston clears his throat. "Catrina, the Bible has things to say about women's and men's appearances. I didn't admonish you in such matters before now because of your illness and your ignorance of the Scriptures, so perhaps I am to blame. But today we'll be joined in holy union before God. I feel the Lord is telling me I must speak to you about your appearance, because when others look at us—"

I'm shaking, holding the words in, but they push themselves out of my mouth. "You're right, Reverend Preston—"

"Please, call me Samuel." He smiles like I'm a child at his knee.

My words keep coming even though I'm thinking they should stop. "I remember God talking about that in the Bible. He was speaking to a man who was named Samuel—like you. He lit into him good for judging someone on their appearance. He told him, 'For the Lord seeth not as man seeth; for man looketh on the outward appearance, but the Lord looketh on the heart.'"

Reverend Preston's eyebrows slide up as high as Henry's. "Well, I—"

"Cat—" Henry's voice is a warning.

But I don't stop. "And I feel like the Lord is speaking to me, too." I clear my throat. "I feel like He's telling me to tell you that He says, 'Samuel, don't make Me repeat Myself.'"

The room turns quiet as death.

Effie's eyes roll to the rafters, and I wonder if it's topsy-turvy up there for her, too.

I hold my breath, waiting for Reverend Preston to make a disgusted noise and walk away. I wait for the sting of Henry's hand across my face.

But those things don't happen.

Instead of storming away, Reverend Preston laughs.

The sound jolts me like sudden thunder.

But everybody else lets out the breath they're holding. Papa and Mr. Lenox look relieved and start chuckling along with

Reverend Preston. Dora still has her hand clamped over her mouth, but now she's giggling, nervous, through her fingers. Only Henry's face looks the same, but with the redness drained out of it.

Reverend Preston holds his side as his laughter quiets. "May the Lord have mercy on me for my pride—for He 'resisteth the proud, but giveth grace to the humble.'"

He stands up straight and pulls his Bible out of his suit pocket. I wonder if he's going to start preaching. "Friends," he says in his deep, liquid voice, "Catrina and I will have many years to read the Scriptures together and for her to learn the finer points of God's will. And I will be faithful in my duty, as God commands husbands to purify their wives, 'even as Christ also loved the church, and gave himself for it; That he might sanctify and cleanse it with the washing of water by the word, That he might present it to himself a glorious church, not having spot, or wrinkle, or any such thing; but that it should be holy and without blemish.' But for now, let us overlook outward appearances—my bride's naïveté, her blunders and blemishes—and turn to the heart of the matter at hand. Mr. Lenox, would you please join our hearts and hands in holy matrimony?"

Oh God. Hurry and get it over with. The angry wound on my arm pounds beneath my sleeve. The heat of it fills my whole body. *Damn you, Stonefield.*

Reverend Preston presses his hand on the Bible and holds it out for me to do the same.

And Lordy, Lordy, Lordy—as God watches, and Henry glares, and Reverend Preston smiles, I do.

25

WHEN ALL'S BEEN SWORN TO GOD AND THE WEDding's over and done with, my darkness comes rolling in. It clings to me, heavy as my vows. I want to fling them both a thousand miles from me. Effie left right after the ceremony was over. I don't think she liked our vows much either.

Reverend Preston rides off with Henry and the men to pick up ale and invite folks to the house for a little celebration and Henry's farewell. I figure the only way to survive the darkness of my own wedding party and all those people is if I'm full of ale, so I start drinking the moment Mr. Lenox rolls in the first barrel and offers to pour.

I down enough toasts to feel like I'm moving slow through a dream world by the time the guests arrive. I don't even care when they look at me strange. When they say things to me, I just nod, because they don't seem real. They're like actors with lines from a play, just not as good as Shakespeare's. By nightfall, I can't even remember why they're all here. Reverend Preston sounds as amusing as the fool in *A Midsummer Night's Dream* who got turned into an ass by Puck the nature spirit. Lord, he thinks he's clever. Even the way he puts his fingers over mine when I hand him his cup feels strange and foolish and makes me laugh. That makes him grin like a dog. His smile looks too large to fit his face. I wonder if he has more teeth than other folks, and I reach out to try and count them, but I miss and my finger brushes across his lips instead.

That's when Reverend Preston decides it's time to say good-bye to Henry and take me away.

But I don't want to go to his home. I hadn't thought about what it would be like to have to live with him, alone. All I thought was how bad it would hurt Stonefield.

I don't want to think about any of it now. I want to stay here with Papa and Henry. I never loved Henry more than I do right now. I think about how I'm wearing his suit, and how he hugged me and Effie and Mother when he unwrapped it on his four-teenth birthday. I hug him now just like I did back then. At first, it feels like I'm hugging a roof plank, but the plank softens the longer I hold it, until it finally feels like the old Henry again.

"Be good, Cat," he whispers. "Be good to Samuel and obey him, and he'll treat you right. He'll take care of you and Papa and Dora while I'm gone." His whisper voice sounds so kind and gentle, like the old Henry, that I want to whisper, too.

"*You* be good, Henry." My words come out slow, stumbling over each other, and I don't even know what I am going to say before the words are spoken. "Make the rebels stop fighting and end the war so the soldiers will leave Stonefield alone. I hate him. But only because I love him so much. If he dies, it will kill me."

All of a sudden, I'm holding a plank in my arms again, and Henry's pushing me away, into Reverend Preston's arms. The room spins. The ground keeps shifting under my feet and the doorframe comes at me and hits me in the elbow. All the faces whirl past me as Reverend Preston guides me out the door where his horse, Faithful, is already hitched to his buggy. I think I'm falling asleep, and Lord, we're already at the parsonage next time I open my eyes. Reverend Preston gives me his hand to get out, but I can't get steady enough, so I put my arms around his neck and let him carry me inside.

I'm so sleepy. My body's made of lead. When Reverend Preston sets me on my feet, I take off all my clothes until I'm naked and hang my jacket, shirt, and pants over a chair. It takes me a long time because the floor keeps sliding away and the walls spin a little bit every time I move. I look for the bed, but none of the rooms I walk into have one.

"It's this way, Catrina." He takes my hand and shows me my room. But instead of leaving, he sits down on the bed and puts his hands around my waist. He sets me on his lap and slides his fingers across my collarbone and down my arm, pushing my hair over my shoulder.

"I'm not yours." I try making the words come out in a serious voice, but when Reverend Preston chuckles at my expression, I feel like I must be saying it wrong.

"Not completely, but soon you'll be all mine."

I laugh at the fool idea of belonging to Reverend Preston. Does swearing to God make something so? Ha. God should know better than to put faith in us humans.

But being so close to a man's body reminds me of how it felt to be next to Stonefield in our secret house. Reverend Preston's legs are strong and solid beneath me and his arm muscles flex as he holds me. The ale makes it so hard to think clear. I try to remember why I did this—so I can stay angry at Stonefield—but Lord, I miss him so bad. If Reverend Preston were to kiss me, I could close my eyes and feel Stonefield's lips instead. It seems a thousand years since I felt him beside me. Reverend Preston puts his other arm around my neck and draws me toward him.

But his kiss isn't Stonefield's. How could I pretend it would be?

I open my eyes and pull away from him. His kiss tastes bitter and his embrace is a tangle of heavy ropes. I struggle free of him and stand up.

The room spins around, and I feel sick. All the ale I drank comes back up, emptying onto Reverend Preston's feet.

He groans and lies back heavy on the bed. After several moments of silence, he sighs and sits up. "I shouldn't have let you have so much to drink—it's my fault." He shakes his head. "You're not yourself."

"*He* was myself and he's gone." I force my eyes to focus on the preacher's blue eyes, but my head feels so heavy and light at the same time, I can't hold it steady. "I never should have done this."

"You don't know what you're saying, Catrina. You need to rest. We'll start new in the morning."

Then, with a heavy sigh, he gets up and fetches a washbasin and water.

I crawl up onto the bed and pull the covers all the way over me so he can't see me. I rub my face hard against the pillow, trying to wipe away his kiss, but I still feel it. I grind my teeth together to rid myself of his taste and bite my lips hard to scrape the kiss away. I think that when the Bible says Hell is a place of wailing and gnashing of teeth, this is what it means. Finally, with the iron taste of blood on my tongue, I give up and let my darkness take me.

26

MY HEAD THROBS WHEN I WAKE UP, AND I'M SO thirsty. The sharp scent of new lumber and fresh white-wash fills the preacher's house. I realize I'm in his bed, but I don't recall why. All I can think is how I long for the comforting smell of Papa's pipe and Henry's coffee that have settled into the nooks and crannies of our musty old house.

I open my eyes. The memory of last night seeps up like old floodwaters that have been hiding underground. Oh Hell. What have I done? It's only been one night since I married Reverend Preston, and already I want to die from it. How could I do this thing?

I can't stay here.

I sit up in the bed and listen. The house is quiet. The bed-springs hardly creak when I stand up, but I cringe, remembering how the preacher heard me leave the Lenoxes' house that one morning, and how he carried me, kicking and screaming, back to the bed and tied me up.

I shiver, still naked, and reach for my trunk, which Henry

and Dora packed for me at the party when I'd had too much to drink. The lid opens quiet enough, but I almost cuss out loud when I see what's inside. My trunk is full of Dora's old dresses. Damn it. I throw them out, flinging each one across the room as hard as I can, and dig underneath, hoping they left me something of my own. But all I find are skirts, underclothes, and fool corsets. I slam the lid shut, not caring anymore whether he hears me or not.

At least I have my suit.

My skin's all goose bumps from the cold, but I don't care. I open the bedroom door and glance around the preacher's house, looking for the chair where I left my suit, shirt, and boots. The chair's there, but my things are gone.

"Reverend Preston?" My voice sounds naked and trembly as my body.

He's gone. It looks to be late morning already. Maybe he put the clothes away for me. I run back to the bedroom and pull open the dresser drawers. But it's just the preacher's things. I'd rather wear nothing than have his clothes touching my skin. Where did he put my suit? I slam the drawers shut, and a note falls from the dresser to the floor.

Dearest Catrina,

I thought it best to let you sleep in this morning, but in the future, I look forward to leading our devotions as we study the Scriptures together when we rise, and again in the evening, before bed. In so doing, I will fulfill my duty as husband and spiritual head of our home and help prepare us for our long and fruitful life, yoked together in Christ.

I usually require dinner at noon, and you may have our supper ready by six o'clock. I ask that no salt be added to the food and that you avoid using onions or garlic, as they upset my digestion. No doubt you are familiar enough with a household to find the things you need for housekeeping, but if you have need of me, I am in the church, practicing my sermon for tomorrow's service.

Your devoted husband,
Samuel

Lord. I rip the paper in half. Then I rip those pieces, too. I rip and rip and rip Reverend Preston's words into tiny shreds and throw them to the floor.

Where the Hell has he put my suit? I run around the house, turning everything over, searching for my clothes. A panic rises inside me. It takes hold and shakes me hard. Reverend Preston hid them. Just like the farmer and the selkie in Papa's stories. The farmer stole his wife's sealskin and hid it so she couldn't escape to the sea where she belonged. She was trapped forever living the life of a creature she never really was. Oh God. My stomach churns.

I throw open the front door and run outside. The October chill hits hard against my bare skin, but I don't care. The farmer buried his wife's sealskin in the dirt floor of the barn. I race to the little barn behind the parsonage. Faithful starts and whinnies when I fling open the side door. She snorts, wide-eyed, at me as I pace the floor and study the corners of the barn, shoving aside her straw and feed sacks. But I can't find anything that looks like it was dug up and covered over.

I sink to the floor on my knees.

"Listen to the words of the Lord."

I raise my head at the faint sound of Reverend Preston's liquid voice, pouring out his sermon for tomorrow from the church sanctuary.

"'And whosoever was not found written in the book of life was cast into the lake of fire.'"

I push myself up. Maybe he burned my suit. How could he do this thing to me? And all at once, it's as if he's thrown a stick of fire on my own self, and I'm burning up. My heart is hot. My body's naked, but I don't feel the cold anymore. I'm swimming through a lake of fire as I run to the church.

"'And I John saw the holy city, new Jerusalem, coming down from God out of heaven, prepared as a bride adorned for her husband—'"

I fling open the front doors. Reverend Preston's face is lifted upward, and his fist is in the air, like he's been tugging at God's coat.

"What have you done with it?" I shout. My voice isn't trembly anymore—my words are roaring flames shooting from my throat.

His eyes are round and stunned, like a catfish yanked from the water.

"Where are my clothes?"

He lets go of God's coat, and his arm falls to his side. His mouth hangs open as he stares at me. I feel his eyes take in my naked body, my dirty knees, tangled hair, my wild fire eyes.

"C-Catrina." He blinks his fish eyes and stumbles toward me. "What's happened to you? Are you all right?"

I shrug his hands away. "Give me my suit," I whisper.

"Didn't you see the clothes Dora packed for you? Here—" He pulls off his own suit coat. "You're freezing. Let me cover you."

I twist out of his arms, away from his coat and its sickening lavender scent. "I want my own clothes." I peer into his eyes, begging him to see me, to understand what it means to me. "Please."

His face hardens, just a little, changing around the jaw and the eyes, like his skin is turning to stone.

"Catrina, you are a wife now. The wife of a servant of the Lord. You yourself have tasted of the goodness of the Lord when He delivered you from your demon." His voice softens and rises, the way voices do when people speak to children or small pets, but his face stays stony. "I understand it will be a trial for you, but it's time for you to put away the things of the past, your careless and rebellious habits of dress and manner. As the Scriptures tell us, if anyone 'be in Christ, he is a new creature: old things are passed away; behold, all things are become new.' It's time for you to put away the old, sinful ways of living, and embrace your new life. That includes dressing like a respectable married woman. I'm sure your father, brother, Dora, and Effie agree with me."

He takes my arm at the elbow and moves toward the doors. "Let's get you inside the house before you catch—"

I yank my arm away from him and walk out the doors by myself, ahead of him. My eyes fill with water. By the time I get to the house, the water has put out the bright fire inside me, turning me dark and cold again. I walk to the window seat and sit down, staring out toward Hudgens Hollow.

The preacher follows me and says things to me—coaxing, gentle things with the voice of a long-suffering saint. But I don't hear words. His voice hurts my head, like a sounding brass or tinkling cymbal. I cover my ears with my hands and stare hard, toward the faraway secret house I built with my true husband in the woods. All day I sit with my arms locked around my knees. Reverend Preston wraps a quilt around me, but I let it fall to the floor even though I shiver and shake. I can't eat the food he makes me or even speak to him—all my words have flown away. Even if I had my seeing stone to lift to my eye, I would be too afraid to use it. What if it had lost its magic to find the beauty in the world—how could I bear it?

I sit there for ages, staring at the woods, and I hardly notice at first that someone is out there watching me back. Then I see the wisps of dark wavy hair from behind an oak tree. The hair floats on the wind, and at first I think it's some kind of netting caught on the bark, but then she steps out from behind the tree. No, she steps *through* the tree. And I realize it's Mother. She's wearing the same thing she wore to the molasses make, her calico dress sleeves undone and rolled up, almost to her shoulders. Her small, tight muscles show hard and round below the sleeves. She looks strong, but delicate, too, like a paper doll that could blow away in the wind. I hold my breath so I won't scare her away by any sudden movement, as if I'm watching a bird or a fawn, hoping she'll come closer.

But the front door opens, and the noise of it startles her. She's gone.

No! I bury my face in my hands. I want her to come back.

I lift my face to see Reverend Preston walking through the door with Effie. I didn't even realize he'd left. The slant of light through the window means it's almost evening now. The preacher will not have had his dinner or supper on time. When Effie enters the room, I don't get up for her. She comes to me, kneeling on the floor beside me, wrapping me in something made of yarn that makes my skin prickle. She pleads with me to stand, to eat, to talk. But I don't speak to her, either. She asks me questions like a good doctor, but I don't want to be doctored. I want my own sealskin back. I sit rigid as a stone on the window seat as she tries slipping her arm in mine.

"Catrina," she whispers. "We didn't know it meant so much to you. They were just clothes after all."

But it's more than that. It's about keeping something that Henry and Reverend Preston want to take from me. It's about all the things I am that people want to change and fix.

I watch a large spider as it crawls up to the rafter and begins spinning. It casts a starter thread out of itself into the great space between the rafter and the window frame in the hope that a slight breeze will carry it across. It throws thread after thread across the gap before one finally catches on the window frame and holds, making a little silver bridge. The spider walks through the great space to reach the other side.

I'm a spider without any silver thread left. I don't know how to ever get across this great empty space around me.

Effie's hand on my shoulder is warm and calm.

"Stop," I say. I don't want to look into her eyes. "I'm not sick. I'm not your patient." I decided I wasn't going to speak to her, but I can't keep the words from coming out. "And you're not even a doctor."

Effie pauses. Her hand starts to lift from my arm. I know that's the meanest thing I could say to her, and I hope she'll leave me again like she did before the wedding.

But even though she must be mad, I feel her come back to me as she lets her hand rest again on my shoulder. "Are you hurting, Catrina?"

I move farther away from her. "I feel fine."

"Maybe your body's not hurting, but do you hurt on the inside?"

My throat swells and it's hard to swallow. Something breaks loose in my heart and I can't be mad at her anymore. "Yes," I whisper. My eyes sting.

She nods. "Catrina, I prescribe this not as a doctor, but as your friend." She moves closer to me and takes my hand, gentle. "Something inside you needs mending. Don't fight it. Don't make the wound worse. Care for it. Find a way to heal."

I turn my arm over, revealing the place where I tried to scrape Stonefield from my skin. My voice creaks like it's rusty. "I don't know how."

Effie's eyes widen when she sees the gouges I've made, but she takes my sore arm in her hands. "Neither do I. But I know you will find a way."

I squeeze her hand back. Just when I think no one will ever be able to reach me again, Effie casts a thread my way and it catches, making a fine silver bridge to my heart.

27

THE PREACHER'S AT THE CHURCH PRAYING FOR ME.
When he brought Effie over, he thought it best to
leave us alone. I'm glad he's not here.

Effie makes a salve and rubs it gentle over my wound and wraps
strips of soft linen around it for a bandage. Then we make tea and
toast. When she's satisfied that I'm feeling better, she leaves, too,
so I can rest. But I don't want to sleep while the preacher's gone.
I can think more clear when he's away. And I know what I need
to do now. I need to make a new sealskin all my own.

I sing Stonefield's song as I work on it.

"Come, live with me and be my love
And we will all the pleasures prove
And if these pleasures may thee move
Then live with me and be my love."

It's late in the evening now, and the room is steamy and
hot, but I don't care. I feel like my body's cleansing itself

from everything that doesn't belong and leaving only the best of me.

> *"There will I make thee beds of roses*
> *With a thousand fragrant posies*
> *A cap of flowers and a kirtle*
> *Embroidered all with leaves of myrtle."*

My heart's thumping hard like it used to in Hudgens Hollow when I made wild work; when I was full of purpose, full of life.

> *"A belt of straw and ivy buds*
> *With coral clasps and amber studs*
> *With gray feather of the dove*
> *Oh, live with me and be my love."*

"Catrina?"

Oh Hell.

Reverend Preston stares at me with his mouth hanging open as I stand naked in the kitchen, stirring a bubbling pot of onion skins. I'm cooking a beautiful dye, the color of amber, the color of Stonefield's eyes.

His face falls. "Effie said you were . . . better. And resting."

"I am better. I can't rest—I have too much to do." I switch spoons and stir the other pot, full of liquid stained with pokeberries I found outside. This will be a rich coral color.

"Are you dyeing something? That's a strong odor." He glances anxious around the parsonage at the mess I've made.

"You don't have to stay." I keep stirring.

"Catrina, what are you dyeing?" He sounds as if he's afraid to hear the answer.

"Felt clasps and studs." The green dress I brought out and hung over the chair catches his eye. For a moment his face lightens, but when he sees my wild work on it, his mouth falls open a little.

"What are you doing to the dress Dora gave you?"

"I'm making it mine."

"It's been shortened—this hem will show your legs. That's worse than wearing pants. Are these leaves you've sewn onto it? And this belt—it's made of straw and vines. And . . . feathers? You can't wear this, Catrina." He shakes his head. "It's not proper."

Lord.

"I won't allow it. People will question whether you are really healed of your evil spirit if you behave this way—"

"It's mine." I raise my voice louder than his. "You can't stop me."

"The Bible says that a wife must submit to her husband in all things." His voice is calm and smooth as always, but I hear something underneath it—something hard and tight that wants breaking. "Perhaps you're not healed from demonic influences as well as I thought. I knew this spiritual battle for your soul would not be easy, but I won't give up on you, Catrina. That would be the same as giving up my faith in God."

Reverend Preston lifts the Bible he carried in with him and opens it. He holds it out, in front of my gaze. I refuse to see the words, and I look past them at the white spaces in between. But then he places something on the pages, and I can't make my eyes not see them. The twisted bindings made of strips of linen that he once tied around my wrists. They lay nestled in the crack of the open book like writhing baby snakes.

"Catrina." The preacher clears his throat again. But his voice is a whisper. "Perhaps the demon has returned to torment you?"

At first, the sight of the bindings sends a shot of fear racing through my bones. But then Effie's gentle words come back to me: *Something inside you needs mending. Don't fight it. Don't make the wound worse. Care for it. Find a way to heal.*

"There's no demon," I say to him, straight. It feels so good to tell the truth. "There never was an evil spirit."

Reverend Preston shakes his head, slow. His blue eyes look sorry for me. "The minions of Satan try to deceive the servants of the Lord." He steps closer and touches his fingertips to my forehead. "Who am I speaking to? What is your name?"

My heart pounds to be let out of the cage. "I'm me—Catrina!"

He reaches for the bindings, but I grab them first. His Bible drops to the floor as he lunges for my wrists, but I'm faster than he is. I hit him in the face as hard as I can with my fist.

As he reels from the shock of it, I run to the stove and throw the bindings into the fire. "I'm me!" I scream. "Me!"

Reverend Preston stares at me. Who does he see? His eyes search me deeper than before. But still, he doesn't quite find me.

He holds his jaw, where my fist has left a red mark. "Shh," he whispers. "Quiet. I won't hurt you." He reaches out slow and cautious, like a person trying to touch a deer. I don't move. He tries to embrace me, but I have turned into a frozen girl, and his arms can't hold me anymore.

It's Sunday. The preacher rises early and heads for the church before I get up. He doesn't leave a note for me this time. He thinks I will stay here. He's probably wondering what to tell his congregation about his new wife, staying home from church on her first Sunday as Mrs. Preston.

But I won't hide here in this place. I'm not afraid of them anymore. And I know what I need to do to heal. I need to face them, let them see me in my own sealskin.

I take my wild work down from where I hung it to dry near the bed all night so no one could steal it from me while I slept. Careful, careful, I slip into my new clothes. I've cut most of the skirt away above the knee so I can walk free of its confines. I used the cut-off material to sew deep pockets to hold my things. The pale green clothes are soft, like a second skin floating over mine.

I walk outside. The twilight month of September is long gone. No more hazy days that linger between summer and fall, and are not quite one or the other. It's autumn. The morning air is clear and sharp with late October cold. This is the month we cut the sorghum stalks and crush them in the press till all the sweet juice is wrung from them. October is when the golden leaves fall to the ground and the spirits who have gone before us sometimes visit us again, when the wall between this world and the next is thin. This is the month my mother died.

I see her. Just for a moment, I see Mother again, near the hawthorn trees. Her image shimmers in the air the way fire bends the image above its flames. Her black hair and pale face look like mine. I reach out to her. I want to tell her I'm sorry—

But she's gone. And instead the air fills with voices from the church as the congregation sings the first hymn. I only hear women's voices. Most of the men have been conscripted. I imagine the men of Roubidoux who were singing hymns next to their wives and children last Sunday shooting guns at strangers now, just miles away in Springfield. Maybe Henry is, too.

I walk to the church and open the door, quiet. Everyone's standing for the hymn and no one sees me. I sit down in the empty back row. Lots of rows are empty—the only men in the church are the preacher, Mr. Lenox, and two farmers, old as Moses. Mr. Lenox, Lu, and Effie are right in front of me. When the hymn is over, everyone sits, and as Effie settles back into the pew, she catches sight of me out of the corner of her eye. She gives me her big smile right away, but when she sees my new sealskin clothes, her eyes grow wide.

Reverend Preston paces back and forth in the front of the church. His eyes travel over the congregation, melting a path with his fiery stare. Most people glance away when he gets to them, because they're afraid he'll see straight into their souls and they'll feel naked in front of the world. But I already know he can't see that far inside of people. His eyes are focused on Heaven so much, I think it's hard for them to adjust to things here below. He doesn't even see me sitting here in the back row.

When Reverend Preston thinks he has the lay of the land, he calls another hymn. I figure out quick which direction he's headed. He gives hints with each new hymn he calls. The congregation sings melodies about their muck and mire. They shout out tunes of deadly sins and earthly temptations. They sing about being lowly worms and wretches, and they do it in pretty four-part harmony.

Finally, they're done with the singing, and Reverend Preston jumps into his sermon about Hell and the Devil. Soon, his preaching settles into a comfy rhythm like a creaky rocking chair going back and forth. Even the *Amen*s and the *Preach it*s that ring out from the congregation every once and again roll over me without a hitch. But the sudden whinny of a horse nearby makes me jump awake. Reverend Preston's sermon keeps going, but there's a rustling among the congregation. Everyone cranes their neck to look out the windows and whisper to each other. Women fidget and fan their hankies faster. Effie just stares straight ahead at Reverend Preston, who doesn't stop preaching for a whipstitch. But at the sound of hooves clopping up the church steps, I twist in the pew and stare.

Stonefield.

Lord. He gallops right out of my thoughts and into the church on Reverend Preston's horse, Faithful. Frank Louis and another man I don't know follow him in on their horses. People gasp when they see them. Stonefield's hair is wild and he's not wearing a shirt. The pistol that belonged to the soldier he shot is stuffed between his back and his belt. The ink circles I drew on his skin are fading, but still plain to see. Reverend Preston's voice stops all of a sudden, as if someone's leaped out of the creaky rocking chair.

Stonefield looks fierce as a wolf as he glances around the church, searching for me. But his eyes don't find me, hidden in the back of the crowd in my strange clothes. I'm afraid to call out to him—afraid of what he will do to me.

Stonefield, I say his name, silent. *Stonefield, I was angry—*

But he doesn't turn to me.

Stonefield?

He can't seem to hear my voice. It's like he's gone to a far-off place.

Stonefield!

And then I remember his last words to me the day the soldiers came. *May a curse fall upon us both.* Oh God. He's far away and I can't find him because of the curse.

"Well, glory hallelujah!" Frank shouts. His hair is greasy and falls in his face as he looks around the church. "Chief, I do believe we got here just in time to pass around the offering plate!"

Stonefield nods. "You better get to it, then."

"Y'all got something to give to the needy? We had our property stolen away from us and our homes burned to the ground by them Yankees, and we're mighty needy at the moment." Frank hops from his horse and whisks off his hat, shoving it under the nose of an elderly woman in the front row. "Don't be stingy, now!" He grins.

The woman shrinks away.

"Ain't you got nothing in the world to give to the poor and desperate?" Frank presses the barrel of his heavy musket against the old woman's knee, and she starts trembling. "You best find something, sweetheart, or you'll be meeting your maker sooner than you thought!"

She lets out a little cry and tears off her bonnet. With clumsy fingers, she pulls two fine green combs from her hair and drops them into Frank's hat. Long silvery strands of hair tumble down her shoulders as she covers her face with her hands and cries.

My stomach turns.

As Frank and the other man force the congregation to hand over their property, Stonefield rides Faithful up to the pulpit, facing Reverend Preston. "I came to hear a sermon on hellfire and damnation. Your Good Book seems full of it. Isn't that what you were preaching?"

Reverend Preston doesn't answer, but slowly closes his Bible.

"Don't let me stop you. Don't you have a message from the Lord for a savage Indian heathen? Keep preaching!"

Still, Reverend Preston frowns at him and doesn't say a word.

Stonefield leans over in his saddle and grabs the Bible from the preacher's hands. He pulls out the pistol, lifts the Bible into the air, and shoots a bullet through the center.

Everyone screams at the sound. Faithful shies and snorts.

Stonefield slams the Bible onto the pulpit and tears the book open. Pointing with the pistol to the hole, he yells, "Right there! Preach it to me!"

I hold my breath, wondering if Reverend Preston will read it or hold his tongue and get shot for it.

He swallows and licks his lips. " 'Blessed—' "

"Louder!"

Reverend Preston winces. " 'Blessed are the merciful: for they shall obtain mercy.' "

Silence. A dark cloud passes over Stonefield's features. The bushwhackers stop passing Frank's hat and turn to look at him. My body's heavy as lead.

Stonefield, please don't. The wound on my arm throbs. *Please hear me.*

But he doesn't hear me. The curse has made us deaf to each other. He snatches the Bible away and fires another shot through it. "Read that!" he orders, throwing it open and pointing to the new bullet hole.

Reverend Preston's hands shake as he draws the book closer. " 'Be not overcome of evil, but overcome evil with good.' "

I slump against the pew. My head's spinning.

Stonefield's chest heaves, and his jaw clenches tight as he brings his fist down hard onto the open Bible. Grabbing as many pages as he can, he rips them from the book. He crumples them in his fist and throws them at the preacher's face.

"I told you to preach hellfire and damnation!" Stonefield shoots a third hole and slaps the pages open. "Now, read it!"

Sweat drips from the end of Reverend Preston's nose. " 'L-love . . .' " His shoulders slump. Glancing up at Stonefield, he reads in a faltering voice, " 'Love your enemies, do good to them which hate you . . .' "

The topsy-turvy words are like blows to Stonefield. He flinches at each one. Reverend Preston's Bible's full of damnation, but Stonefield must be a bad shot—he's missing every time.

"'. . . as ye would that men should do to you, do ye also to them . . .'"

Stonefield, please listen.

"'. . . forgive, and ye shall be forgiven . . .'"

Stonefield's eyes turn glassy wet. He shakes his head and lifts the pistol. This time he points it at Reverend Preston.

"Stonefield, no!" I cry.

My voice shakes him, and he almost drops the gun. His eyes find me.

Please don't.

But if he hears my inner voice, I can't tell. If he's speaking silent words, they're not reaching me.

His face wrenches in pain. His eyes glisten wet as they roam over my unfamiliar clothes. He reaches into his pocket and pulls out a handful of something colorful and frayed. Pieces fall to the floor. Then he flings them out toward me and they float to the ground. Feathers. My feathers that hung above our secret house.

All broken.

"Well looky here." Frank Louis is staring at me with his hungry animal eyes, just like that time he spied on me while I was swimming in the creek.

My hands tighten into fists.

"Ain't this the Dickinson gal?" He wipes his mouth with his

sleeve. "I never thought I'd see a wild little vixen like her in a church meeting. Did you go and get religion, honey?"

I stare bullets at him, wishing I could shoot his eyes out.

"I think I'll take her with us. I could use a little feminine company—know what I mean, Chief?" He laughs and reaches toward me.

Reverend Preston's voice is shaky but deep. "You will leave my wife alone."

Frank laughs. "Wife? This witchy little thing is your wife now?"

The preacher's words have turned Stonefield into a statue. He stares at me as if I've just shot him with a bullet.

Frank steps toward me. "If I'm going to do some stealin' from the house of the Lord today, I might as well steal me the preacher's wife, too."

"No." Stonefield's voice is like God shouting the Commandments down from the mountain. Everyone stops moving and turns to look at him. "Not her." He glares at me. "I don't want her near me."

Frank swallows hard and then shrugs. His eyes glance over me to Lu. He brightens. "Ah, looky here. I believe this darkie used to take a shine to me. I guess her rich white daddy must own the church, or she'd be singing hymns from outside with the mules like the rest of her kind."

Lu's whole body bristles. Her chin goes up like Effie's does when she knows she's right. "My heavenly Father's the one who owns this church and He's the one who wants me in it."

Frank laughs. "She'd look even more pretty if she didn't talk so much, but we can fix that."

"Don't you dare touch me!" Lu shouts.

Stonefield isn't looking at Lu. He's staring at me. And before any of us realize what's happening, Frank lunges toward us.

Lu screams and grabs hold of Effie.

Frank pushes Effie backward to the floor and throws Lu over his shoulder, nimble as a weasel. I grab hold of Frank's leg and hang on with all my might to keep him and Lu there. He keeps walking, just like Papa used to do when Henry and me would each hug one of his legs and sit on his feet. The other, burly bushwhacker plucks me off like a tick and shoves me into Effie, who's struggling to her feet. Her features are stretched wide with fear for Lu.

Mr. Lenox doesn't seem to notice the gun pointed at his head. He rushes at Frank, throwing punches. Frank aims his gun cool as cucumbers and shoots Mr. Lenox in the leg. Lu screams louder, and Effie catches her father as he falls against the pew.

We search the faces of those around us for help, but the bushwhackers have their guns pointed at Reverend Preston and the old men. Mr. Lenox struggles to get up like a coon caught in a trap, but his leg's bleeding bad. His face is ashen. I think he'd bite his own leg off to get free of it and save Lu if he could. But he can't. Nobody else moves.

The burly man helps Frank bind screaming Lu, tying her up and slinging her over his horse as if she's a sack of corn.

Stonefield's eyes never leave me the whole time.

"Please don't," I beg him.

But instead of answering me, he grabs the preacher's Bible and throws it hard. It whizzes past me and slams against the back wall of the church.

As the pages flap, Reverend Preston lunges for Stonefield, to knock him from the horse.

Stonefield pulls the trigger, and the preacher falls to the floor, bleeding from his shoulder.

As everyone shouts and flees for cover, Stonefield turns and rides Faithful out of the church with Lu's frightened screams trailing behind him.

28

FRANK AND THE OTHER BUSHWHACKER GALLOP AFTER Stonefield like a tornado. They've stolen some of the horses that were tied up outside the church and have driven off the rest so no one can give chase. Reverend Preston's collapsed behind the pulpit, and Mr. Lenox is fading, too.

Effie presses her father's bleeding wound with her coat and ties it up around him tight with the sleeves. She shouts orders for another woman to do the same for Reverend Preston. Everyone but Effie is sobbing and helpless and doesn't know what to do. But I know what to do. I run to the door.

"Yes!" Effie calls to me. "Catrina, run to the depot in Rolla—tell the outpost to send soldiers after the men to save Lu."

I do run to save Lu. But not to the depot to get the soldiers who want to kill Stonefield. I know where he is hiding. I run to the cave.

There's no flutter of gold wings or rustling of leaves in the thickets this time. I slow my steps and peer through the tangle of bushes that guard the hidden ravine. It's already noon, though

I ran as fast as I could. Sweat drips down the back of my neck; I'm out of breath.

I hear the men before I see them. Three men I don't know and the bushwhacker from the church gather around a small copper still, making moonshine near the stream. Stonefield's not with them. Neither are Frank and Lu. Maybe they're in the cave—I strain to see through the dark opening, but I can't tell. Right then, Frank swings his legs out over the ledge and jumps to the ground. He walks over to the still to join the bushwhackers.

He stokes the fire under the still while the others cut wood, bring water from the stream, and wash out jars. They're busy as ants at a picnic and don't even notice when Napoleon comes up to the bushes to sniff me.

"What are you doing here?" I whisper as he wags his tail. "Go home to Papa." But I know he's here because he wants to be with Stonefield, like I do.

The men are getting noisy. Looks like they've already finished a run of whiskey making, because most of them are on their way to getting drunk, and they've started on another. Frank is Roubidoux's coppersmith and owns his own still—most likely he made this one. An older, heavyset man with a shiny bald head rubs his hands together and stares at a clear fruit jar as it fills up with moonshine trickling from the end of a copper pipe. Frank pours some yeast and a sack of sugar into a barrel of corn mash. He's mixing it up to ferment and distill into more alcohol.

"We'll let this here mash set and bubble for a couple days,"

Frank says. "When it's got the kick of a mule colt, it'll be ready to cook!"

The man with the shiny head raises the jar of whiskey. "This batch is nearing its last run. This here's just low wine of no account—" He's about to dump it out when Frank pounces on him.

"Are you fritter minded, Joe? That there white lightning is crystal clear, double run, and three times twisted!" His feathers ruffled, Frank pours some into a tin cup and fetches his gunpowder horn to pour some of that in, too. Joe almost pops his buttons as he watches Frank light fire to a stick and dip the end of it into the cup. The whiskey-gunpowder mixture bursts into flame, and Frank's grin stretches from ear to ear. "See?"

Joe huffs, then takes a swig from the fruit jar. His eyebrows rise, and he stands there, blinking. Finally, he gives a little cough and says in a weak voice, "You call that whiskey?"

Frank bends over double and laughs. "Well, it sure ain't gravy!" He slaps his thigh.

I want to shove the whiskey gunpowder down Frank's throat and light it. I want to hit his handsome face over and over and over with my fists until his outsides are as ugly as his insides. I want to call out for Stonefield. But I don't do any of those things. What has he done to Lu? Where are they? I make up my mind to climb through the thicket and sneak over to the cave while they're not paying attention. But soon as I reach out to part the bushes, something hard pokes me between my shoulder blades and I hear the sound of a gun being cocked.

"Turn around real slow-like, or there'll be a new face in Hell tomorrow," the owner of the gun drawls in a deep voice.

I do as I'm told. Before me stands a great bear of a man. "Hey, fellas!" he shouts. "I found me a little rabbit hiding in the bushes!"

"Well, bring it down. We'll cook it for dinner!" Frank answers.

The man pushes me down the slope, through thorns and thistles that tear at my sealskin clothes. Frank's grin looks like it's too big for his face. "She couldn't stay away after all."

Joe snorts. "You better hope she don't have fangs and claws like your nigger gal. The womenfolk don't seem to care so much for your good looks once they get to know you."

Frank has a big red slash mark down the side of his face. Lu.

A sound of movement comes from the woods. Stonefield looks like a wild man walking out of the trees. His dark wavy hair sticks out in all directions. He wrestles a soldier's army cap down over it and walks toward us real stiff. But when he sees me, it's like I'm a ghost come to haunt him. He turns pale and stops dead. His face twists up like he's in pain.

"I don't want her here." He turns and heads to the cave.

"Stonefield!" I cry. "Wait. We haven't spoken in so long. And now—your words—they hurt."

" 'I am not bound to please thee with my answers.' "

Hearing him speak in his old way of quoting Shakespeare, but in this strange distant voice, cuts me deep to the bone.

He spits in the dirt. "I'm a savage, remember? Like you said, 'You know how people feel about Creek Indians.' You and Henry and the damned 'people' have made it clear that I don't belong with you and that I don't belong here."

His words spark my anger again and my own words bubble up before I can stop them. "What do you expect, stealing the preacher's horse and riding it into the church. Then you go and shoot people and steal Lu away. No wonder they think you're a savage!"

His eyes are fire now. "I knew you thought it, too." Before I can protest, he yells, "So go on back to your husband the preacher."

I wince as if he slapped me in the face. "Please, Stonefield, you have to leave—they'll kill you as a traitor—"

"*I'm* the traitor? 'Though those that are betray'd do feel the treason sharply, yet the traitor stands in worse case of woe.'"

Stonefield. I did it because you wanted to leave me. I wanted to hurt you as much as you hurt me. But if you don't go right now, they'll kill you.

The curse blocks my silent voice. He keeps walking away. I start to run after him, when a shrill whistle sounds from the woods. Two men on horseback gallop up to the thickets at the edge of the ravine. The other bushwhackers jump to their feet—all except Joe, who's had too much whiskey to notice.

"There's a troop of Home Guard Unionists on horseback," one of the riders calls. "Heard about them yesterday—they're from Germantown in St. Louis, headed to Springfield!"

"How many?" Stonefield comes back, already loading his pistol. It seems like he and Frank are in charge of the other bush-whackers.

"Fifteen. And a wagon of supplies and guns!"

Frank makes a whooping sound. "Them supplies and guns will be ours before the day is done! I'm feeling like taking back a little of what Union soldiers stole from me. Vengeance, boys!"

Stonefield saddles up Faithful. All the men get busy. Joe puts out the fire under the still, shaking his head and muttering, "Only two runs. It's a cryin' shame . . ." The others bring out the horses, and the burly man takes hold of me. He smells like sweat and liquor.

"Should I tie her up and leave her with the other one, Chief?"

I glance toward the cave.

Stonefield takes a loop of rope from his saddle. "I'll tie her up, but we'll bring her along. The soldiers won't be looking for ambushers if they're looking at her instead."

Lord. What's he going to do with me? He looks so stony and cold, I'm afraid to have him touch me. My heart beats like galloping hooves. My whole body quivers like Faithful's nervous hide as he winds the rope rough around my wrists in front of me and heaves me into his saddle. I never thought he'd bind me the way the preacher did. He pulls himself up behind me and, to take the reins, he wraps his arms around me. I smell the familiar scent of his skin and want to sink into his embrace, only it's not an embrace. His arms are rigid. They don't want to hold me. The big man rides beside him and slaps the horse's haunches, making Faithful jump and nicker. He yells, "Let's ride!" and everyone takes off.

I grip the saddle horn with my tied hands, trying to hang on as we whip through the woods, the rest of the bushwhackers racing along with us. When we reach Springfield Road, we gallop alongside it, hidden by the trees and sticking to the brush. There are nine bushwhackers altogether. The wind tears through my hair and whistles in my ears. It lifts the back of my shirt. I feel the cold weight of Stonefield's pistol pressing against my thigh. After about five miles, he slows down and motions for the men to guide their horses over to the side.

"Make sure she's tied up good and tight, and get her set down in the middle of the road. She's our decoy."

"No!" The words burst out of my mouth. "Stonefield, wait—"

The burly man lifts me off the horse, away from Stonefield, slaps a handkerchief around my mouth, and ties it firm. He sets me down hard on the road and winds a rope tight around my arms and legs till I can't move. He lays me down in the middle of the road.

Stonefield, Frank, and the men turn and leave me, coaxing their horses up the steep hill lining the road to the low bluff. I can see them make it to the top. Stonefield holds up his hand for them to slow down. The men vanish from my sight for a little while, and when they come back to the edge of the cliff, where I can see them, they're on foot. They each take powder, lead shot, or bullets from the saddlebags and load their guns. Joe's face is almost purple and just as shiny as if he'd glazed his forehead with grease. He and some of the other men fumble for their flasks of whiskey and guzzle the drink down.

Frank signals for them to take positions. They crawl to the edge, partly hidden by brush, and peer down at the road, about thirty feet below them. All the men are watching the bend in the road, listening for the approaching soldiers. All except Stone-field. His face is turned toward me. My heart's hammering. What's going to happen next? I focus on him and listen hard for his silent voice, but all I hear is a low rumble of hoofbeats in the ground. They're coming.

I try to turn, but I'm tied so tight, I have to rock my whole body to move my position just a smidgen. If only I could get enough momentum to roll farther away—Lord—I'm afraid the horses will stampede me before the riders have time to see me, let alone rein them in. The ropes cut into my wrists and arms. I can hear the horses right around the bend, but it sounds more like a trot than a gallop. I glance up at the bushwhackers and see the sun glinting off their rifles.

Right then I see out of the corner of my eye the leader of the riders coming round the bend. I push myself into a position where I can see better. Following the leader are two groups of six—one group riding in front of a supply wagon, and the other behind. Two men ride in the wagon. None of them are looking up at the bushwhackers—all their wide eyes are stuck on me.

When I see their blue coats and caps, my heart thumps in my ears. I imagine Frank picking one out and wetting his lips as he takes aim. I clench my eyes shut and brace myself.

CRACK!

A gun fires from the bluff. I flinch. The leader falls from his horse, landing in front of me with a heavy thud.

Mercy, mercy, mercy.

The bushwhackers let loose, their shots exploding in the air like popped corn. Blue caps dot the ground.

I want to swallow, but my throat's a parched riverbed. I try again to roll away, but a hot poker of pain jabs my right shoulder—I've been grazed with lead gunshot. I duck my head and curl into a ball as the noise of shots ricochets off the bluff.

Oh Lord.

Am I going to die here on this road?

My shoulder's on fire.

My head's pounding.

The hurt I feel from Stonefield, the pain in my arm, and the blood from my flesh wound all flow together over me.

The blast of exploding bullets rattles my skull like hail pounding a tin roof.

The world spins. I dig my fingers into the earth and hang on.

Finally, the shooting stops and all is quiet.

I'm alive. My fingernails are deep in the dirt, and I feel stuck to the ground. I lift my aching head. Dirt and small pebbles are pressed into the side of my face.

Stonefield stands on the bluff. His gun arm relaxes at his side as he gazes at the road. All the bushwhackers stand up.

"Woo-eee! Would you look at that!" Frank whistles. "I can't aim for shucks when I'm sober, but when I'm drunk, I sure can shoot me a mess of soldiers!"

The burly man grunts and shakes his head. Joe, his face flushed, struggles to his feet. They both disappear into the woods and bring the horses back with them. Stonefield takes Faithful's reins, jumps on, and rides off. The rest of the men hurry after him. He gallops through the woods, down the hill, and around to the road.

Oh God. My stomach lurches. The dead men's bodies lie twisted over each other, looking like a pile of dirty washing scattered everywhere. Oh Lord, their bodies are limp and empty, like Mother's was when she fell to the ground.

There's blood all over the road. My breath catches in my throat, and I turn away.

I listen to the bushwhackers' heavy breathing and grunting as they dismount and start pulling dead bodies into the woods. Finally, I open my eyes real slow, afraid of what I'll see. Stonefield's squatting beside me, peering into my face. His own golden face has turned ashen. But as soon as he sees I'm all right, he stands up to help the men.

Joe's passing by me, pulling a body. I keep my eyes away from the dead soldier's face and look at his boots. They're small, about my size. Something in my chest flutters like a trapped bird.

Frank leans over the last dead body on the road, the man who'd been the leader. He slides his knife from its sheath and kneels near the dead man's head with his back to me. When he stands, he's clasping something in his fist. A sour taste rises to my throat. Frank spits on the man's face. "That's for your damned Union Army burning down my house and barn and kicking me off my own land. You ain't gonna be giving any Federalist orders now, are ya," he mutters.

I watch him tie the scrap of hair he's holding to his horse's mane. All the life drains out of me when I realize what the trophy is that now dangles from the horse's neck. The blond scalp of the dead man.

"Get out your knife, Chief—you can cut the scalp of Joe's

man like a true Indian savage." Frank nods toward the body Joe's pulling. "Ain't that what your people do to their enemies?"

Stonefield glares at Frank. I can tell it makes him mad that he knows as little as Frank does about what his own people do or don't do. My chest tightens, my hands go numb as Stonefield steps toward the body. *Don't do this thing. Frank's the savage, not you.*

Joe drops the soldier's feet. They slap against the ground.

A low moan from the man makes me start. I stare at the dead man who is not dead. He isn't a man, neither, but a boy. Younger than me. The boy clutches at the bleeding wound in his side and groans. He stares wide-eyed at Joe and Stonefield like a scared rabbit stuck in a spring trap.

Stonefield points his pistol at him.

"Nein! Nein!" The boy gasps. "Nicht schiessen!"

Howls of drunken laughter explode from the bushwhackers. "What's a matter with him?" shouts Frank. "Is he drunk, too, or just plain stupid? What kind of crazy talk is that?"

"Him? Why, he's one of them fool German-talkers from St. Louis, ain't he? I hear a whole slew of them live up there," Joe says. "He can't help talking that-a-way—he don't know no better."

The boy looks from Joe, to Frank, to Stonefield with anxious eyes. "Nicht schiessen," he repeats.

The bushwhackers burst out with fresh laughter at the strange tongue. The boy glances around at the dead soldiers and sees the scalped body of his leader. His chest heaves, and his face goes white.

Stonefield takes two steps toward him.

The boy's eyes dart over the bushwhackers, searching for pity. When he notices me, he locks on to my gaze.

I look up at Stonefield. *Please.*

The boy follows my gaze and pleads, "Hab Mitleid!" straight at him.

I can feel Stonefield's stare burning a hole through my chest.

The men roar with more laughter.

The boy holds out his hand toward Stonefield, his eyes desperate. "Hab Mitleid!" he cries.

Have mercy.

Stonefield's eyes flicker over to me and then back to the boy. For a moment, I almost think I can hear my name. But then his face clouds over and I hear nothing.

He cocks his gun.

I drag my face against the ground to push the gag out of my mouth, and I manage to croak, "No, Stonefield. No."

He doesn't move his pistol away, but his hand starts to shake. His mouth trembles like he wants to say something but can't. His gun is ready to fire, yet he still doesn't pull the trigger.

"Damn it, Chief." Frank spits in the dirt. "I thought you was a true Indian savage."

The crack of a pistol splits the silence.

The thud of the boy's lifeless body follows, but it's Frank's gun that's smoking, not Stonefield's.

My own body gives out, and my head falls to the dirt. The world spins out of control. I can't breathe. The men's voices sound like the buzzing of flies.

The boy's feet were so small.

My stomach lurches and empties on the ground.

"That there soldier was a puny little rabbit, weren't he?" Frank laughs.

The burly man snorts. "Let's get out of here. We ought to take what we can and head back to the cave before we leave the county. We need to get, before them church folks send for some Yankees to come after us from Rolla."

Joe, still a little drunk, mumbles, "I hope this little one's ghost doesn't follow us to Mexico when we hightail it out of here. I'm plum worn out from being chased, ain't you?" The rest of them mutter their agreement. "Chief, you sure you don't want to stick with us, instead of stopping in Indian Territory to join the Creeks? If the Union soldiers don't track you down first, them Confederates might force you to join their army. But if you stay with us resisters, you stay free for sure—we don't take orders from neither side."

Stonefield stares off into the woods. I remember what he said about the group of Creeks who hope President Lincoln will grant them asylum so they can stay neutral.

He glances at me. "I'm not changing my mind."

29

THE RIDE BACK TO THE WOODS IS A HAZE. I'M faint, and drift in and out of consciousness. When I come to, I'm being thrust onto a rocky cave floor by big grimy hands. Now the hands are gone, and it's just me in the darkness. I hear the bushwhackers' voices and then the sound of their horses as they ride away.

The floor's muddy. My whole body's numb from being tied up tight in one position. I can barely move; I'm so cold. The pain from the scattered bits of gunshot that grazed my shoulder has lessened, but I still have the sour taste in my mouth from retching up my breakfast. The young soldier's image haunts me.

Lord. Water drips onto my cheek and tickles my neck.

"Catrina?"

My heart skips. "Lu?"

"Oh, Catrina." Her voice has lost its creamy sugar—it's brittle and broken like crushed herbs. She sounds so far away.

I reach out as best I can with my fingers and extend my legs, fumbling in the dark for her. "Lu, where are you?"

No answer, just low moaning. A cold dread seeps into my bones. I struggle to move toward the sound of her voice. "Lu, are you all right?" I stop moving so I can listen for her reply.

"I don't know." Her voice is small, like a child's. "I don't know!" she whimpers.

Lord, oh Lord. I push myself through the mud toward the sound of her weeping. "What did Frank do to you?" I remember how he shot the boy, and hot hate rises up in my heart. "Where did he hurt you?" My arms are tied down against my sides, but the tips of my fingers touch the lacy material of Lu's dress. It's a piece that's been torn loose. I take hold of it and climb my fingers up to find Lu. Her skin is icy and she's trembling like a rabbit. As soon as she feels me touch her arm, she leans against me heavy, like she's drowning, and her cries come pouring out in a flood.

I let her press against me hard. Her hands are tied behind her back, or she'd probably grip me, too. Her body quakes and trembles as the sobs rack and heave through her small frame. I wait for her to quiet. "It's all right now, Lu," I tell her, soft, like Papa does to soothe a spooked mare. "Frank's gone. You're all right."

"No, I'm not," she whispers. "I'm not all right."

I struggle to move out from under her and touch her hand with mine. I hold it strong but gentle like Effie would.

"He—" she tries to say, and then I feel her shake her head.

"You don't have to tell me if it hurts too much to say it."

"He took . . . he stole something from me. I screamed and screamed for him not to, but nobody tried to stop him. He just took it." Her body shakes again with fresh sobs. "It hurt more than anything, ever."

Lord, I can feel what she's telling me the way I felt when Reverend Preston tied me to the bed and tried to force part of me away from myself. I grip her hand so hard she gasps. I loosen my hold and move closer to her again until we're side by side, our shoulders touching.

"Catrina," she whispers, "I don't know what it means."

"It means he's a sack of dirt, a pile of shit, a—"

"I don't know what it means to be like this. You saw him mistreat me once—but this is so much worse." She keeps talking through her sobs. "Catrina, am I still the same person? I don't feel the same."

I don't know how to answer. How much can be taken away before a person isn't herself anymore? Is there one most important part of a person—the part that would change everything if it were taken away? If the curse cut the bond that holds me to Stonefield, and he floats away from me forever, will I still be me? I can't bear to let that happen.

But Lu fought hard to keep what was dear to her—I remember the slash down Frank's face—and still she couldn't stop it from happening. My darkness inside me grows blacker than the cave.

"Lu, I don't know."

She slumps a little, next to me. She turns so quiet, I feel alone again. I can't tell how much time has passed in the dark stillness. I feel suspended in nothing. I know Lu's here with me, but I don't feel her any longer. I wonder if this is what it would be like for Aphrodite floating in the night sky if the rope that connects her to Eros got cut.

I think about the baby floating inside me—how it's a part of me and maybe the size of a gooseberry, connected to me by a little cord. I wonder when it won't be me anymore, not even a speck, but all its own self. When it's taken from my body and the cord cut, will it still be a part of me? Or will I have lost that most important part? I think of my wild work in the woods, how I create a rain girl and the rain slowly steals her away. But the real girl always stays.

"Lu," I whisper.

She doesn't reply, but I hear her sniffle.

"I think you're still you. You have to want to be hard enough, and then I swear no one can take you from yourself."

I feel Lu moving back toward me. Her fingers stroke the tips of mine. At first I think she's showing me tenderness, but then something cold and smooth fills my open hand. A knife.

"I want to go home."

"Lu, how—"

"It dropped from his belt when Frank was—" She can't finish. "I found it on the ground in the mud after he left. I tried cutting through my own ropes, but couldn't do it. I'm so stiff and it hurts to move. I can't get the angle right."

Lord, how I want to hug Lu. I wrap my fingers tight around the knife handle and together we cut ourselves free.

When we climb outside, it's almost as dark as it was in the cave. We have maybe an hour of daylight left, and it's hard to hurry through the woods with our stiff limbs and sore bodies.

Despite all she's been through, Lu manages to keep up with me. Maybe it's because she wants to get home with every fiber of her own self. Every step I take drains life from me, because it pushes me in the opposite direction of Stonefield.

No one's at Papa's, so we go on to the Lenoxes'. Effie and Dora come running from the lit-up porch when they see us. Papa's there, too. He gets up from a rocking chair like it's difficult, and walks toward us. They must have been keeping watch.

"Heavens; oh my Heavens, my Heavens!" Dora squeals.

Effie's eyes are red and puffy. She embraces Lu and grabs me into her hug, too. I never felt Effie shake before. Like God was playing a washboard up and down her spine with a thimble.

"I thought—" Effie pulls in a deep breath. "I thought I might never see you two again." Her laugh sounds like a sob. "I'm so glad I was wrong!"

Dora's hands are on her face, like she's scared she might have to cover her eyes at any moment. "What happened to you both? Oh, don't tell me." She covers her ears.

Effie looks into Lu's eyes and I can tell she knows what has happened to her sister. She puts her arm around her shoulders. "Come inside with me, Lu. I want to take care of your wounds."

Papa reaches me and takes me into his arms. He smells like coffee and soap and pipe. "My Cat. I was so afraid I'd lost you, too."

I bury my face in his chest.

When I've hugged all I can hug, we go inside, too.

Later, after I'm clean and fed, I find Effie sitting near the bed as Lu sleeps. I sit down beside her and she gives me a small smile. "I'm glad you're well." Her smile fades. "Lu told me what happened to her. She also said she might never have been able to leave the cave if you hadn't been there to help her." Effie rests her hand on mine. "What happened to you?"

I remember the bullets and dying soldiers, the scalp Frank cut and the boy he shot. I shake my head and close my eyes.

"I understand." Effie nods. "The Union soldiers will be asking questions about the bushwhackers. They'll want to know where Stonefield, Frank, and the others are headed next. I thought if you could tell me anything, I might be able to help them in their search."

I can't tell her they're headed to Mexico, because Stonefield will be traveling with the men until he gets to Indian Territory. I want them to catch Frank, but not Stonefield. Even if I never get to be with him again, if he got killed because of me, I'd want to die, too.

"I don't know." I turn away from her so she can't see from my face that I'm lying. I stare out the window into the darkness. "Don't ask me."

"All right, Catrina. I know it's been a difficult day."

I'm so grateful she's not going to call me out for lying, I feel my body relax—I didn't even know I was so tense. "Effie, how is your father?"

Effie's face tightens up like a hem thread pulled taut. "Father's out of danger now, though he's lost his leg—the doctor from Rolla was sent for and he finished the amputation just before you arrived." She clears her throat. "It will take a while for Father to recover, but he was in good health, so there is reason to be optimistic and hope for the best."

I bet she stayed in the room when that doctor cut off her father's leg, to learn everything she could about the surgery, even while it hurt her to see it.

"I'm sure you are wondering about your new husband's health as well . . ."

I don't answer. I hope the preacher's arm was cut off, too; then he'll never be able to hold me down again.

"I was able to remove the bullet with little stress to the surrounding area. It missed the bone, and you'll be happy to hear that he'll certainly be back to normal soon. He's anxious to hear word of you and plans to pray in the church continually until you return." She clears her throat again. "On their way home, your father and Dora will drive you to the parsonage."

"The parsonage is not my home."

Effie lifts her chin. "It is now."

"It will never be my home."

"Catrina, it became your home the day you said 'I do' to Reverend Preston."

"They're just words. I don't belong to him."

"Words are powerful things, and so is a person's free will. You used both when you married Reverend Preston, and now you need to go make the parsonage your home with him."

Hell. Why does she always think she's right? Can't we both be right in different ways? My rightness suits me thousands better than hers does. I want to argue with her, because I hate when she acts like she knows more than me.

But I'm worn out and feel like something got broken inside me back on that road, and then it cracked even more, seeing Lu in the cave. Now all my thoughts keep leaking out the crack and I lose them. I can't think straight enough to give Effie a hard time. So I go, because Effie wants me to, and because I don't have any fight left in me tonight.

When I walk through the door, a single lantern is lit, but the preacher's not there. Nothing's changed since I left. The kitchen is still a mess from when I made my own sealskin, the pots of dye on the stove and spools of thread on the table. The new dress now hangs from me, dirty, tattered, and ruined. I want to close up this day like a book I hate. I want to shut the covers hard and throw it across the room. But something draws me to the church instead. Like the unfinished story is gnawing at me and I just can't sleep until I find out what happens.

Lit candles flicker in the two front windows. They've burned down to stumps. I walk, quiet, back outside to the front doors of the church and lean in to press my ear against the wood. I hear a muffled sound like moaning or low sobs coming from inside. I stay still for a long time, but nothing happens, so I push the doors open, gentle—they don't even creak—and find Reverend Preston, lying prostrate before the Lord. I read about that in the Bible—prostrate before the Lord—and asked Papa what it meant. He said it meant to lie on the floor with your face to the ground like a dead man before the Almighty. I know the preacher is alive, though, because he is quivering and murmuring.

"Please, Lord," he begs. The flickering candlelight casts eerie shadows over his back. One arm is in a sling and he has a bulky bandage where Stonefield shot him.

At first I think the reverend's praying to God about me, asking Him to keep me safe and bring me back to him. But he isn't.

"Please speak to me." He groans. "Why do You stay silent, O Lord? I don't understand. Why can I no longer hear Your voice? What have I done? Do not remove Your presence from me. Where are You? What shall I do without the voice of Your Spirit to direct me? I am lost! I am nothing without You! Please, O Lord. Speak to me!"

But the Lord can't hear him or isn't listening, because Reverend Preston lets out a moan full of such pain and anguish, it makes my knees buckle. I'm scared thousands more than I was lying in the road during the ambush. Right before my eyes, the thing most dear to Reverend Preston in all the world is being ripped away from his insides. I didn't know God could be so cruel to folks that aren't even heathens.

I walk closer and drop to my knees beside him. "Reverend Preston," I whisper, "are you all right?"

He turns still for a moment as he realizes I'm here with him. He doesn't ask me how I am or what's happened. He just keeps prostrating and moaning to the Lord as he did before. I never felt so sorry for anyone as the preacher, because I know what it feels like when the secret voice of the one you love most in all the world is taken from you. It hurts worse than a thousand pokers of fire set inside your ribs. And it leaves a deeper scar.

30

ALL NIGHT, I LIE ON THE FLOOR NEXT TO THE moaning preacher as we drift in and out of sleep. In the morning, my back is sore. I open my eyes. Reverend Preston is staring at my sealskin dress with bloodshot eyes. He sits on the step below the pulpit, one elbow on his knee and his chin in his hand. He must have run his fingers through his hair many times, because it stands on end.

"Reverend Preston?"

He doesn't ask me to call him Samuel. He doesn't say a thing.

"Reverend Preston, what's happening?"

He slips the wilted lavender from his pocket and crushes it between his fingers. "I truly do not know, Miss Catrina." The pieces fall to the floor. "I thought the Lord wanted me to come to these hills and start a church, help establish a town. I heard His voice so clearly, guiding me to Roubidoux and to you, but I must have misunderstood." He hangs his head and stares at the floor. "I've displeased Him somehow." He unties the sling from around his neck and with a grimace of pain, he flings it away from him to where it lands beside his Bible. I don't think he's touched the book since Stonefield shot it three times and threw it against the wall.

"What else are the humiliating and crushing events of these last several days, if not punishment from the Lord? And this war—it's His wrath upon us all for displeasing Him. He has withdrawn from me. From us all!" His whole body shudders as if he wants to weep but is trying to hold back. "Without His guidance, I am forced to guide myself until He speaks to me again."

He straightens his shoulders. "I've decided to go away for a time." The blue of his eyes no longer looks like the hottest part of a flame. The color's turned a dull gray. "Faithful is gone."

At first I don't know what he means, but then I remember Faithful, the horse that Stonefield stole from him.

"I'll sell the buggy and buy another horse."

"Where will you go?"

"The Missouri State Militia has been asking any men of the area who aren't enlisted to join—they hunt out Confederate guerrillas. The branch in Rolla has formed a group to track down the bands of outlaws who have been terrorizing the area. I'm sure that will include the group who caused us such grief here in Roubidoux. I'll leave tomorrow."

Something catches in my throat.

"It's a noble cause—to seek justice. If I cannot be a minister of God to the people or a true husband to you at this time, then there is no reason for me to sit here and do nothing while outlaws run loose."

Oh God. My heart throbs like the burning wound on my shoulder. My whole body starts trembling at his words. I can't think.

Reverend Preston looks me in the eye for the first time since I arrived at the church last night. "It may not be possible to send letters by post during my travels, but if I can, I'll inform you of my situation by sending messages however I am able."

He turns to leave, his shoulders slack, his hair tangled. Every inch of his clothes is wrinkled. He reminds me of a broken piece of porcelain that has so many tiny hairline cracks that one more will make it fall apart completely.

I can't let him hunt down Stonefield. My darkness comes flooding into my body like a rushing muddy river over my head.

"Stop," I say. The word is loud in the quiet church.

He pauses, his back still to me.

"Don't do this, Reverend Preston."

He turns to me. The surprise of my resistance makes his weary features wake up.

"You can't. I love—"

A hopeful question rises in his eyes as he takes a step nearer. I take a step back.

"I love Stonefield. If you hurt him, you hurt me. If you kill him, you kill me, too."

Reverend Preston's mouth falls limp, but his eyes widen. He seems frozen in place. Then he shakes his head, stunned. "That outlaw? The Indian?" He looks like I just told him that I'm in love with Napoleon the dog. He shakes his head again, unable to take it in. "But that was before, when you were guided by the evil spirit. You changed. I—God released you from the savage's hold on you."

"You can't go hunt him down. My child—you'll be killing the father of my child."

His chest rises and falls like someone's pumping a bellows into his lungs. I think he's going to burst. The blue flame of his eyes rekindles. When he speaks, his voice starts low but grows louder, like a rumbling train headed straight toward me.

"I wanted to seek justice and that's exactly what I will do. If anyone deserves to be hunted down, it is that scoundrel! I know this even more certainly than I did before." He turns to leave.

"No!" I grab hold of him. His body is shaking. So is mine. "I won't let you do this." I shove him away from the doorway and block his path.

"Please step aside, Miss Catrina."

He moves forward again, and I push him. He takes hold of my wrists, forcing me away from him as he flinches from the hurt in his wounded arm.

"No!" I scream in his face. As soon as he lets go of me, I grab his injured arm as hard as I can and twist it. He moans in pain like a bellowing cow.

The horrible sound startles me. I look down at my fingers, tight and so white, gripping Reverend Preston's arm. My hands don't even seem like they belong to me. I feel like I'm in a bad dream.

"Catrina," he whispers. "Let go. Let me go."

As soon as I release my hold, Reverend Preston pushes past me, over the threshold, slamming the door shut behind him.

All my darkness inside presses me to the floor. All the air is being sucked out of me. I gasp and gasp, but I can't remember how to breathe.

31

EVEN WITH THE PREACHER GONE, THE PARSONAGE IS still not my home. I know the truth—the woods are my only home now. When I pledged my soul to Stonefield's—using my words and my free will just like Effie said—I made that vow to myself and to him, not like the lie I told to God and the reverend when I married the preacher. Stonefield is gone, but the secret house is still our home.

Sometimes I eat the food Effie and Dora leave for me at the parsonage, but mostly I eat what I find in the woods. At first there was watercress, wild onions, walnuts, chanterelles, and persimmons, but now food in the woods is getting harder to find. When I grow so hungry I feel faint, I find a page of one of Stonefield's books where he wrote a note in pencil in the margins and I tear each word out and place it on my tongue. I imagine his voice saying the word inside me. I feel it dissolving and becoming warm liquid in my mouth, becoming part of me as I swallow, like when Jesus told His men to break off a piece of bread and eat it because it was His body. After I've eaten enough, Stonefield's words fill me up and my stomach finally stops growling.

I keep busy making wild work and sending messages to Stonefield. I cut my name into pieces of bark and send them down the creek so he will see them and have to think of me. First, I whisper a charm over them so they will find him and so they will cut me into his heart like a sharp knife when he reads them. Once, before the mourning doves flew south, I caught one in a net of knotted yarn so I could tie a tiny scrolled message to its leg. For ink, I used the blood that blossomed from my arm as I picked off the scab where I'd scraped his name from my skin. I pray the dove will reach him.

Always throughout the days, I watch for Mother. I see her more and more, now that I spend most of my time in the woods. Sometimes she appears through the trees, looking for me. If I lie still long enough for it to feel as if the moss has begun to grow over me and the tree roots to entangle me, then I might be lucky enough to catch a glimpse of her. She never sees me. But if I hold my breath, she grows clearer and brighter for a moment before she fades away.

Sometimes I watch the farm from the woods and wait for Dora to go a-visiting. When she leaves, I step inside to see Papa and read to him in front of the fire. He scolds me for how dirty and skinny I've become. He wouldn't understand that the dirt I've rubbed into my skin is necessary. It's from the spot on the ground in the secret house where Stonefield used to sleep. At first I lay in the space and sank down a little into his piece of earth, but I needed to take it with me when I got up, so I stuffed the moss in my pockets and pressed his dirt into my skin, all over my body.

Papa reminds me that Effie will be leaving for the Congo in the spring, and says I should go visit with her to hear all about her plans, but the Lenox house seems as far away and unreal to me as Africa now. Mostly, Papa is quiet and rocks in his chair, his gentle eyes on me. I know he sees Mother in me when he does that, and it opens the door to my darkness. That's when I kiss his forehead good night, and run back to the woods to look for her myself.

One month after the preacher set out with the militia, a letter arrives. But it's not from Reverend Preston; it's from Henry to Dora. Dora is waiting for me at the parsonage to open the letter and read it out loud in my presence. I don't want to hear it. I go inside and close the door on her instead of inviting her in, but she just opens it again and walks in behind me. She fusses about the mess in the house and fans away the smoke from my pipe as I light it up.

No one's ever doted over a couple pieces of paper the way Dora is, making a show of opening the envelope with a special knife and waving the pages like a fan as if she might faint from the excitement. If Henry is able to write a letter, then he's still alive. That's all I really need to know. I'm sure and certain Henry won't include any of the interesting things that happen in the army, so as not to scare Dora. I sit cross-legged in the preacher's red velvet gentleman's chair and smoke my pipe, half-asleep, hoping she'll just leave.

Dora frowns at me over the letter. "Good gracious, Catrina, how unladylike."

I glance down at the drawstring trousers and long tunic I made. I got the idea from a picture of Chinese women's clothes I saw a long time ago in Mr. Lenox's book about the Far East. I embroidered ivy buds along the hems. Everything is stained and dirty now.

"Maybe you should go read the letter out loud from the kitchen so you won't have to see me. You might have to raise your voice, though." I blow a smoke ring in her direction. "But I doubt it."

"Oh, Cat, now you're just being silly." She waves my words away with the pages. "Now hush, so we can find out what Henry wrote!" She smooths the papers straight and clears her throat. "November 14, 1861, Fort Rolla, Missouri—"

"Fort Rolla?" I interrupt. "I didn't know he was so close. I thought he was sent to Springfield." I set my pipe down on the table next to my fiddle.

"Well, goodness, now, let's just wait and listen to what he says." She straightens the papers and reads Henry's letter:

My Dear Wife,

I hope this finds you well. Since I finally have a quiet moment while the boys are smoking and supper is over, I thought I would write to you about my time away these last several weeks, which have been quite eventful. Of course, I will not mention anything too unpleasant so as not to disturb you.

"I knew it." I roll my eyes and keep smoking.

"Shh." Dora keeps going:

Under Maj. Gen. John C. Frémont, our boys set out to Springfield to clear Maj. Gen. Sterling Price's Confederates from the state of Missouri. On October 25, we engaged them with this shout to our troops: "Let the watchword be 'Frémont and the Union!'" We beat them back and claimed the victory. Afterward, our troop evacuated Springfield under Maj. Gen. David Hunter, and withdrew to Fort Rolla, where I am stationed now.

Upon our arrival in Rolla, I was informed of the savage goings-on of the group of resisters led by the Creek Indian drifter whom my father once harbored. I am grateful to God for keeping my sister safe. Please express my sympathies to the Lenox family for the hardships they were subjected to in my absence and assure them that I pledge to bring this individual to justice if his path ever crosses mine again. I was pleased to be informed that our fine Reverend Preston has taken it upon himself to join the county militia in this very spirit of justice to search him out. I do have deep concerns for my father and especially my sister being left without the preacher's care, but I trust that you, my wife, will do your best to help in his stead as we all do what we must in these trying circumstances.

But as to the subject of the reverend's mission, I have some confidential information for your eyes only. Please be so kind as to not share this with my dear sister, as I fear it will have an ill effect on—

Dora stops reading and blinks at me over the top of the page, wide-eyed. "Oh!" She fumbles to fold the letter. "Well broom me out! I best read the rest of this at ho—"

I leap out of my seat and snatch the letter from her hands.

"Catrina Dickinson, you give that back!" She tries to grab me as I dart away, but I don't have any long skirts for her to catch hold of. "That letter is for my eyes only. You heard what your brother said!"

I stand on the chair so she can't reach the letter as I read it out loud.

Please be so kind as to not share this with my dear sister, as I fear it will have an ill effect on her fragile state. You may be interested to learn that while in Springfield, we received word of a—

Dora fetches a step stool, but I kick it over before she can step onto it.

"Witchy!" Dora's crying now. Her face turns red. "Catrina, please!"

. . . we received word of a large group of Creek Indians who have left Oklahoma Territory and are traveling northeast toward Fort Row in Kansas to flee the Confederates and seek asylum on the word of President Lincoln. The group consists of almost a thousand men, women, and children being led by a man named Opothle Yahola, and were said to be about two hundred miles

southwest of Springfield. We had orders not to interfere with them.
I tell you this because Stonefield and the bushwhackers were last
seen headed toward the very path in which these Creeks are
advancing. Stonefield may very well take up with them if they
are to meet. This means he may return north with them in our
direction, instead of traveling farther south with the outlaws. This
is a great concern to me. If word is received from Reverend
Preston—

I stop reading out loud and continue to myself without speaking, so Dora can't hear.

If word is received from Reverend Preston, I ask that you
copy the information I have given you here and include it in a
letter to him if he provides an address where he can be reached.
Samuel will know what to do.

Lord. My heart's pounding so fast.

"Catrina," Dora whines, "if you're going to steal my very own letter, the least you can do is keep reading it to me!"

"I lost my place." I run my finger over the part where Henry asks Dora to write the preacher about Stonefield, skipping ahead to the end. "Oh, here it is."

I know things have been difficult since the conscription, with
our horses taken from you and few friends left in Roubidoux to
help. I have been concerned for you and Father being able to find

workers for the harvest after I left. Please do write to keep me informed.

Dora makes a slight whimpering sound. Everyone's crops are rotting in the fields; there's no one to help bring them in. Papa's down to his nest egg savings and making coffee with ground-up acorns. I swallow hard and keep reading:

I have had a good deal of sickness this past month, but our late victory has given new life to our boys. I rejoice in the hope that the war will be brought to a speedy termination. It is enough to make anyone rejoice who has a heart for his country. Give my well wishes to Father and Catrina, and keep me and these brave boys in your prayers.

> *Your faithful husband,*
> *Henry Wells Dickinson*

Dora starts crying again. "He's been sick for a whole month and I never knew!" She paces in front of the window, staring out toward the woods as she dabs her nose with a hanky.

My stomach growls and I rest my hand over the slight but firm thickness forming around my middle in front. My body's trying to knit together a baby with what little food I give it.

Without me noticing, Dora's turned around. She grabs the

pages from my hand and stuffs them down the front of her bodice before I can snatch them back. "This letter is my own personal property!" She sniffs. "And I know you skipped parts when you were reading!" She blows her nose. "Just wait until I write and tell Henry what you've done."

"Go ahead and tell him." I pick up my fiddle. "How do you think he'll feel to know that the one simple thing he asked of his dear wife—to keep something confidential—was the very thing she failed to do." I run the bow across the fiddle, making the strings screech as loud and shrill as I can.

Dora clenches her hands over her ears. "Stop that!"

"I bet he'll wish he'd told Effie instead." I rub the bow again to make another screech.

"Oh, please stop that!" Dora cries. "You should be ashamed of yourself, Catrina Dickinson!" She turns away, her face wet. I know she won't tell Henry now.

I stare out the window. The trees are bare. Brown dead leaves pile up as high as a person's knees in some parts of the woods. A frost hangs in the air. Soon it will snow. I picture Stonefield camping out in this bitter cold with those Creek Indian families. I wonder how many months it will take such a large group of people to walk all the way from Oklahoma Territory to Kansas. Will their journey take them anywhere near Roubidoux? Will I be able to sense it when Stonefield passes by? If I call in my silent voice every day for him to come back to me, maybe one day he will answer.

The chance that he might be just a day's journey from where

I'm standing, instead of way down in Indian Territory where the preacher's looking for him, makes my heart thump too hard. My chest hurts from how swollen and bruised my heart feels.

The door slams. Dora's left. From the window, I watch her run away as I play a nervous wild tune on my fiddle to match the rhythm of her racing feet and my anxious pulse.

32

IN DECEMBER, MY STOMACH BEGINS TO SWELL AND MY breasts turn tender. When I run my hands over the hills and hollows of my new body, I imagine Stonefield's fingers touching me.

When it snows, I take my fiddle to the secret house in the woods and I play for the stone guardians. They still stand, but parts of the stone house are crumbling. Dried weeds line the perimeter of the house and shoot through the blanket of snow where the roses and mint once carpeted the ground.

After I'm warmed up from playing music, I make wild work by collecting icicles, breaking them into pieces, and reconnecting the melting parts bit by bit into small arcs. I press the arcs against trees, curving the loops of ice round and round the trunks until the woods are filled with shining silver spirals.

At twilight, I lie down in the middle of the stone circle house. My body makes the shape of a girl in the snow. I imagine that the most important part of me pulls loose from her and flies across the hills and valleys, the gray fields and green cedar woods, to the place where Stonefield lies on his own spot of snowy ground.

Come to me, Stonefield.

I lie down inside his body and we become warm. We melt just a little as we press together and become connected.

When the dimness in the sky grows greater than the light, I return to my own cold body in the secret house. Then I race to the parsonage, outrunning the falling dark that always threatens to swallow me.

I don't hear from the preacher until the new year, when the creek has frozen over and the crows arrive in the hollow. They caw and caw from the direction of Stone Field. The letter, addressed to me, arrives on the coldest day in January, slipped under Mr. Lenox's front door.

Effie and Lu deliver it to me at the parsonage along with a supper of bean-and-ham-hock stew. They hope I will open the letter and read it to them, but I fold it up and push it deep into the pocket of my trousers. All through supper, the cawing voices of the crows fly around inside my head. Their black wings flap against my heart.

Inside my pocket, the preacher's letter has turned into a heavy hand, pressing on my thigh. When they leave, I take a deep breath, pull it out, and open it.

Christmas night, 1861
Shoal Creek, Oklahoma Territory
Near Missouri's southwestern border

Dear Catrina,

Though we did not part in peace, I do beseech you to harken unto the words of this letter, for they are written in the spirit of deepest sincerity. I am not proud of my behavior toward you and my Lord, but, through His grace and mercy, He has forgiven me and once again, He speaks to my heart! He has revealed to me that it was my own selfish passions which drew me to you and away from Him. Though it was His plan that we should marry, He desired I come to the union seeking His kingdom first. If I had only placed the yearning for spiritual union above my selfish longing for an earthly one, I would never have received such punishment from God. I have been called to care for my bride as Christ loved the church. Because of my impurities, God requires that I be cleansed first, so I might then purify you.

Despite my transgression, the Lord has forgiven me. Not only has He transformed my savage and unclean heart into something pure and white as snow, He has blessed my travels and led me and the men of the militia to the murderous band of bushwhackers we have been devotedly pursuing all this time. We overtook them just days ago, deep in Oklahoma Territory. The heathen, Stonefield, was not among them, but in return for clemency, his fellows quickly betrayed his plans. The rest of the militia has headed back toward Rolla to take the outlaws home for trial, but I remain. The Lord has given me a new mission.

He told me to seek the heathen on my own and serve God's justice upon him. The outlaws confessed that the Indian broke off from them near Round Mountain in early December when they encountered a large band of Creek Indians headed north toward Kansas, near the Missouri border, fleeing Confederate troops. The chief welcomed him into their group, as they expected to be engaged in battle soon and needed all the assistance they could get.

I have picked up the unfortunate Indians' bloodstained trail from just such a battle and have gone ahead of them to this place, Shoal Creek, where they plan to make camp, though Confederate troops continue to pursue them. Tonight, the night of our Lord's birth, I wait with both my pistol and rifle loaded for the Lord's direction and will see how His divine will shall play out when they arrive with the Stonefield Indian among them.

I hope, dearest Catrina, that my words will bolster you in the knowledge that your husband is faithful in his devotion to the Lord and to justice, and will carry that devotion into the marriage that God intended for you and me. I trust He has spoken to your heart, too, since I have been so fervently praying that He will give you understanding and repentance, as well.

It is getting late on this icy Christmas night, and there is much to anticipate in the morning, so I shall close with my love and blessings in the Lord.

Your faithful husband,
Samuel Preston

My hand trembles as I set the letter on the table and pick up the preacher's table knife, which Effie used to slice the cornbread at supper. I stab the pages over and over again. "God can keep your love and blessings!" I cut them until the pages are ripped to shreds. "I don't want them!"

I've never been so mad at God. Why does He always take to meddling with folks' hearts so?

The baby inside me moves for the first time. The quickening feels like a butterfly tickling my insides with its fluttering wings. *Come back to me, Stonefield,* I call to him as I dip the ripped letter into the fire and watch it burn down to my fingers before I let it go.

Come back.

33

MOTHER NEVER HAD THE CHANCE TO TELL ME what a heavy burden it is to carry a child inside the belly for months and months. And I never had the chance to tell her what a heavy burden it is to carry a secret love inside the heart, swelling and kicking under the ribs for release.

I sometimes wonder if Stonefield ever thinks of me. But even if he thinks of me only half as much as I do him, that'd be at least ten times a day, and it's now been almost two hundred days since I last laid eyes on him. The burden of all the moments I've passed without him weighs heavier on my heart than his child pressing against it.

I hope he's suffering as much without me as I am without him. I hope he can't sleep for the ache. Lord, I want to kill him like he's killing me. I wish I could sink to the bottom of Roubidoux Creek, but Effie won't let me. You'd think she was the one who had vowed to love me through sickness and health rather than the reverend. With me too ill from throat sickness these last couple months to even visit Papa, she's trapped me here in the parsonage. She keeps me away from the woods and mostly in bed, trying to make up for the fact that she failed to notice I was pregnant in the first place. She can't bear to make another mistake in her doctoring and has determined that before she leaves for the Congo, she'll be my salvation.

But Lord, maybe I don't want to be saved.

"Stick out your tongue," Effie says as she pushes me back onto the bed. She leans over my stomach, which rises above my breasts, round and high like the baldnob hill above the church and parsonage. With a flat stick she presses my tongue and peers down my throat. "It's getting worse."

I hate my throat sicknesses. They didn't use to be this bad when I was little. I want to ask Effie if she knows why, but it hurts too much to use my voice.

"I'm afraid it's turned into rheumatic fever." She exchanges the cooling rag on my forehead for a fresh one. "Is breathing difficult?"

I shake my head no, though I have felt out of breath lately. But it's just from the baby's weight pressing on my lungs. I know Effie's worried about me and the baby from the way her eyes linger on my stomach as she sets her stethoscope over my heart. She's listened to Papa's heart like this many times over the last eight months and every time, her jaw sets a little tighter. She says his heart doesn't beat as strong as it should—probably weakened from the rheumatic fever he, too, had when he was young.

Lu comes in with a cup of broth. It's about the only thing I can swallow. I almost drop it when she hands it over, and broth slops onto the blanket.

"Goodness, you're so clumsy, Catrina. I've never seen a person with such a knack for messing things as you."

Lord, I don't even have the energy to glare at her. But her voice has lost the creamy sweetness that used to cover up her sourness toward me. Now when she talks to me, it sounds like she's skimmed the icing off and doesn't use any spoiled words, just plain honest ones.

Before we get the mess cleaned up, the front door flies open and in bursts Dora, her face red and splotchy. She's so far along, she looks like she's hiding a watermelon under her dress.

Effie jumps up and runs to her. "What are you doing here, Dora? You shouldn't be exerting yourself like this."

Dora's gasping for breath, her hair falling out of her pins.

Effie leads her to a chair. "What's wrong?"

Oh God, please don't let it be Papa.

"Broom me out." Dora gulps in air like a catfish sucking up pond water. "That Devil man." She fans herself with her hand. "That treasonous bushwhacker savage."

I hold my breath.

Dora almost spits out the words. "Stonefield's back!"

Stonefield.

I struggle to a sitting position and catch Effie's eyes. She knows what I'm thinking. Lord, Lord. To see him after all this time! But does he want to see me? Is he still angry?

I slide my legs over the side of the bed.

Dora keeps talking between her huffing and puffing. "He's the one stealing from our pantry and eating the eggs and milk! Mr. Dickinson says he told him he can take whatever he needs, but I think the Devil man has a hold on him, just like he bewitched Cat when he first showed up in the field. And what if he tries to see Cat? Mr. Dickinson told him she's settled and she and Samuel are expecting a child, but who knows what he'll do."

Oh God. He'll think it's the preacher's baby.

Dora stops for a moment to catch her breath. "Oh, I hope Henry hurries and gets here soon! He needs to catch him before he does something terrible!"

Henry?

Effie's eyebrows lift in surprise and she asks my question for me. "Henry's coming home?"

"Yes." Dora's still huffing and puffing. "I mean—he will. When he gets my message. Shouldn't take long—I gave it to your father just now at your house. I told him it was urgent and he said he'd take it to Henry at Fort Rolla first thing tomorrow morning. Surely Henry will get permission to come after him— Stonefield's a violent resister wanted by the Union Army!"

Lord, he'll kill him.

She stops to catch a breath, but she's so agitated, she can't stop talking. "In the letter I got from Henry in April, he said that the Creek Indians who were trying to make it to Fort Row, Kansas, have nearly all been killed by Confederates. Most of the ones who reached the fort didn't live through the winter. So that's probably why Stonefield headed back to Roubidoux—to secretly cadge supplies from poor Mr. Dickinson!"

Effie motions to Lu. "Help Dora and get her some water— she needs to settle down."

Lu glances at me and runs off to fetch some water. I can see the fear in her eyes. She's remembering the last time she saw Stonefield.

My head's turned into a heavy ball of lead. The walls move, like they've come loose from the ceiling. I find my trousers and tunic and slip them on. The soft cool fabric feels good against my skin and I stand up taller. If Dora can travel between the farm and the parsonage, so can I. I'll use the Lenoxes' carriage out front. Maybe Effie will understand when she finds out later—I have to see Stonefield.

But Effie frowns at me, her forehead all knotty, as I walk slow across the room to the door. "What are you doing? Get back in bed, Catrina."

She knows I can't speak from the throat sickness. I grab a pencil and scrap paper from the end table. The front of the paper's covered in Reverend Preston's handwriting—notes for an old sermon called "Prepare to Meet Thy God." I turn it over to the blank side and write to Effie, *Is there a new law against folks using their own outhouses?*

"The pan is clean. It's under the bed—you can use that."

Lord. She's going to make God jealous if she keeps trying to boss the world. I write, *I need fresh air.* I stuff the paper and pencil into her hands and open the door before she can say anything else, but she puts them down and walks right out with me, closing the door behind us. The sweet smell of honeysuckle hangs in the spring air. Red columbines have grown up against the side of the parsonage. A hummingbird darts away as I reach down and pick a flower to slide behind my ear, waiting for Effie to go back inside.

"You're sick, Catrina. You can't go to your father's house."

Oh Hell. I place my palms on either side of her face and draw her toward me. I close my eyes, rest my forehead against hers, and think the words to her. *I have to see Stonefield. I thought you of all people would know what it means to me. I might not have another chance, Effie!* I press my head harder, as if I can push my thoughts into hers. *Please try to understand.*

Effie rests her hands over mine. "I do understand," she whispers. "I understand why you need to go, but *you* don't understand why you need to stay."

Did she hear my thoughts? *Why are you trying to stop me from being happy, Effie?* I turn to go. I don't need her damned carriage. I'll walk to the farm, even if it takes all day and makes my ankles swell up like tree trunks.

"You need to stay because of your father."

I stop and turn back to face her. *Papa?*

Her eyes look the same way they did when she told me about saying no to Henry's proposal.

No, you're wrong, Effie. It will be fine. I start walking again. *Papa will understand.*

"It's not that your father wouldn't understand . . ."

I stop, stunned at how well she can hear my thoughts. *What is it, Effie?* I still don't turn to face her.

She doesn't say anything.

I sigh and cross my arms over my chest, waiting, as I stare at the distant cliff above Roubidoux Spring. Up there somewhere is the cave opening—my secret place, but I can't see it. I ache to be there now. Two hawks soar over the valley.

When Effie finally speaks, her voice is so soft I can barely hear her. "Catrina, your father's heart has grown so weak this past year." Her voice changes—like something inside her throat is cracking. "If he's exposed to your rheumatic fever . . ."

I close my eyes tight, trying to shut out her arguments. Papa's had it before. And he gets throat sickness all the time. I start walking, faster this time. I'll try not to get too close to him. I just want to see Stonefield.

". . . it will kill him, Catrina."

I shake my head. That can't be right. How can she be sure that my presence at the house will be dangerous to Papa? I look back over my shoulder at her.

"Is that a chance you're willing to take, Catrina?"

Lord, Lord, Lord. I'm all torn up inside. I want so bad what I can't ever seem to have. I scream at the sky before I can stop myself, and the force of it rips my throat like knife blades. I'm still walking, even though I know I can't go any farther. My legs don't belong to me. I can't feel them. It seems like I'm stumbling over the edge of my secret place and plunging down the side of the cliff, but I'm only falling to the dirt on my hands and knees.

"Catrina!" Effie cries and runs toward me.

Lu joins her, breathing heavy. "Heavens, Catrina, are you all right?"

They try to hold me up.

My head's swimming in the swirling waters of Roubidoux Spring.

I hear the parsonage door opening and Dora calling out.

My legs are wet. A dark spot spreads over my trousers. Water and blood trickle over my calves and ankles and darken the dirt. The fire in my throat and my head spreads through my whole body.

I can't go to Stonefield, but his child is on its way to me.

34

Y MOANS SOUND LIKE A PANTHER'S IN THE WOODS.
With every wave of pain, the noise scrapes my
throat. I never knew pain like this existed—like someone's
twisting my insides up to wring every last drop of life out of
me. The waves come more often now and last longer. I clutch
Effie's hand till each one passes. But she lets go soon as they're
over, because I'm bleeding. Every time my body clenches and
shudders, the bedsheet gets wetter. Effie's good at keeping her
worry inside, but Lu and Dora aren't. Each time they clear away
the bloodied linen, their eyes look like they'll pop out of their
heads.

I keep my eyes on Effie. Just watching her calms me. She acts
like she's caught thousands of babies before and this one will
be no different. I never saw her so determined as she is right
now. She smooths the hair away from my face and gives me her
middling smile. "The baby looks ready, Catrina. Do you feel
like you need to push?"

I nod. My throat's swollen shut.

Dora whimpers. "I feel foolish as a farmer at a quilting bee. What should Lu and I do, Effie?"

"Help her to the edge of the bed. Let her hold on to you for support."

They help me into a squatting position, holding me on either side.

Effie kneels on the floor in front of me, waiting to catch the child. "Catrina, remember all our talks about what you'll need to do and what will happen?"

I nod. We read a whole book about it together, but I never imagined it this way. And it's too early. This wasn't supposed to happen for a couple more months.

She reminds me as she squeezes my hand, "Rest between contractions so you'll have the strength to push through the pain."

As she speaks, the pain comes rumbling toward me and I push through it. I groan and squeeze Dora's and Lu's arms tight as a vise grip. Then the pain leaves me, and I go limp, gasping like a fish out of water. So dizzy. But seems as soon as I get a rest, the pain comes rolling back in and I'm pushing again.

Finally, Dora cries in a wobbly voice, "Oh, Effie! The baby's head!"

Lord-a-mercy.

"Goodness gracious!" Lu's fingers dig into my arms. "Push that brat out, Catrina, then we can all take a rest!"

Sweat drips into my eyes, stinging. I push one more time, screaming like a screech owl, and, Lordy, Lordy, I'm finally free of it. Effie catches the baby. My body stops working. My hands release Dora and Lu. I'm crumpling onto the bed, folding up, finished.

Effie's holding a red, wrinkled creature. "Catrina, you have a daughter."

Lu squeals.

The room spins.

I'm slipping away.

The last thing I hear is a murmured "Well broom me out!"

35

THE SUN IS DIM OUTSIDE THE WINDOWS NOW. I swim in and out of sleep, but every time I open my eyes, Effie's by my side. She says I have not been fully awake for a whole night and now it's late the next day. I've lost too much blood and my fever's too high, but Mr. Lenox left this morning for Rolla to get Henry, and will fetch a doctor, too. She says I am in grave danger. Effie always dishes out the truth. If she lied to me I would see it on her face.

Effie, does Stonefield know?

She nods. "Hold on, Catrina." She squeezes my hand. "He'll be here by evening. Just keep holding on."

I don't know if she means Stonefield or the doctor. She gives me a little morphine so I can tolerate the pain, but it makes me even sleepier. I see Mother standing over me, and then Stonefield outside my window watching me. I reach out my arms to him. *Come to me.* The next time I open my eyes, he's gone.

My daughter lies beside me, quiet. She has no breath, no heartbeat. She never made a sound. Soon they will take her away and bury her in the dark womb of the earth near my mother. My eyes make tears for her, but they get lost inside my body somewhere and do not fall.

Before they take her, I name her in my mind. I name her after my best friend and my mother. I slip Lu's name in there, too, to make it sound pretty. Effie Lu-Ann's face is pale, but I imagine her eyes are dark and deep like her father's. I want to keep looking at her, but I can't make my eyes stay open.

I hear the front door of the parsonage burst open and Lu cries out. I struggle to wake, but the morphine pulls me back down into its deep sea. Oh God, oh Hell. Every time I almost break the surface, I go under again. I try to ask Effie what's happening, but my throat feels like knives have shredded it and nothing will come out.

An angel of light stands in the bedroom doorway. He's come for me. Lu tries to stop him, but he pushes her away and stands beside my bed. He reaches toward me and touches the spot on my neck where my seeing stone used to rest. I think he will fly me to Heaven, but his face turns dark as death.

Stonefield? I'm sinking again.

"Catrina," the angel says to me. "They said you're dying. Don't do this. Don't go."

Stonefield. I push at the darkness and try to swim to the surface.

"Did you ever love me, Catrina?" he shouts. Tears turn his eyes wet.

Always.

Can he hear me or are we still deaf to each other? A shadow

falls over me as he comes near. He has my seeing stone and is tying it around my neck where it belongs.

"Stay with me, Catrina!" he cries. "Don't you dare leave me!" He takes my hair in his fingers the way he used to. To try to catch me.

I'm sinking.

The angel picks me up from my bed.

I can't move. My body does nothing I tell it to. I'm not even all the way inside myself. I think I hear Lu sobbing. This dream feels so real. I never saw Effie cry before. She tells the angel to put me down and that it's too late—that I've gone to a better place—but he doesn't listen. As he carries me out the door, I slide deeper into my dream, like Ophelia slipping into the river. I'm floating away on the current with him.

The dream man, the angel, kisses me. It makes me think of the first time, when his kiss made my soul rise to the surface, trembling for release. His lips join mine, but I don't feel them this time, because I'm hovering between my body and his. From here I think my soul and his are almost close enough to touch. He lays my body down gentle on a bed of hay in the back of Papa's wagon, and climbs to the wagon seat. Faithful whinnies as Stonefield snaps the reins and takes us away.

It's nearing twilight. The hills form a black rolling line against the sky. Bats swoop down between the trees, and frogs chirp along the creek bank. The smells of river water, black walnuts, and wet cedar fill the air. I think if I let go of myself, I will fill the air, too. I've slipped loose, but still I hold on.

Stonefield's shoulders are shaking. His whole body heaves and shudders as he drives the wagon away. Soon, shouts rise up behind us, and the sound of galloping hoofbeats follows. Stonefield whips the reins harder, and Faithful quickens her speed.

The hoofbeats are beside us now.

"Stonefield!" It's Henry. "Pull over! Where are you taking—"

"Leave me alone!" Stonefield kicks out at him to push him away, but Henry catches hold of him and lunges forward off his horse and into the wagon, pushing Stonefield down against the seat.

"Why are you doing this?" Henry shouts. His eyes are red. "It's too late—we've lost her!"

Stonefield swings wild and hits him in the face.

Henry grabs him and they crash against the front of the wagon, startling Faithful, who bolts forward at an even faster pace. They get thrown backward, over the seat into the wagon bed beside me. Henry pins Stonefield to the floor. "I'm after my sister, not you. You have to stop." Sweat drips from his forehead.

Stonefield's chest heaves as he tries to breathe; he turns to look at me.

But Henry's still staring at him, pressed against the wagon bed.

Look at me, look at me, look at me, I chant inside to Henry. I know that if Henry lets go of Stonefield and turns to me, he will finally see me.

And he does. Lordy. Henry turns his head. His fingers let go. His body softens. His eyes find me. The most important part of me, hovering here. And for the first time in so long, my brother finally sees me.

The wagon jolts as it hits a stone, and Henry gets thrown off balance. He struggles back up and climbs over the seat to find Faithful's reins and guide the wagon to a halt. We've come to the edge of Stone Field. Henry sits still for a minute, catching his breath as he looks out at the rows of rotten brown sorghum stalks standing forgotten in the field. Sprinkled among them are snatches of green—little sprigs of tender new sweet sorghum grass that have sprung up from fallen seed of the old crop. He turns to Stonefield, who still lies beside me in the wagon, never taking his eyes from me.

"I know you came back and risked your life to help my father." Henry climbs out of the wagon.

"I didn't come back for him. I did it for her." Stonefield doesn't turn his eyes from me.

Henry says nothing.

The stillness of the night beckons me. I want to slip into the twilight where I belong. Up above us in the cliff is my secret place. A dark figure moves in the cave opening in the bluff, watching us, but Stonefield and Henry don't see.

Henry glances around at the fireflies that have arrived in the hollow. "I remember once"—he swallows, like it's hard to speak—"Cat went to the corn-husk dance wearing a muslin dress our mother made." He gives a laugh that sounds more like a quiet sob. "Even when she was little, she didn't like to be told what to wear. Cat wouldn't wear the dress until she'd made it her own. So she caught fireflies and quilted them into the skirt." He looks over at me; his eyes are wet. "When she stood still, the fireflies would fall asleep and it looked like a white dress with black polka dots, but when she moved or danced, they lit up like she was full of stars."

Stonefield climbs into the front seat and picks up the reins. "I'm taking her with me."

"I can't let you do that," Henry says. But Stonefield slaps the reins and Henry gets shoved to the ground. We bolt away, toward the center of the field. We're almost near the black rock. I think of the song from that first day in this very field where it all started.

> *Come, live with me and be my love*
> *And we will all the pleasures prove*
> *And if these pleasures may thee move*
> *Then live with me and be my love.*

His song was an invitation. A promise. He's keeping his promise.

> *There will I make thee beds of roses*
> *With a thousand fragrant posies*
> *A cap of flowers and a kirtle*
> *Embroidered all with leaves of myrtle.*

As we reach the black rock, the dark figure up in the bluff crouches in the opening of my secret place. The preacher. He has a gun.

A belt of straw and ivy buds
With coral clasps and amber studs
With gray feather of the dove
Oh, live with me and be my love.

The air seems to quiver as if it holds the charge of an approaching storm. I feel it inside me. The gun fires from the cliff like a lightning bolt striking Stonefield near the heart. He falls to the floor of the wagon as Faithful races through the field, taking us toward the woods. There's a dark red stain on the seat where Stonefield sat.

36

I'VE LOST TRACK OF TIME. BUT TIME DOESN'T MATTER anymore—nor does distance nor place.

I think I hear someone whispering my name, but now the noise sounds more like the gurgle of Roubidoux Creek and the wind rustling the walnut leaves. I almost think if I were to wake from this dream-sleep, I'd see that I'm really in Hudgens Hollow after all.

As I think it, I realize it's true. I'm in our secret house in the woods.

Lord. Maybe I've always been here. Maybe it's the room in the parsonage that was a dream. I feel myself sinking into the layers of leaves and moss and dirt beneath me.

I feel as if I'm pulsing to the thrum of life all around—tree roots sucking water from deep inside the ground; animals burrowing tunnels; stones eroding; seeds sleeping, humming, dreaming, waiting. I lie here like a daughter in the arms of the earth.

But I still hear my name being murmured in my ear. It's

Stonefield. I am both in his arms and hovering above him as he holds my lifeless body. He's wounded bad, but somehow he's driven the wagon to our home in the woods and laid me in our secret house. Henry and the preacher haven't found us yet.

The light of a small grease lamp flickers in the dark. He's decorated my hair with leaves. His own hair is long and dark and curls on his neck. His eyes shine amber in the light with a wildness I remember from the day I first saw him in Stone Field.

"Catrina." He runs his fingers over the healed wound on the inside of my arm where I scraped his name from my skin. The scar has faded to a soft silvery mark. Then he traces the small scar on my forehead from the day the people in the church crowded in on me, but I don't feel his touch. I'm outside my body, barely holding on to it.

Blood stains his shirt, his arms. "I went away to find myself among my people, but my people didn't know me, just like your people never really knew you. You and I don't seem to belong anywhere. Except with each other." He touches my cheeks, my lips.

It's true. The day I almost killed him in Stone Field was the day we each came alive.

He glides his finger over my chin and down my neck. "I longed to be back in your arms—the only place I ever felt truly known."

He holds my seeing stone between his fingers. I think of all the beauty in the world contained in such a small gift. And how I threw it away and he gave it back to me.

His voice is quiet, like a whisper. "One winter night you came to me. I lay on the hard cold ground, and you flew to me like a dove."

I remember the night I lay in the snow inside the secret house while my spirit traveled to Stonefield.

"You rested over my heart and kept me warm. When you left me, I knew I had to stay alive until I could get back to you."

My soul longs to touch his soul. I almost can. Lord, I feel the warmth of it so near. If only I could hold it, I would let go of the cold girl on the ground and become something bright and burning.

Slow, like he's almost too weak to move, Stonefield pulls a book from our wooden chest. He opens and reads, " 'We know what we are, but know not what we may be.' " He closes his eyes and lies back down next to me, weak from the bullet inside him.

I say to him in my silent voice, *To be or not to be. That is the question.*"

He whispers, silent, back to me, deep, deep, deep inside me, *Then the answer's "not to be," if it means I can be with you.*

Stonefield's book slips from his hands and lies open between us. The pencil marks of all the little parts he underlined weave across the pages like a thread connecting us.

The lamp flickers and dies, but now we can see the stars shining above our secret house. I let go of the cold girl and reach for Stonefield.

Author's Note

"He's more myself than I am.
Whatever our souls are made of, his and mine are the same."

WUTHERING HEIGHTS BY EMILY BRONTË TELLS THE story of the Earnshaws, a farming family living on the moors of Yorkshire, England. Young Catherine Earnshaw and her dark-skinned foster brother, Heathcliff, become inseparable companions and spend their time running wild together over the moors. As they grow up, familial resentments and social expectations cause Cathy to decide to marry Edgar Linton, a man of higher class. But Cathy, struggling with her decision to marry Linton, confides to the servant Nelly the spiritual connection that she believes exists between herself and Heathcliff. Cathy reveals a recurring dream to Nelly:

Heaven did not seem to be my home; and I broke my heart with weeping to come back to earth; and the angels were so angry that they flung me out into the middle of the heath on the top of Wuthering Heights; where I woke sobbing for joy.

For Cathy, the "heath on the top of Wuthering Heights" is, of course, Heathcliff. She has the intense belief that her own soul is intricately tied to another's in part through the landscape they grew up on. When I set out to write *Stone Field*, I was interested in the struggles and joys of a troubled and passionate person like Cathy, so I created a character, Catrina, who feels her soul is bound both to Stone Field, the place, with its surrounding hills and hollows, and to Stonefield, the person.

Wuthering Heights takes place in the isolated Yorkshire moors of Northern England, a setting that Emily Brontë was intimately familiar with. This inspired my decision to set *Stone Field* in a remote wild environment to which I feel a deep attachment—my childhood home. I grew up among the hills and valleys of the Ozarks on my grandfather's land, which was nestled in the countryside that stretches between Rolla and Newburg, Missouri.

Following the Missouri Compromise in 1820, Missouri entered the Union as a slave state, which kept the peace for a time, but its people were divided during the Civil War, with some fighting for the Union and others for the Confederacy. Missouri, a border state, had its star on both flags, had separate governments representing opposing sides, and waged its own miniature civil war within its borders as neighbor fought neighbor.

As a child, I heard stories of Bushwhacker Bill Wilson, the brother of Napoleon Wilson, my grandfather's great-grandfather. Bill resisted enlistment by the Union soldiers and sought revenge when they burned his house and barn during the Civil War. I swam in the same creeks as Bill and Napoleon and went spelunking in the caves where Bill once hid from the soldiers. My grandfather's and mother's graves now lie in the real Hudgens Cemetery, the old graveyard where Napoleon Wilson is buried.

Although *Stone Field*'s setting was inspired by a real geographical area, I created the fictional town of Roubidoux Hollow and invented other fictional locales, such as Lanesville, where Stonefield was a schoolteacher. Some of these sites were placed in personally significant areas; for instance, I imagined Roubidoux's first church to be on the spot where my grandfather attended a one-room schoolhouse when he was a child. I also sometimes renamed or repositioned landmarks such as springs and creeks to better suit the story I wanted to tell.

Rolla, in Phelps County, Missouri, was an important site during the Civil War. The southwest branch of the Pacific Railroad had recently been extended to the town of six hundred people and ended there, becoming a busy depot for arriving Union soldiers and supplies on their way to the early battles in southwest Missouri.

Missouri was a slave state but had relatively few slaves. An 1880s history of Phelps County says that in 1861 there were only about one hundred slaves in the whole county. A brief biography of a white missionary to the Congo in the 1800s who married there and brought back eight black daughters when his wife died, inspired Effie's and Lu Lenox's stories.

Stonefield's story was based on the various experiences of many displaced Muscogee Creek Indians during the Civil War as well as accounts of mission schools and orphanages in the Western territories. In September of 1861, Creek Indians in Indian Territory (present-day Oklahoma) received a promise from President Lincoln that the United States government would assist them and protect them from Confederate forces. The letter directed their leader, Opothle Yahola, to move his people to Fort Row in Wilson County, Kansas, and pledged refuge and support there.

Stonefield seeks out the Creek Indians who are headed north at this time in order to join them. But by November, 1,400 Confederates, including pro-Confederate Indians, pursued the fleeing Creeks to convince the chief and his followers to support the Confederacy or to "drive him and his party from the country." An estimated two thousand of the nine thousand Muscogee Creek people were killed from the battles, diseases, and harsh winter conditions, leaving a "Trail of Blood on Ice" during their journey to Fort Row. The survivors arrived in December to find that the fort lacked medical support and supplies. Many died that winter under bitter conditions.

To learn more about life in the Ozarks during the Civil War, read the accounts of those who experienced it firsthand. "Community & Conflict: The Impact of the Civil War in the Ozarks" at ozarkscivilwar.org is a fascinating collection of primary source documents—photographs, letters, journals, and other artifacts—that portray people's struggles in everyday life during the devastation of the American Civil War. The project is a collaborative digitization effort to document the war in the Ozark region from 1850 to 1875. To find out more about the Muscogee Creek Nation, past and present, please visit the official website, muscogeenation-nsn.gov.

ACKNOWLEDGMENTS

*I*T TAKES A VILLAGE TO MAKE A BOOK. THE MAYOR OF my little village is Erin Murphy, a brilliant agent and dear friend—thank you for believing in me. I would also like to thank the people at Roaring Brook Press, especially Katherine Jacobs. What a delightful experience to have someone with whom to discuss the imaginary people inside my head as if they were mutual friends. I appreciate your astute insight and shared vision.

Others in my village who have helped me on this journey include Debby Vetter, editor of *Cricket* magazine, who published many of my first stories and whose editorial guidance taught me to appreciate the collaborative effort involved in producing good work and fostered in me the desire to write books. I am also thankful for Miciah Gault, Bethany Hegedus, Caroline Carlson, and *Hunger Mountain, the VCFA Journal for the Arts,* for connecting with my work and publishing various short stories and novel excerpts, the first being an excerpt from an early version of *Stone Field*.

Some wonderful people read various drafts along the way. Thanks to Cheryl Klein for her generous and thoughtful notes on an early version, and for introducing me to Francisco Stork and his work. I am grateful to have had him as an early reader. Thanks to Francisco, also, for giving me my own magic seeing stone—a reminder to always find the beauty in the world.

I am grateful for writer friends who read and critiqued *Stone Field* at various stages: Jennifer Duddy Gill and Elizabeth Reimer (Weird Martian Gnomes!), Sarah Williams, Rose Green, Sarah Shantz, Suzanne Kamata, Raynbow Gignilli, Jeannie Mobley-Tanaka, and Tanya Goulette Seale.

Bridget Gallagher, Jan Marlese, Lisa Jones, Allison Savage Atas, and Ellena Gibbons—thank you, dear friends, for your commiseration, art therapy, and laughter. And thanks to Hector Escalante and Wanda Wright for your encouragement at my day job, reminding me that I can do this.

I also want to credit those whose ideas directly inspired some of my own: Michael Ondaatje tells of his grandmother sewing fireflies into her gown in his memoir, *Running in the Family*, which inspired me to imagine a similar dress for Cat. The poem "A Noiseless Patient Spider" by Walt Whitman inspired the scene where Cat has similar observations. The work of nature artist Andy Goldsworthy had a tremendous influence on how I formed my ideas about Cat's "wild work." And thanks to Zac Spurlin for letting me steal his description of a piece of sky being carried in a mirror.

I appreciate the assistance of Michael Price, Local History Reference Associate at Springfield-Greene County Library

District, in answering my questions. If there are any inaccuracies in this text, they are due solely to my own mistakes or stubbornness.

My family is familiar with this stubbornness of mine, and I am grateful they have patiently endured my dogged determination to write and publish this book, and cheered me on during the long journey. Thanks to my parents, who always filled our house with love and books. Much love to Alexandria, Noah, and Josh for keeping me supplied with hugs. Alan, I never had to convert you, because you believed in me from the beginning. Thank you for everything. I'm a lucky gal.